· · · · · · · · · · · ·

GRUESOME

© 2014 Donald Brown

Gruesome! A Novel Drawn from True Crime

ISBN 978-0-9883893-7-3

Library of Congress Control Number: 2014932929

Borgo Publishing
3811 Derby Downs Drive
Tuscaloosa, Alabama 35405
www.borgopublishing.com

Cover illustration and design by Paul Looney, Tuscaloosa, Alabama.
Book text design by Randall Williams, Montgomery, Alabama.

Printed in the USA

GRUESOME!

Five Women, One Killer.
A Novel Based on True Crime.

Donald Brown

To Mary Jo —
remember the
many Christmases,
Don, 2014

ALSO BY DONALD BROWN

(as author)

*Forward Ever: Sesquicentennial History
of Birmingham-Southern College*

Tuscaloosa: Yesterday, Today, Tomorrow (with Hannah Brown)

Tuscaloosa Sketch Book

*Saints, Servants & Sinners:
A History of Tuscaloosa First United Methodist Church*

Timeless Service, 90 years of the Tuscaloosa Rotary Club

Portrait of Birmingham, Centennial Year

Taming the Black Warrior

*Chamber Perspectives,
Chamber of Commerce of West Alabama, 100th Anniversary*

(as co-author or editor)

Foundry Life (with Paul Singleton)

A Cry for Help (with Henry Tyler)

Tearing Down Walls: A Woman's Triumph (with Mary Jones)

Profiles of Alabama Pharmacy (with Alabama Pharmaceutical Association)

Our Heritage (Illges-Barnett and related families)

(as contributor)

Tuscaloosa: Centennial Memories, Millennial Hopes

View from the Hilltop

I Wish I Was in Dixie

FOR THE COUNTLESS CO-WORKERS
WHO TAUGHT ME A NOBLE PROFESSION

. . . .
Prologue

It is a festered and forbidding gash in dirt, this hole whose depth disappears in darkness, its opening surrounded by rotting brush and slithery muck that clutches at you like tentacles.

Once it was a life-giving water well, this hole hiding in a thick forest of towering pines. Now, and forever, it is a symbol of death. Her murder.

As a young reporter, untested by violence, I was sickened by the sight of this hole and its crude wooden ladder that seemed to rise out of hell, through the blackness and jut into the soft daylight. On that winter morning I muttered, "How could he? His wife!"

"Holy Jesus!" the photographer with me gasped in the spooky stillness and to the black birds calling one another from high in the trees. He steadied a shaking hand and began shooting a scene whose fullest meaning would be some of the hardest words I ever put into print.

Giving self-interested sources, patient legwork, predictable bullshit and firsthand knowledge their due respect, even the best of us—and I was far from that—sometimes don't grasp the totality of what we're covering. This story, I think I never did. But what I will tell you is as close as I could get to the truth of what happened, who caused it, and why, in Henderson County, Alabama in the new year of 1959.

THE WELL AND THE body in it were the crux of everything. But with more experience, or if anyone at all had been willing to share the bigger picture, I might have quickly learned that this story was as much about the political and social clash of two families as it was about violent death. In particular, two men, friends turned rivals, each determined to bring down the other.

The opponents were Bill Tomlinson, the county's powerful probate judge, and Seth Yielding, the ambitious chief prosecutor of Henderson and three other adjoining counties. The pawn was Bill's younger brother, John Ed Tomlinson, charged with the first-degree murder of his wife, Jo Dell.

Talk in Butler, the county seat, said that John Ed and Jo Dell were in the process of a divorce over his mistress, and that he killed his wife to remarry and make sure he would keep their twin boys and two daughters.

County residents took sides; they couldn't avoid it. Those with allegiance to the most important family they knew sided with the Tomlinsons. Others stood with Yielding and Phillip Hunter, his political mentor. An old-timer put it this way: "Jo Dell's death gave Seth the fuel he needed to even a lot of scores. He viciously pursued that case. And John Ed's reasoning for burying Jo Dell in a filthy well never satisfied anybody."

It took three trials—over three years—for Seth to gain a conviction that stuck. That alone kept people divided and created bitterness that lasted for decades. I covered trials two and three, and during that time got close to a woman whose soft sexiness brightened a very hostile setting. We measured risk against need. In doing that we learned a lot about ourselves.

After John Ed went to prison, Seth challenged Bill for probate judge in 1964, but lost by 108 votes. Seth then resigned as prosecutor and "jumped the river," townspeople said, crossing the Tombigbee River to relocate in neighboring Grove Bluff where he gained prominence as a defense attorney. Bill ran for Congress in 1966, lost, and never campaigned again.

Time and death did their work and today the bitter blood is mostly an afterthought in Henderson County. But of the old folks left, many say they still hear the echoes—the men and their ambition, the women involved, murder or accident, three juries and one gruesome image.

Forever more, the well.

GRUESOME

Chapter 1

When we kissed goodbye and parted, I knew we'd never meet again. Love is like a dying ember, only memories remain. Through the ages I'll remember blue eyes cryin' in the rain.

Willie's song played in my head that day because a country road can be like a jukebox love song, often waking what is best left asleep. I'm traveling two lanes of worn west Alabama asphalt that stretch all the way to Mobile, but the past will stop me long before the swells that softly lap the sugary Gulf beach at our renowned redneck Riviera.

Why am I doing this, bumping over pitted paving, crawling behind a flatbed straining under its massive load of lodgepole pine logs? This hasn't been a story for several decades, and I've crossed the last peak of a reporter's career that carried me up challenging mountains. George Wallace's "segregation forever" inauguration. Apollo 11, first humans to the moon. The funerals of the four children murdered in the Birmingham church bombing. Martin Luther King's campaign that brought Birmingham to its knees. The disappearance of three civil rights workers in Mississippi. The death of ex-slave Josh McCord, who claimed to be 117. Viola Hyatt, who axed apart her two lovers. The Challenger disaster. The nothing-like-it rush of countless other page-one stories; voices, faces, events, most long-preserved in cluttered closets of memory.

What, then, pulls me back to Henderson County and into a conflict long-settled, but whose wrath split this place and its people for decades, and reverberated across Alabama? I was just a neophyte of twenty-three then,

3

shaping into a pretty good reporter, the bosses said. But in reality I didn't even realize what I didn't know. For starters, my notebooks didn't contain violent death, a Klan rally's fury, telephone threats, or the mandate to get out of our town. My work was mostly human-interest stories, and the occasional severe weather. It seemed I had a flair for covering people and storms.

They sent me anyway to this foreign country of southwest Alabama, where I'd never been, for the second trial of a powerful man already convicted of murdering his wife and sentenced to life in prison. But the first verdict had been reversed on appeal due to errors by the judge. I would write of number two ending in a hung jury. It's not over, said my hard-nosed city editor; go back for number three.

Certain stories take up permanent residence within a journalist, some as pleasant memories, some you'd like to forget. Most others come and go like the daily editions. This one has had a special place because it became a learning experience that marked me, professionally and personally, in ways no other did. Now it had stirred from the dust of decades, calling my name again. I have answered, and I know why.

Because she called.

· · · · · · · · · ·
Chapter 2

"Mr. Anderson?" the voice asked.

"Speaking."

"You covered the Tomlinson trials in Henderson County years ago."

It was a statement, not a question.

"Yes."

"I'm Sarah Tomlinson, John Ed's second wife." She paused for the connection to register. "We never met. But all that is past history now, and I'd like to talk to you."

"This is quite a surprise," I replied. "What is it you want to say? You know, it's been a long time—a lifetime, almost—since all that happened down there." Surely I had seen her before, but couldn't yet put a face with the smooth voice that reminded me of the mellowing effect of good wine.

"I read everything you wrote, and kept much of it," she said. "But everything didn't come out at the trials. There's a lot you don't know."

"Perhaps not," I countered. "But what does it matter? It's long over."

She persisted. "Yes, it's been many years, and those who knew most about everything have taken it to their grave, including my husband. In the time I have left, I want you to know it, too. I live at Bladon Springs—maybe you remember—a little way south of Butler. Will you come? Is next Wednesday a good time? About two?"

I glanced at the calendar. "Yes, I'll come," I replied, surprised that I would agree so quickly. But reporters play hunches, and this was the person—the mysterious other woman—whose name and reputation were dragged through the mud of the trials, who was branded as causing her rival's murder, but who was never called to testify or ever came to court that I knew. Sometimes my hunches had paid; often not. I would check this one out.

"I live at 610 First Street, on the east edge of town. I'll be waiting. And thank you."

· · · · · · · · · ·

Chapter 3

In the week between the call and this drive another thought welled up again that I had long lived with, but too often repressed. Personally and professionally, I have dealt with life's wrong turns—including the several I have caused—just by accepting them, showing few feelings, closing a door and moving on, seldom looking back. That's how I grew up.

That is part of why this story was a turning point for me. Once I wrote, "Why did Tomlinson—in the twenty-four hours after his wife's death—give four answers to [her] whereabouts? . . . Why did he wait four days to tell of the shooting, which he said was an accident? Why did he give a fish fry, and invite couples to his home, on January 30, the day he later said he buried

Jo Dell in an abandoned well?" The man toted heavy baggage to his show-down with justice, I once thought. And at the time I carried plenty myself.

I WAS FOUR WHEN my mother abandoned me and her marriage, and moved away from my Florida birthplace, back to Birmingham, her hometown. Grandmother-father-stepmother raised me for eight years, but when I decided at twelve that I wanted to live with my mother, my father put me on the Dixie Flier to Birmingham and watched the overnight train carry me out of his life. For twelve more years I just didn't exist; through high school and college, marriage, work, the birth of two sons. The few times he wrote he would sign the letter, "A. R. Buchan," as if it was business correspondence. I don't remember ever getting a phone call. I had hurt him deeply, and damned if he'd forgive me for it. So I grew up believing my daddy just didn't care.

My mother lived in a housing project in downtown Birmingham, sold dresses at Loveman's department store, and in 1941 married a poorly educated outdoors man who worked rotating shifts in the powerhouse at a steel plant. He built them a four-room concrete block bungalow across the tracks in North Birmingham, setting it back against the alley that bisected the block so he could grow a front-yard garden. He added a second bedroom for me when I came, and for a while tried to shape me in his likeness: hunter, fisherman, occasional moonshiner; bought me a shotgun. But it didn't work, none of it was me, which he resented. I was in my senior play. His comment about it, "not worth a shit." But he liked that I could sing country songs and play the guitar he had bought me at a pawn shop one Christmas. He'd put me on the back of a flatbed truck when country music personality Joe Rumore brought his radio show out to the neighboring O. Z. Hall Ford sales lot. He wanted me to become a singer up there in Nashville, to give him something about me to brag on. Wishful thinking. In an adolescent decision I have long regretted, I let him and my mother talk me into adopting his name. That, to my father, was the ultimate insult that burned any remaining bridges. I considered changing it back as an adult, but my career was built as Anderson. So I didn't. My sons did, and I was glad when they asked.

Both my mother and stepfather had affairs during my teenage years, and one night he waited in that concrete block house holding a loaded sixteen-gauge, hoping her lover would come around. Her affair was with a gambler who ran a nearby pool room. He and his wife were longtime friends of ours. When my stepfather refused me his black Packard sedan for dating, Claude, the friend, let me drive his sporty hard top in exchange for favors. My stepfather's affair was with someone down in Panama City, Florida, where he would go to deep sea fish, among other things. I never met the woman.

My mother and stepfather eventually divorced. My last words to him, on a Birmingham street corner, after the final settlement, were, "I've tried to be a good son." I never saw him again. Years later, someone told me of his death in Panama City.

Friends over time have talked proudly about growing up with their dad—ball games, vacations, each other's company, which triggered no such recollections in me. School, and work that started at age fourteen, replaced what passed for home life. An average student in both high school and college, nonetheless I excelled as newspaper editor at both levels, and was senior class president in high school and college. My steady girl and I married as college juniors, which gave me the example of her sound upbringing and a strong family unit. Still, I didn't trust a relationship to last beyond someone leaving. Insecurities of always needing to prove myself and win admiration were stored deep within me.

On a Father's Day weekend, I took the initiative to reunite with my father, locating him in North Carolina, in retirement from Florida. I phoned to tell him he had two grandsons. It was a reunion with hesitant steps and without promises, but over several years, until his death, we managed a quality relationship, considering that I was the son who had left home and he was the father who had disowned me. We rarely reopened the past, cautious not to scrape wounds that would never fully heal. But he adored my two little boys, and they became the lasting bridge between us. They loved to visit granddaddy and ride the tractor around his pretty yard.

A decade later, summer 1973, hardly believing it, I watched my mother and father remarry after being apart for thirty-two years. Her third husband and his second wife had both died, and they reconnected one Christmas when, while visiting Birmingham, he was hospitalized. The ceremony occurred at a small Methodist church in Brevard, North Carolina. They had four years together in the Smoky Mountains before he died at age seventy-seven. During that period I divorced, became a part-time father to my boys, moved from a daily newspaper into public relations and magazine work, and in 1973 I, too, remarried to a captivating divorcee with three daughters.

JOURNALISM ALWAYS LAID CLAIM to me in one form or another: reporter, magazine editor, public relations director, free-lance writer, and the last fifteen years back in the daily news business as executive editor of two Alabama newspapers owned by the New York Times Company, in Florence and Tuscaloosa. I couldn't count the times, as I entered those buildings, that I would detour to walk by those sleeping sentinels, the massive presses, already loaded with tons of newsprint and waiting for the start-button to wake them. For another day I would be responsible for inking that white paper with the best stories and pictures available from all our resources. No idea what they might be, but thank God for the privilege. I never dreaded going to work. Not a day.

The calling dominated the other worthy parts of my life; wife and sons, family, church, and anything else of relevance. Living to work, ever reaching for approval and the higher bar were ingrained choices that drove me until my last night as an editor, when an unfit publisher (later fired) and I parted company.

Insecurity grew a wall between me and others that I believed would be a shield against disappointment and hurt. I wrote guidelines on my wall: don't be totally open with anyone; don't expect a lasting relationship; be self-driven, don't need anything from anyone; figure that someone will always leave in the end, and it might be you. The guidelines seemed to summarize the culture that shaped the person I grew to be, and colored many of my decisions.

This story, in particular. was formative. It seasoned me against criticism and rejection, and I grew more confident in myself and my work. Years later

I realized that the experience had worn down my wall to let me examine my baggage and understand myself better. I haven't finished yet: why my mother left me, why my parents divorced and what else loosed all that followed. I never asked them; now they are dead.

IT MAY SEEM ODD, but as an impressionable teenager I found degrees of solace and security in the newsroom of Alabama's largest newspaper. Reporters and editors, mostly older men, liked the energetic copy boy who showed up every Saturday by seven, worked a twelve-hour shift, retrieved coffee and doughnuts from the first floor lunchroom, sent edited stories to composing, occasionally took obituaries and on football weekends organized the scores for Sunday's edition, among countless other duties. I marveled at those with the skills to produce printed pages from blank newsprint. I wanted to learn how to do it.

Some of those men had women on the side, drank like fish, and would work with a cigarette or cigar on their lips. Perhaps the best writer of them all was our sports editor, who had tucked the kid under his awesome talents and taught him the basics of sound reporting. He wrote me a letter at a pivotal point in my youth. What he said included, *You grew because you worked at it, and you must continue to do so in all the good years lying ahead of you. The only limits will be those which you place upon yourself.* I later lost that friend. He followed the path walked by his own father, suicide. Tormented by inherited depression, he shot himself at home, just back from a road assignment.

When the elevator opened on the second floor, I saw fulfillment. It was a spacious room, six rows of desks on either side of a center aisle, on each desk a black Underwood. Executives' offices and particular departments lined the perimeter, editors worked at the front, and two six-foot floor fans flanking the elevator doors would blow away anything not weighted down. I was drawn to that life and to the camaraderie of those men and the few women among them. They became mentors and most encouraged me. If work sent them away, I was confident they would return. I became as dependent upon those relationships as any other. In hindsight it was what I needed, but the rear view is oftentimes the clearest picture.

WHAT DOES IT MATTER NOW?

Going back to the Tomlinson story won't answer that question, but as I drove I thought it might help me fill other gaps. Or, like many hunches I've played, it may prove to be a dead end. Regardless, I'm here, at the address. As if posing for a spring photograph, she is rocking gently in a swing hanging from the ceiling of a full-width, columned, shiny white front porch accented by urns of graceful ferns and brilliant red geraniums.

Sarah Tomlinson, I thought, talk to me.

. . . .

Chapter 4

Sarah met me on the steps and, gripping my hand gently, said, "After all these years we meet." I looked into warm brown eyes and the easy smile of an attractive, small woman—close to my age, I guessed—whose facial lines were holding firm and seemed relaxed, considering the nature of our meeting. Her chestnut brown hair, tinged with gray, was cut short for the long summer ahead. She wore a scoop-neck blue sundress that hinted of cleavage, and a choker gold necklace from which two entwined hearts hung daintily. The second Mrs. Tomlinson would still turn heads, mine included.

"My call surprised you, but I'm glad you decided to come," she said as we sat, she in the swing, I in an oversized rocking chair.

"I was intrigued by the call, and it was worth the drive just to finally meet you," I answered, not saying what else I was thinking, ". . . but tell me something I don't know already."

"Excuse me for a moment. I've made lemonade. Let me get it," she said.

Sarah Tomlinson was no more to me than a vaguely familiar face, someone you think you might have met somewhere. Instinctively, I wondered if she would really tell all she knew, or play a polite, ladylike game on the occasion of a new face visiting. Alone for that moment, another image flashed into focus in my brain, long tucked away inside my wall. For an instant, I could see and hear Lindsey. I even looked around expectantly, but as a ghost vaporizes, just that quickly her image was gone.

Sarah returned with a frosty pitcher and tall glasses. As she poured, I said, earnestly, "Thanks for the refreshment. Now that we've met, I'm anxious to hear your story." Such disarming courtesy nearly always served me well, and co-workers sometimes teased me as being a "silver lips."

We sipped icy lemonade, chatted idly, and could have been neighbors whiling away a warm afternoon. Then her face turned from soft to serious. "My husband died May 23, 1979. He was just fifty-five. Another time, I'll take you to his grave. It's out in the country, far from where Jo Dell is buried. I, too, will be with him one day. I moved back here after his death.

"I was a pretty young widow, mid-twenties, slender, shoulder-length brown hair, and a figure that I knew men talked about. My husband, Kenneth, was an independent logger and had died in a tractor accident. Left me to raise our three little girls on a pittance of life insurance and little else. That he was working on John Ed's land didn't mean anything. I didn't know John Ed at the time.

"Then it just happened. I took up with a married man who had a reputation, who pleasured me as no one ever had. Willingly, I became his other woman, with his promise of a future together. That decision defied local behavior, or that's what they said. I didn't care.

"John Ed was very sure of himself. He knew he could catch most any woman's eye. Lean, muscular, six feet and a few inches tall, he favored his father, Mr. John. The woods had given him a rugged look to go with his tousled dark hair, hazel eyes, and the easy smile and hearty laugh that were the best of his nature. Khaki shirt and pants, work boots and a tractor cap were his trademark wardrobe, except Sunday. He lived for logging and a good time. Held his whiskey better than any man I'd ever known.

"I knew he'd been married for fourteen years, and had seen him, Jo Dell, and their four kids plenty of times. So what? I thought. If he wanted me, it was mutual, and I was his for the taking. We couldn't keep the affair quiet for very long—not in this county, not who he was—and everything seemed to explode in the winter of 1959 when Jo Dell was shot dead, left in a well, and John Ed was charged with murder and put in jail. In no time talk spread that I was the cause of it all."

I interrupted—"Were you?"—having never heard any of this from Sarah herself.

"Everyone said so, behind my back and even to my face. 'The whore who broke up his family, the bitch who didn't shrink from murder.' The Sunday hypocrites had their way, but I shrugged them off and went about my business. Held my head up and looked straight back into their pious eyes. The county consumed itself with gossip and lies, mostly about me. No sympathy for anyone except Jo Dell and her children. I hated it for his kids, too, motherless and all, and for what my kids were hearing. But I believed what John Ed told me the first time I saw him in jail.

"'I'm innocent, Sarah, I swear.' He held my hands through the bars and looked straight at me. 'It was an accident, honest to God! We were arguing over the divorce, really going at each other. She took my rifle from the truck and pointed it at me; said I'd never have the children. She was going to shoot me. I grabbed at the rifle and we struggled for it. It went off and she fell dead.'

"Mr. Anderson, of course I believed him. Why wouldn't I? His heart was filled with love for me and our children. He never would have ruined our hopes and plans for a future together by killing Jo Dell deliberately. But everything we had and wanted seemed to be crumbling. I couldn't think straight for a long time, but even if I had, I still couldn't have imagined how awful the future would prove to be for everyone touched by the killing and all that followed."

Sarah's voice gradually had softened as if she had begun speaking to herself. Her face grew tired, and she shifted her gaze from me to the expanse of green lawn and toward the quiet street. Leaning back in the swing she closed her eyes, took a deep breath, and sipped her lemonade, as if resting her soul for the remainder of a painful journey.

Chapter 5

On a freezing evening of February 1, 1959, John Ed sat at his mother's polished oak dining room table with her and his brother. He said, voice trembling, "Bill, mama, Jo Dell is dead. She's not at the beach house. She's in the woods down the highway, in a well. I put her there four days ago."

Probate Judge William Tomlinson took a quick breath, not believing what he was hearing. His eyes widened and his mouth opened, but he couldn't say anything for several seconds. Rose Tomlinson moaned in agony. Finally, the chief public official of Henderson County spoke with soft intensity. "My God, John Ed! What happened? Tell us what happened."

"It was an accident," his younger brother by four years replied, leaning forward and trying to compose himself. "I had found her with a man at a motel in Citronelle that morning. We left her car there and were driving back, arguing. We turned off the road to have it out. She got the rifle that I keep in the truck, and I thought she was going to shoot me. I grabbed for it and we struggled. It went off and she was shot dead."

Bill Tomlinson sat rigidly in an antique cherry dining chair, arms folded, stunned at what he was hearing. *Jo Dell? Cheap motel? No!* But his mind was racing and instinctively he went to the closest phone and dialed. "Bill Tomlinson here. I need the sheriff now."

When a Tomlinson called, Sheriff Lonnie Hutton moved. In twenty minutes, lights flashing, he had sped to Rose's house in Silas.

Typically composed, collected and smoothly diplomatic, Bill Tomlinson at this moment was pale, drawn and blunt. "Lonnie, there's been an awful accident. Jo Dell is dead."

Hutton responded in a whisper. *Shit!*

The judge continued, "She and John Ed were out in the woods over the weekend. She was shot and killed. He dropped her in a well and covered her up. A terrible decision made worse by the tragedy. I have just been told all this."

"Whereabouts is she?" Hutton asked, looking at John Ed.

He answered, "Out in the Tom Everett tract. The well's out there."

"You gotta go with me now," said the sheriff. Bill Tomlinson nodded his permission, and they walked outside to Hutton's car. John Ed got in the back seat, where prisoners sat, and they went to the county jail in Butler. They walked in, past the night deputy without a word, and back to the four empty cells. "In here," Hutton said, unlocking a door. As he left the jail, Hutton told his deputy sternly, "What you've seen don't leave this office."

THE LATE AFTERNOON SUN was hiding behind a thick blanket of clouds being pushed onward by a sharp northwest wind. Waning daylight slipped away quickly on this February 2. By dusk the temperature was in the forties and a misty drizzle had begun. Before long, sleet mixed with the rain. And the plan to recover Jo Dell Tomlinson quickly materialized.

John Ed was let out after his supper so he could lead a group out to the site. There were nine: the widower, his brother, Hutton and deputy Horace Ford, funeral home director Uriah Park, and four uneasy Negro diggers that Hutton had rounded up. They arrived in the judge's truck, the sheriff's sedan, the four-door belonging to one of the blacks, and Park's station wagon, which doubled as a hearse at times. They followed John Ed's light to a jagged hole that looked to be three or four feet in diameter.

Above them a cluster of tall pines moaned in the wind. Around them sleet rattled through branches and onto shivering bushes. Their boots sank slightly into thickening mud. Their kerosene lamps and flashlights illumined the opening.

"She's in there," John Ed said softly.

It was about 10 P.M. The sleet slacked a bit. With a spitting camp fire and the lamps piercing the darkness, the diggers, working in pairs, began removing the mud in the well a shovel full at a time. Scared near to death, and spooked to be searching for a dead body, they dug steadily, filling pails that were dumped, and finally lowering a crude wooden ladder into the depth to dig deeper into the slime. When one pair stopped to rest and get warm around the fire, the other pair replaced them.

Just past midnight, somebody hit something solid. "Careful, now," said Bill Tomlinson and the sheriff, almost as one, as if what was there was alive.

Gradually the form appeared, submerged half in dirty water, half in mud. Looping a rope around a leg after several attempts, the diggers pulled her slowly out of the muck; a gruesome sight so caked in filth as to almost be unrecognizable.

"Lawd hep us!" the diggers gasped. Trembling, they backed away into the cold shadows, away from the fire, not wanting to see the awful doings any closer.

John Ed stood silent and didn't move, his face as solemn as stone. His brother whispered, "God in heaven!" She was laid on the ground, wrapped in plastic sheeting, and zipped into a body bag by Hutton and Ford, then lifted into the station wagon.

As rain doused their fire, the group went back to their vehicles, working no more at the well site, just glad to leave a place whose horror, to a man, would haunt them for years. Park headed south to Mobile and the regional hospital, where the body would be washed and the state medical examiner would perform an autopsy to formally determine the cause of death. And, finally, Mrs. John Ed Tomlinson would be brought home to Butler, to the Riggins Funeral Home, for further preparation. Plans would be made for the viewing and funeral at her church, First Methodist, while the investigation of what had actually happened was begun.

. . . .

Chapter 6

The funeral was a countywide event, same as the fair and the homecoming game. It drew a cross-section of the whole of Henderson County. Many knew her, many more didn't but came anyway out of sympathy and curiosity—whites and blacks, those educated and well-to-do, and those who weren't; shift workers at the paper mill and nine-to-fivers, those who earned a pay check and the monthly recipients of welfare-by-mail. It prompted a few dozen of the regulars who shopped at the popular Wilkes General Store on the downtown square, which Jo Dell's mother ran, to dig deep and chip in a dollar each for a wreath of white roses and black ribbon that hung on the double doors just under the "Closed" sign.

Cheeks rouged, lips discreetly red, auburn hair combed just the way she wore it, her expression peaceful, the corpse of Jo Dell Tomlinson lay in a copper-looking metal, open casket that was all but encircled by stanchions of sprays and baskets of blooms. Agnes Richey, self-appointed church pianist, played from her limited repertoire of hymns—"In the Garden" and "Softly and Tenderly," among them—to the slow shuffle of curious and mourners whose line filled the center aisle, stretched across the narthex and out into the sunshine of a rare pretty February afternoon.

"She was a wonderful mother and such a good soul. Why, everybody loved her."

"I just thank the Lord she's here and out of that awful well. How in heaven's name could he have done that? It's the worst thing I've ever heard of."

"She's so pretty in that navy suit; it's just the right color; and I like the way they did her hair. Isn't it sweet, she's wearing her WMU pin. And I reckon that's a family ring on her right hand. Probably her mother's."

Such comments flowed softly from one individual, one family, one group to another along the continuous column that took two hours to pass the thick brown brocade curtain, pause at the casket and pay its respects—with a gentle hug, grasping her hand or a whispered comment—to Annie Pearl Wilkes, who would bury her thirty-six year-old, only child later in the day. As if guarding these proceedings, she sat in the minister's chair, almost within reach of the casket, under control but bearing weariness beyond her fifty-nine years. Brother Henry Harris, the First Church minister, stood by Mrs. Wilkes, a surrogate family member in his preaching dark suit, greeting the visitors as Mr. Wilkes would have done had he been alive. Solemn-faced officials of Riggins Funeral Home closed the curtain just before 2 P.M. to give the family a final minute or two. Mrs. Wilkes stroked Jo Dell's brow, caressed her cheeks, then closed her eyes and bowed her head.

He wouldn't call it a congregation because it wasn't Sunday church, but Brother Harris, as he stepped toward the pulpit, thought to himself, "Lord, I wish I could see a crowd like this other than at Easter or at such a heart-breaking funeral." Annie Wilkes remained in her chair next to the pulpit, front and center, gazing out into the sanctuary, the symbol of irreplaceable loss.

"Beloved family members, sisters, brothers and friends," Harris said, eying the Negroes clustered in a back corner, "grief is etched into our souls today, etched into our hearts because a dear woman, admired and respected by hundreds of people in our community, lies before us, her earthly life ended." Lowering the pitch of his voice to his best stage whisper, and flicking a glance at the Tomlinson family members filling the first pew, he then added, "And she shouldn't be here." Gathering himself again, he continued. "But our Jesus, who himself rose from the dead, calms us in these moments, saying 'I am the resurrection and the life. She who believes in me shall never die.'"

For fifteen more minutes, guided by Mrs. Wilkes's suggestions, he expounded on Jo Dell's virtues as a wife faithful to her marriage vows, a woman committed to fulfilling the needs of her husband and four children, a leader in community and school, and someone who loved the Lord with her whole heart. Mrs. Wilkes nodded to the certainty of his remarks, and blotted tears as Agnes Benson, soprano in the choir, sang "Precious Lord," her voice quavering with vibrato and emotion.

Around 4 P.M., the sun thinning, long shadows reaching down from the old oaks that embraced the small cemetery, and the breeze chilling those gathered, Jo Dell's casket was lowered into an opening much more respectable than the one she had been pulled from a week earlier. She would rest in the Wilkes family plot in Memorial Gardens, a popular space within the Butler city limits. Her father was already lying there, in the rectangular space measured for three graves and edged with red brick. As this burial occurred, Mrs. Wilkes, in a resolute voice loud enough that the fifty or more friends could hear, said, "I'm coming soon, sweet daughter, and we'll all be together again."

"Life eternal. Jo Dell has claimed her reward," Brother Harris said at the grave. He paraphrased the assurance found in Revelation: Blessed are the dead who die in the Lord. The Spirit says they rest from their labor, and their works follow after them. Harris had book-marked one other passage of scripture, feeling led to do it for his own peace; but it went unspoken as he closed the short ceremony by shaking the hand of each member of the two families, who had finally sat together in folding chairs facing the casket—all Tomlinsons except for Mrs. Wilkes, and her sister and brother-in-law from Mobile. But one Tomlinson was absent. John Ed didn't join the mourners or the curious of his own choice. Instead, he took a nap in jail, a few blocks away.

The Old Testament verse marked by Harris, in Galatians, read, "Whatsoever a man soweth, that shall he also reap."

· · · · · · · · · ·
Chapter 7

Gus Robertson's fish camp, twenty miles out of Butler, at Bladon Springs, was closing early that raw evening. The Tombigbee River, a short walk from the main building, had been choppy all day, and by dark had turned ominous. The boats still on the water were coming in, the fishermen wet and shivering, their hopes of catching catfish, crappie and bass lost in an icy wind.

"I was out there when it all went down, and had no idea," Sarah said as we sat on her porch. "By six, we were gone. I drove to my house in Bladon Springs, and to my girls, Mary Lou, Pat, and Suzanne. I assumed John Ed was at home with his family, but I expected him to come by the next morning, as usual.

"Our affair started there at the fish camp one summer. He liked to come out there at dawn for coffee with the early guys. We met on the days I opened the place, started talking and right off he said he was sorry that my husband had died logging on his land when his tractor flipped on an incline. He always spoke kindly and left me a nice tip. Maybe he could tell by the way I warmed to his looks, the remarks, the first touches that I was hungry again for affection. He began showing interest. A woman senses the heat building.

"Fishing slowed quite a bit during wintertime, and I didn't go out there as much. So I invited him to come to my house for coffee. The rest happened pretty fast. In no time we were making love in my bedroom, before the kids woke up. It was tender but hot, if you know what I mean; the best I'd ever had. I still shiver thinking about it. But it was more than that. We fell in love; no escaping it. We couldn't help ourselves."

. . . .

Chapter 8

The working folks of Henderson County had to scratch to find a decent paycheck. There was the timber industry, backbreaking and dangerous. And the big paper mill on the outskirts of Butler. Or the chemical plants down state highway 43 on toward the coast. They could also travel an hour west, into Mississippi, for whatever prospects Meridian or Waynesboro held. Always, they could farm—usually soybeans, peanuts or cotton—as share-croppers mostly on land they rented. Black Belt soil produced strong crops.

The county's natural qualities matched others in southwest Alabama: miles of rolling plains for hunting quail, doves, deer and turkeys; the fish-rich Tombigbee flowed into the Alabama River below the county before finally emptying into the Mobile River and Mobile Bay; and thousands of scrubby acres good for little else but to nurture seedlings and grow them into lodge pole pine trees sixty feet high or more.

A young migrant came out of Mississippi and into this part of Alabama, Jonathan Tomlinson, who showed up in 1928, ten dollars in his khakis, released from home by his mama who wanted her boy to have a better life than hers. He, too, had hopes of finding prospects for a brighter future. But it was hard times over here, too, Depression and all, so he worked any job he found, boarded cheap, ate rounds of bologna and hoop cheese, and saved most of his meager earnings.

Within a year Jonathan had almost six hundred dollars hidden in his room, and began to look seriously at how much of the vast plains that stretched all around him the money would buy. Poor ground, maybe, yet out of it came those stately pine trees, nourished mostly by sweltering sun and God's rain now and then. For five dollars an acre, Mr. John, as he liked to be known, bought his first one hundred acres of young trees, and still had money hidden.

His trees grew steadily as years passed and he continued working odd jobs and keeping his seed money replenished. The road to success grew surer, too, as did his reputation for quick temper and tough action. Stories were told that he shot dead more than one man, and the local weekly once wrote that he killed a black man, tied the body to his truck, and dragged it around the town square. As his mama had taught him, Mr. John Tomlinson didn't suffer fools.

Mr. John came to court a strong-willed woman who once had told him, "I don't shy from long hours or hard work." Rose McMillan hailed from south Henderson County, the Silas community, and grew up in the long hours of a small family grocery and gas station. She married Jonathan and helped him day and night. Bossy and difficult at times—as he was—nonetheless she was smart and ran their business of buying land and growing trees. Bore him two sons, raised them strictly, had them christened Methodists. Like her or not, and some didn't, her presence increased along with his and she became perhaps the county's most important woman.

Land and trees equal money if you own enough, and the Tomlinsons did. By the 1950s they had bought or leased several thousand acres. Their decisions were making them rich, and with wealth eventually came the power to control the county and elect one of their own as probate judge. Their influence could defeat any politician they opposed, and it would decide who else would be big players, or who wouldn't.

The sons, particularly John Ed, learned early that harvesting trees wasn't complicated. It was really not much more than twelve-hour days of exhausting work with sharp saws and heavy machinery; work done by strong men who would sweat and bleed for twenty dollars a day. John Ed had taken it all in on the Saturdays he rode with his father out to the woods.

Mr. John's death of a heart attack in 1954 deprived the county of its patriarch, and cast the mantle on the sons—Bill Tomlinson, business and politics; John Ed, timber. Too young for the responsibility and lacking a business mind, John Ed succeeded with Rose's guidance. He self-appointed himself a lord of timber in southwest Alabama. No one questioned, openly.

SIX DAYS A WEEK, in good weather, blacks would gather at dawn at the feed store in Silas, and wait for the white boss to arrive in his pick-up. First business of most days.

"Mornin' men; who wants to cut trees and make money?" He'd look them over. "Climb in," he'd tell the ones he wanted. The process reminded him of stories about slave times, told by his father, when black men and women, and often children, were paraded on the auction block while buyers from the plantations eyed the build of the men, and coveted the breasts and asses of the women. Appraising the flesh walking before them, the white bosses then bargained and bought what they needed, or wanted, to work the fields, keep the house, and especially to give them pussy.

John Ed liked to know, barely one hundred years later, that he could wield some semblance of that power in the Black Belt, that statewide strip of dirt across lower Alabama that was particularly fertile for field crops. He routinely carried a dozen or so men out to the woods and left them in charge of his foreman, Woody. Strength, endurance and cash money drove the crew to work until they nearly dropped, and take only a five-minute break every three hours.

These men peed and shit in the bushes, squashed chiggers that latched onto their bodies, and killed rattlers as thick as their forearm. They pushed and pulled eight-foot saws with razor-like, inch-long teeth through pines two feet around that seemed sky-high. Then they skinned the fallen timber clean of branches and skidded them out to the trailer with six-foot sides. Most cuts and sprains were ignored. Broken bones sent them back to a doctor in Butler. The white boss hauled the crew back to Silas at six, and gave each man a twenty. Hard-earned.

Chapter 9

As the Tomlinsons grew more important, so did another local family, in other ways. The Wilkeses owned the main general store in Butler, easy to find there on the courthouse square. They sold everything from flannel shirts to souse; good location, steady traffic. Even in hard times, when money was so tight, they helped their customers. If a man couldn't pay right away, the Wilkeses would carry him over for a few weeks. Word spread and business grew. Jo Dell, their only child, worked most days after school and on Saturday. Miss Jo, as customers called her, was a pretty teenager, with warm eyes, a chatty manner and sparkling smile. Her manners and courtesy made every person feel welcome. Jo Dell and the Tomlinson brothers were in school together; she and John Ed in the same grade, Bill a senior. The brothers liked her.

But Miss Rose turned herself in another direction about Jo Dell. She was polite to the girl, but wouldn't hide the fact that she didn't care for her, and urged John Ed to date around. Maverick that he was, John Ed did the opposite, and in their senior year at county high he and Jo Dell were going steady.

"You will not marry her!" Rose told her youngest son, her tone a command, not a request. He replied, just as forcefully, "It's my life, mama. I love her, and if she'll have me, I will." Despite his mother's objection, John Ed and Jo Dell, not long out of high school, were married in the Butler Methodist Church in September 1945, as Henderson County celebrated the end of World War Two and mourned the fighting men and women who did not come back.

People mused that John Ed had married up to snare Jo Dell; but to Rose, she wasn't good enough for her boy. The marriage produced two lovely daughters and handsome twin sons, grandchildren that Rose adored despite her coldness toward their mother and to the Wilkes family, which also wasn't in her nature to conceal.

BILL TOMLINSON DIDN'T DEFY or disappoint his mother. Whereas John Ed never was much for studying and rejected the notion of college, Bill graduated from the University of Alabama, and from its law school, just as Rose wanted him to. As she hoped, he married well socially to a beauty from Meridian, Nancy Lewis; then established a Chevy dealership in Butler whose sales were high, new and used models. Most everybody sensed that if Bill developed political ambitions the family would see them fulfilled. Ultimately, he did and they were. At age twenty-eight he was elected probate judge, as a Democrat, unopposed. Nobody had the nerve or money to run against the Tomlinsons.

Bill and Nancy lived in Butler in an antebellum house with wide porches, high ceilings, and fragrant magnolias. John Ed and Jo Dell built south of town, a sprawling, brick ranch-style house set back from the highway and half hidden by pines. Rose, the family matriarch, stayed in her home in Silas after Mr. John's death. Silas was little else but a feed store, and the small grocery and gas station that she owned. She and her sons were not more than thirty minutes apart, and were as tightly knit as they were powerful. Rose made sure of it.

One of Bill's classmates in law school was Seth Yielding, who also came from Silas. Seth's father, Marcus, ran a small insurance office in Butler. The Yieldings paid their bills and tithed to the Baptist church, but didn't have much left over. Family wealth hadn't eased their only child's way through the University of Alabama. Seth chose the Capstone because he was ambitious, and paid his way as a waiter and working other part-time jobs. In his senior year, to finish on time, he borrowed three thousand dollars from a bank and paid it back in full, on time.

Seth inclined to be more like Bill. Knew him better than the younger John Ed, considered him an arms-length friend and a rival. After law school, Seth opened a law practice in Butler and soon established himself; made his parents proud, doing better than they ever had. But he still felt twinges of jealousy over Bill's wealth, him being probate judge, and the Tomlinson's social prominence.

Seth began to calculate his own chance of gaining public office and aligned himself politically in a different camp than Tomlinson. In time, he ran for circuit solicitor of the Sixth Judicial Circuit, chief lawman of four counties. He was elected as a Democrat by a large majority, and now had power and prestige to match Bill's. He also knew the Tomlinsons had not opposed him, but if they had he would have lost.

THAT FEBRUARY DAY, AS John Ed told Bill and his mother about Jo Dell, Bill could see what was coming. "You'll stand trial and Seth will prosecute. He'll be after your ass, but more than that he'll be after us, the family." He spat the words out. "You've given him his best chance to bring us down. Think on that, little brother."

· · · · · · · · · · ·

Chapter 10

"**H**ey, let's get some whiskey!" John Ed was a happy man and wanted all to know it. "I'm getting a divorce. Jo Dell's agreed to terms," he told those who'd come to his party on the day after Christmas, sounding carefree and relieved for the first time in months. The crowd of twenty or more friends was drinking beer and frying catfish at a popular hangout, Gus and Sarah's fish camp and boat landing on the Tombigbee River. A fire crackled sharply and a slender, ten-foot, long-needled pine, strung with colored lights and tinsel, still displayed season's greetings.

"Sarah, honey, how 'bout you and Barbara going to your house and getting us some whiskey," John Ed asked. "We gotta celebrate. I'm free!"

The women, close cousins, left in Sarah's fifty-six Chevy to drive the eight miles to Sarah's house. "Did you know it?" Barbara Evans asked Sarah as they rode.

"Just awhile ago he told me," she answered. "I didn't think they'd work it out. She doesn't want to give him up. But she realized that she couldn't keep him. Can't give him what I can. Ours is a real spark; actually, a pretty strong flame."

"So what's going to happen now?" Barbara asked.

"First, the divorce, with me left out of it, I hope," Sarah replied. "Then, the usual: let time pass, have the blood tests, get the license, and do it. Make decisions about where we live and all that."

"And Robert Whatley?" Barbara said. "Everyone thinks y'all will be married. You're supposedly engaged. What about him? Does he think he's still in the picture?"

"I reckon," Sarah sighed. "I'll handle Robert. He won't stand in our way."

Sarah took two fifths of Bellows bourbon from her cupboard and a fifth of the vodka she liked. It was going on 5 P.M. and the women got back to the party to see lights shining warmly through the windows of the building that served to sell bait, fishing gear and short-order food.

"All right, set 'em up," John Ed ordered. Sitting at a wooden table, he pushed aside a platter of fish and hush puppies, and started filling a dozen shot glasses. Most of the men and a few of the women gathered around eagerly reached for one. Sarah filled her own.

John Ed stood, his face a reddish hue from too much drinking over Christmas. He raised a juice glass that held twice what the shot glasses did, filled almost to the brim. "To freedom and my new life!" And he whispered, "And to my new wife." He downed the full glass as if it was water, and uttered, "Oh, yeah!" as the eighty proof hit bottom. Sarah did the same with her vodka. Everyone ate, talking and laughing mostly about the holidays and prospects for the New Year 1959. But they cursed the local Negroes who they said were joining a growing movement, and who wouldn't stay in their place. There were murmurs of having to deal with that. Then they revisited the plentiful beer and the bourbon.

Now, it was almost 8 P.M. A cold wind whipped off the river and chilled the big room whose bare pine floor and split timber walls were warmed only by the oak and hickory logs blazing in its massive stone fireplace. The crowd began drifting away, telling John Ed as they did that they hoped it all worked out. It was the right thing for friends to say, but in reality some didn't care whether it did or not. John Ed had picked the fight that was about to start.

The logs burned down, turning to crimson coals, and the last few couples sat around a table near the waning heat. His belly full of bourbon and libido heating up, John Ed took Sarah's hand and led her to a cluster of chairs closer to the fire's remains. He spoke to her softly, still holding her hand. He wanted to run a fingernail gently down her neck, and nibble an ear lobe, as he had done many times, but this place was too public. Not yet.

"I love you, baby," he said in a low voice. "Hold tight to that as things develop over the next few months. I'm going to fight for the kids, and with mama's and my brother's help I can get custody. You stay quiet and keep up your routine, no matter what is said or what happens. This is the first step toward us being together, and we're going to make it. I promise you, we'll make it."

Sarah, John Ed, and Barbara were the last to leave, about 9:30 P.M. They gathered the plates and glasses for Hester, the cleaning woman who would wash them the next morning, then they banked the dying fire and locked up. Barbara watched her friends clutch in the darkness, and wondered if their passion would survive what lay ahead.

"I feel you against me, big and hard," Sarah whispered.

"Honey, I want you bad," he replied.

"Come early tomorrow. I'll be waitin'," she said.

Sarah and Barbara left together. John Ed drove home, the bourbon, passion and cold mixing to mess with his head. He thought about Jo Dell, the kids, and the coming fight to dissolve his marriage. Uneasiness crept over him, causing him to shiver down into his bones.

· · · · · · · · · ·

Chapter 11

Comfort food called to Jo Dell. Nothing else did in the lonely house. John Ed was out with his friends, *and her,* still partying. The kids had been fed and put to bed. Etta, the good-as-gold housekeeper, had been gone since 4:30 P.M.; she didn't like to drive after dark. Neither Jo Dell's mother nor Miss Rose had called. Strange not to hear from either one, she thought.

Neither the television nor radio was on. She didn't want the noise, and had grown tired of carols on the stereo. Lamps lit the living room, den, and foyer, but cast creepy shadows on the walls. The Christmas tree, a spruce whose star touched the ten-foot ceiling—decorated for three weeks—was dry and dropping needles, yet still glowed cheerfully with blinking lights and favorite ornaments, but she didn't notice. The kitchen was bright, but the dining room was dark. The house was spooky quiet, and in it Jo Dell was not only alone, she felt lonely, distanced from her husband, the family, even the children and life.

She hadn't gone with John Ed because she didn't feel like drinking and chatting, or being pleasant—especially to Sarah—even though she would know everybody who gathered at the fish camp. She'd seen enough of them during the holidays and wasn't in the mood for any more racy jokes and racist conversation. Just my husband alone for an evening, she said to herself. Kids asleep, fire burning, tree lights shining, wine and bourbon, casual conversation. Maybe the start of new closeness between them that she knew was slipping away.

John Ed wouldn't have it. He had told her, "Aw, honey, I want to step out for a little while, loosen up, have a few drinks with our friends. Too much family-family over Christmas. I need to socialize some. If you don't care to go, okay. I won't be late." With that, he tossed on a car coat over his khaki shirt and pants, was out the door and gone in the pick-up. That was four hours ago.

Something else gnawed even deeper. John Ed was pressing her for a divorce, ready to throw away fourteen years together and the family, the life they had built. She resisted his pressure, but in the times it had come up had said point blank, out of self-protection, that he would never get the children except under a strict visitation directive.

"Forget about it!" she had told her husband. "Your family's power and money don't matter. They won't help you, because if you fight me on that I'll tell the court about your girlfriend. Don't think I won't, and your charade will be over."

He had answered softly, "We'll see about that, Jo Dell."

It wasn't mentioned again over the holidays, but the schism between them was widening, the marriage falling apart, and Jo Dell felt powerless to stop it against the pull of another woman.

Familiar things became solace that night. She changed into her favorite flannel gown and light blue chenille robe; then grilled a sandwich thick with melted cheddar cheese and added cold sweet milk, dill spear, and slice of dark fruitcake. After days of rich food, the tasty variation was welcome. She ate in the kitchen's brightness, and was almost finished when she heard the pick-up roll to a stop in the carport.

"I was lonesome tonight, you should have been here." She spoke without looking up, and saw his cap and jacket land on a chair.

He replied in a voice slurred by whiskey, "I had a good time without you. It was a good party."

"And your girlfriend was there?"

"Sarah was there. She's nothin' more than a good friend to both of us, and you know it."

"You're lyin', John Ed."

"Shut up about it," he said, and left the room.

John Ed stripped to his underwear and went to bed in the guest room, several steps away from his and Jo Dell's bedroom, where she would sleep. But he couldn't relax and drop off into peaceful sleep. He had lied at the party, lied to Sarah. Jo Dell hadn't agreed to anything. Their situation was in knots. It had to be untangled, once and for all, and it was up to him to figure it out and get it done. Alone, in the darkness, he thought about it and began to form a plan. He muttered to the darkness, "She ain't gonna stand in my way." And, finally, he slept.

Ten feet away, down the hall, Jo Dell laid in their bed, where they rarely slept together any more, her mind cluttered with her future and that of her children. She knew, beyond a doubt, that the Tomlinsons would band together against her if she fought the divorce and child custody. They would run her down as an unfit mother because of her problems since the twins' birth, and try to drive her away from the children in shame. Her body shook with silent sobs and tears filled her eyes. Then a biblical image took shape: she, as David, against the Goliaths of Henderson County.

Instinctively, Jo Dell prayed about the overwhelming odds. "Oh Lord, give me the courage to fight for what's right, the strength for the approaching battle, and the faith to trust that with you on my side, I will win. My little children need me more than anyone, and I need them, as well, to be the whole person I want to be. So I ask, Lord, for you to guide me through each step of this ordeal, empower me with wisdom and sound judgment, and may your will be done. Thank you for hearing this prayer. Amen." Feeling calmer and more comforted than she had all evening, Jo Dell went softly to check on the twins, Johnny and Jesse, and the older girls, Melissa and Margaret. Back in bed, she quickly fell asleep

THE REST OF THAT week and through the New Year holiday, John Ed and Jo Dell seemed to be the typical married couple. He was particularly careful, calling Sarah only if he was out, to say how much he was missing her. He went to her house only once, the morning after the party. Jo Dell bundled up the girls for a day trip to Tuscaloosa, lunch at Morrison's and a Disney matinee at the Bama Theater. The family went to church together, and to Rose's house afterward for lunch with Bill and Nancy.

John Ed and Jo Dell considered spending New Year's Eve at the beach house on Dauphin Island, but the weather turned bleak and cold, and they decided not to make the three-hour drive. Instead, they stayed home, built a fire, listened on the radio to Guy Lombardo's orchestra serenade the new year at the Roosevelt Room in New York City, and drank a bottle of vintage cabernet sauvignon. They retired before midnight to the same bed, exchanged a ritual kiss goodnight, but did not make love. They had not had sex in weeks. Neither did they exchange a Happy New Year.

. . . .

Chapter 12

Tensions mounted again in mid-January. John Ed was leaving before sunup to see Sarah; Jo Dell had resigned herself to the deteriorating situation, and felt trapped in part by winter doldrums, and unable to break loose from the house and children, or from her unhappiness. Issues flamed the night that Rose came for supper and to keep the children, while Jo

Dell went to a band mother's meeting at the high school.

Rose found her daughter-in-law nervous and despondent, cranky with the kids, and self-absorbed. The onset of depression, she thought. John Ed would not be home for supper, Jo Dell said angrily. "He's out at the hunting club with the boys. See, Mama Rose, he doesn't even care that you're here."

Rose measured her part of the conversation carefully, so as not to appear overly warm and sympathetic toward Jo Dell. She had no motherly feelings for the woman, and would not be hypocritical about it. Henderson County gossiped cruelly about hypocrisy, even more so than one's perceived family problems.

"He's basically the same man now that you married fourteen years ago," she said. "That's not to say there haven't been changes. We all change to some degree as we grow older. I certainly have, and, I've noticed, you have as well, particularly since last fall. Is it just the kind of hormonal fluctuation that some women have as they approach menopause, or is something more serious wrong?"

Jo Dell wasn't sure what Rose knew or didn't know, what John Ed might have told his mother, or what Rose suspected about the marriage from her own observations. She feared that any of these scenarios could be used against her in a custody battle; that alone made her wary as she listened to Rose. Also, having experienced Rose's coolness and aloofness for years, she could read her well.

Looking away as if in thought, Jo Dell didn't reply right away, and when she did evaded the question. "I'll be late for the meeting if I don't go on. We'll talk further when I get back." That would give her time to think carefully.

She wouldn't say too much and would try to bait Rose a little to learn some of what she knew. That was Jo Dell's plan as she arrived home about 9:30 P.M. To her surprise and slight disappointment, she found the children tucked in and Rose already in bed in the guest bedroom. She was just finishing a cup of tea in the den when she heard John Ed's pick-up in the carport.

"How was it? A real macho night, I'm sure. Well, Rose missed you, and was surprised you'd leave when you knew she was coming."

"Damn, I forgot she'd be here. But I had told you this supper was on; you knew it."

"Obviously, you forgot that I had to go out, too. Or it didn't matter. You know, John Ed, you act increasingly like everything in this house revolves around you. But it doesn't."

"Just shut up, will you? I don't want to get into it with you." John Ed still felt the warmth of Sarah's body from the hour they'd had together after he left the hunt club early. He'd said Jo Dell wasn't feeling well and he'd best get home early. Damned if he would let an argument chill the glow of sex with Sarah.

She didn't stop. "We're going to get into it because I want to. We have to! I can't stomach this pretense any more." Angry and trembling, she whirled and left the room. He stood in his tracks, muscles tense, face grim, thinking maybe she'd gone to the bathroom, and that she'd be right back.

She was, carrying John Ed's sixteen-gauge, double barreled shotgun, loaded, the way he kept it. With a steady hand, she leveled it at her husband.

· · · · · · · · · ·

Chapter 13

"**W**hat the hell are you doing? God Almighty! Put it down!" John Ed shouted.

Jo Dell looked hard into his deceiving, lying eyes. Voice firm and rising, she said, "If you want your whore, by God, you can have her! If she's worth wrecking our marriage and losing your children, take her! But make no mistake, John Ed, our divorce will be on my terms. And you'd better be ready to give up a lot of money, this house, and the children!"

Before John Ed could reply, his mother burst into the room, awakened by the shouting. "My God, what's happening? Jo Dell, what in heaven's name are you doing? Don't shoot him, for God's sake!"

Not shifting her gaze from her husband, Jo Dell answered, softly and ominously. "This has been coming on a while, Rose. John Ed doesn't want me any more. He's taken up with Sarah. She's his newest whore. Fucks her every chance he gets. Probably did tonight. In case you haven't noticed, we haven't had a relationship, much less a marriage, in months. He looks right through me as if I don't exist, or doesn't look at me at all. We hardly ever talk. I don't know what he wants from me, I really don't know. But I'll tell you this: I'm through being the brunt of his games. I've told him tonight that he can have his whore, but that he'll lose a lot in the process, including the children. I'll take them and be gone. You'll never find me. And if he thinks I'm not serious, this shotgun says I am."

John Ed pleaded with his wife. "I'm beggin' you, put the gun down. Please! For God's sake, somebody could be killed!" He slowly extended an arm toward Jo Dell. She didn't lower the weapon.

"Please!" he whispered, and grasped the barrel gently, not forcefully or threateningly. Jo Dell didn't flinch or change expression, but relaxed her grip on the stock and the trigger guard. John Ed eased the shotgun from her grasp and took it across the room. He leaned it on a book case. As calmly as if she had just served tea to guests, Jo Dell turned to leave the room. She looked back at her husband and said, "This doesn't end anything. It's just the beginning."

MARGARET, THIRTEEN AND THE oldest child, stood at the door to her room. "Mom," she sobbed as Jo Dell held her, "the shouting woke me up. It sounded awful."

"Daddy and Mother had an argument," Jo Dell said. "Adults sometimes do, and it can be very unpleasant. It may happen again, but, regardless, I will look out for you and your sister and brothers. I love you all more than anything, and you are the most important persons in my life. Whatever happens, that is the truth. Let's go to bed now. We can talk more in the morning. I'll sleep with you, if you want."

"Yes, please."

Chapter 14

"John Ed, she scared me to death. Is it that serious?" Rose asked when they were alone in the den. "Is there going to be a divorce?"

"I think so, mama," he replied. "Jo Dell hasn't been a wife to me, really, since the twins were born, and particularly since her surgery in November. She's fidgety and nervous, upset much of the time. I've had to find companionship outside of the marriage. She didn't give me a choice. I met Sarah—she's a widow—and have become very attached to her. But what happened tonight came totally as a shock. I never thought she'd go off the rails like that. I had hoped we could work things out, but not now."

Rose heard John Ed's lame rationale for his affair and dismissed it. Quickly, she calculated exactly how she would respond, and precisely what she wanted him to hear. She spoke as coolly as if this was a business arrangement. "Son, I'm sorry as I can be. It's never pleasant when a marriage ends. I know you'll provide for Jo Dell, as well you should. But after witnessing that outburst tonight, I believe she is dangerously unstable. For the children's sake, they must stay with you, and we must not lose sight of that fact."

"Thank you, mama." He unplugged the Christmas tree and they went to bed. John Ed slept alone, the scent of his woman all over his body.

The previous night was not mentioned at breakfast the next morning. Jo Dell cooked eggs and sausage for John Ed, who had decided it best not to go to Sarah's. He left quickly after eating, saying he had errands and business in Butler. Rose had toast and coffee, gathered her things, hugged Jo Dell loosely, said, "call me," and went home. The children were sleeping late, which was welcomed.

Left alone, Jo Dell poured new coffee and replayed the episode in her mind, hardly believing that she had actually shown such strength, resolve and plain guts in that confrontation, when it wasn't her nature to draw a line and take a stand in her own behalf. "Who would believe it?" she thought, a slight smile crossing her lips. Soon the girls were up, hungry, and the twins needed feeding, which moved their mother into more routine matters. Etta would arrive at most any time.

John Ed knew now that his wife would be adversarial and a tough fighter, but wasn't about to let her take command of the situation, or exercise any leverage with respect to a settlement or the children. He had decided during a mostly sleepless night to act decisively.

· · · · · · · · · ·

Chapter 15

Stuart Putman, who said he could handle anyone's legal business successfully, had a particular reputation for divorces. His office was two blocks from the courthouse, on Reed Street. Low brow work like that didn't gain him access to the finest circles of his profession in Henderson County, who gave Sunday afternoon parties on their big boats on the river, and who could go missing on a pretty Friday to play golf at what passed for a country club nine-hole course. But Putman took his snubs in stride, straight to his bank, in fact, where his accounts reflected that divorces, bankruptcies, repossessions and other minor messy work paid pretty damn well.

"Mornin', Stuart," John Ed said, finding the secretary out on an errand and the man himself at a cluttered desk with peeling veneer. The room sported cheap paneling, linoleum flooring, three chairs that looked like they had been salvaged from a dentist's office, and window blinds. Nothing matched, including the occupant.

"Mornin' yourself, John Ed, and a belated Happy New Year, my friend." Stuart was in worn tan corduroy pants, blue plaid sport shirt, and black cardigan sweater. He wouldn't show himself in court today. "I must say, you've surprised me with this visit. I don't owe you, do I?"

John Ed got right to the point. He wasn't in the mood to make small talk. "I need your help, Stuart," he said. "Me and Jo Dell are getting a divorce. I want you to represent me and get me a fair settlement. I also want custody of my kids."

At the last statement Stuart bit into his unlit, hand-rolled, imported cigar and sat upright in the room's only comfortable seat. "I hope you've got some ammunition, John Ed. And I also hope you're clean."

"Clean, I reckon, is relative. Jo Dell thinks I'm screwing around with Sarah Davis, which I am, but she hasn't caught us. And she can't prove anything. As for ammunition, she pulled a shotgun on me last night and said that everything would be on her terms. My mother was there. She heard it and saw it all."

"I think we can work with that," Stuart said confidently, suddenly more relaxed. "I do, indeed. But you and Sarah need to stay apart publicly till this is over. We don't want Jo Dell producing any evidence. And don't y'all separate unless it's her who walks out. When do you want me to file?"

"Any time. Soon. I want it over with."

Stuart stood, extended his right hand over the desk, and the two shook hands. He liked Jo Dell, and had always thought that John Ed's best day was when she married him. But business was business. And this divorce, he thought, was the boost his scatter gun practice needed; also, the bombshell whose shock waves would shake up Henderson County for years.

"I'll handle it," he said firmly.

· · · · · · · · · · ·

Chapter 16

Annie Wilkes answered the phone. "Mama," said Jo Dell, "could you come over today? The kids would like to see you. I would, too."

Mrs. Wilkes heard noticeable anxiety in her daughter's voice and knew immediately that something was wrong. "It's ten o'clock, now," she replied. "I'll come about twelve and we'll have a sandwich together. All right?"

"Good, mama; I'll see you then."

Over hot tea and sandwiches of leftover turkey, Jo Dell told her mother everything. They embraced and cried together.

"Jo Dell," said Annie, "you've been wronged in the worst way, and good men don't treat their wives like that. People who know you, our friends and neighbors, will judge John Ed for what he's done, and they will see you for the fine Christian woman you are—faithful wife, loving mother, loyal to your church, leader at the girls' school, someone widely respected and loved. Your God-given strengths will see you through the ugliness you'll face. They, and the Lord." Annie then added a warning, "But you'll need a strong lawyer. John Ed will fight, and the family will be determined. Someone like Jerry Wade, up in Livingston. Family man, Christian, good reputation, won't be intimidated in court."

"How do you know him, mama?"

"Friends of ours up there hired him for a civil matter, and he won. They speak highly of him. I'll get his phone number, if you like."

"Yes, ma'am, I'll talk to him."

Two mornings later, John Ed already gone out, the girls in school and Etta at the house, Jo Dell drove alone to meet Jerry Wade. "If John Ed asks, tell him I'm out for a little while," she told the housekeeper.

It was just over an hour's drive north, giving her time to ponder her and the children's future, also the uncertainty so deeply entrenched that she was prompted to level a shotgun at her husband. "I'll tell Mr. Wade everything," she said aloud to herself. "I have nothing to hide or to be ashamed of."

Jo Dell was back home by 4 p.m., feeling more secure and strengthened than in months, particularly by the attorney's last words to her: "Mrs. Tomlinson, I'll take care of you." No one had said that in so long. As she drove, she said aloud, "Mr. Wade, you're just who I need."

Neither wife nor husband mentioned their legal steps to the other. Instead, they tried to maintain an air of civility and normality for the children. Often the house echoed with empty conversation that had neither meaning nor purpose. Meanwhile, Jo Dell told her mother, who responded, "We'll stand together. You will win. It's God's will." And John Ed told Sarah that the process had started—the truth this time—but swore her to secrecy.

Chapter 17

The Thursday morning of January 29, 1959, came with heavy frost, forbidding overcast, and thirty degrees. At breakfast, John Ed chanced a new strategy on his wife. Carefully made and well rehearsed in his head, the plan was ready.

"Could you go with me out to the woods?" he asked Jo Dell.

"What for?"

"There's some acreage near the Everett tract, close to an old well, that I'd like to plant in seedlings. Wanted you to look at it, too. It's nearly time to set them out, so we need to decide."

"All right, but you'll do it regardless, I'm sure."

They left in the pick-up and headed southwest on state highway forty-three. Some five miles below Silas, John Ed turned onto an unmarked dirt road, rutted and muddy from winter rains. He went a quarter mile, then drove through a tractor opening in a barbed wire fence that ran alongside the road, and bounced the truck across an open field matted with winter-withered sedge grass. At the edge of a thick stand of mature pines, he stopped.

"The field and beyond is what I had in mind. Should be fifty acres or so." As he spoke, they got out, zipping their coats higher, boots squishing into soft earth and rotting pine needles.

"State forestry plant them?" she asked.

"I think so. The county agent should work things out. One day our kids will harvest them."

"Fine. Suits me," she said, turning to get in the truck. She stopped abruptly when John Ed said, "Speaking of the children, you know I'll expect custody."

Jo Dell whirled around to face her husband. Fury turned her soft eyes into narrow slits and erased the beauty of her mouth and cheeks. "Like hell, John Ed! That's why we're out here, isn't it? Not seedlings. Divorce! I'm telling you, our kids will stay with me because they should be with their mother, and because I'll raise 'em a damn sight better than you and your mistress, and however many kids she has by who knows who?"

John Ed didn't shout back or even raise his voice. The plan. "You can't win, Jo Dell," he said point blank. "When it comes out that you're depressed and despondent all the time, that Etta is more of a mother to the twins than you, and that you actually threatened me with a shotgun in the presence of Rose, the game is over. And you lose. Unfit mother."

The finality of that last remark brought warm tears coursing down Jo Dell's cold face. She blinked to clear her blurred vision of the man close in front of her, whom she despised for his betrayal and lies. She opened her door as if to get a handkerchief to wipe her eyes, but turned back holding his thirty-thirty rifle that always hung behind the bench seat. Holding it waist-high, she leveled it at his stomach.

Calmly but emphatically, she said, "You think you're a big shot, John Ed; but you're not taking my children. I'll see you dead first. I ought to shoot you right here, right now, but—"

Before another word formed, John Ed struck like a rattler hitting a hand too deep in broom-sedge. In one motion, he grabbed the barrel and yanked it away from her body. "No!" Her cry pierced the frosty stillness, echoed from the canopy of trees, and woke flocks of starlings and crows that smeared the sky with frightened flight. Hands still on the stock, she pulled back with all her strength, but it was no match for his. "Damn you to hell!"

He twisted the rifle until it turned upward, then pushed its muzzle downward toward Jo Dell's torso. They struggled for perhaps ten seconds before the blast, which ricocheted through the hundreds of trees around them and off the leaden floor of the heavens. The bullet tore through her coat and white cashmere sweater, into her left breast and across her body. She lurched back against the truck and slumped to the ground, whispering, "Oh God, John Ed."

Chapter 18

He leaned the rifle against the truck fender. Squatting, he felt for a pulse but it was nothing more than a symbolic gesture. Her eyes were wide with shock, but unseeing; the sweet face frozen in pain. He was already a widower, and knew it. She was thirty-six, his wife of fourteen years, both of them now free.

John Ed then spoke gently to the body, departing from the plan. "It was going to be a showdown, honey, sooner or later. Me or you. It came quicker than I expected. You shouldn't have got the rifle, but I figured you might. Bad enough the first time. Your last mistake today. My promise to you is that I'll be a good father to our children. Raise 'em right. They'll always love you."

He got back in the truck, started the engine to get some heat going, and sat still for several minutes, thinking through his story and the plan. He smoothed it out, put the truck in gear, and slowly drove back to the highway. He left Jo Dell lying just where she had fallen. "I know who to talk to, and what to say happened," he told himself. "Hell, I may not even be charged. But if I am, I doubt the grand jury would indict me. 'Course, I could go to trial, but I'll know everybody on the jury, and they'll turn me loose. By summer, it'll just be Sarah and me." Nonetheless, he began to feel nervous and queasy.

Stopping at his brother's office at the courthouse, he found the probate judge busy and unable to see him. After thirty minutes, pacing the outer office at times, he left and went to the county's vehicle shop, where he arranged to borrow a small bulldozer the next day. He would not use his own. "I've lent it to another logger," he told the shop manager.

A Negro he knew only as Leroy was there, sweeping the garage. "Could you help me out a little tomorrow?" John Ed asked. "We'll put a little dozer on a lowboy and go down to the Everett tract. I need to move some dirt. Should be back by lunch. Ten bucks if you can."

"Tank ya, suh," Leroy said.

THEY LEFT THE VEHICLE shop at eight, pulling the lowboy and dozer. So far, so good. Jo Dell was down at Dauphin Island for a quiet weekend, he had told the girls and Etta, who would stay the weekend at the house. He'd taken Jo Dell's car to Sarah's. At the edge of the woods, they unloaded the dozer.

"Wait here," John Ed said, his face grimaced. "I'm not feeling so good and I'll be right back." He drove the dozer toward where he had left the body, out of Leroy's sight. There she lay. He lowered the bucket, scooped her up encased in mud and pushed on for several feet, through the rusted remains of a low wire fence that had once marked the well. Lowering the bucket, he dumped the stiffening form and nudged it into the hole, its inside slick from rain. She slid quickly, twelve feet, he reckoned. Then the muffled sound stopped, and it was quiet again. Very quiet. A mound of soft dirt and rotted leaves was nearby. He filled the bucket twice and shoved the loads into the hole, filling it to the top. That done, he went back to the truck. He and Leroy loaded the dozer, and drove back to the county's shop.

"Thanks for being there in case I needed you," he told Leroy and paid him the easiest money he'd made since Christmas. When the time came, he would explain, "I panicked, I fell apart, I lost my senses." He would wring his hands, fight back tears, and say, "I don't know why else I would do something so awful." The terrible accident had made him temporarily insane. Leroy had seen it, but of course would never be mentioned as being there unless things turned for the worse.

That was the plan and the story.

. . . .

Chapter 19

The girls missed their mother. She had been gone four days, and John Ed knew his excuses had run out. He had partied one night over the weekend, taken a car to Mobile for her to drive back from the beach, and coasted the rest of the time on pretense. On Monday, after school, Margaret and Melissa asked their father, "Daddy, when's mama coming home?" He called Etta into the room.

"Sit down, my darlings. I don't know how else to say this. Your mother and I went out into the woods last Thursday morning to look at where we wanted to plant new pine seedlings. We started arguing about something, and she got real mad. For some reason she took my rifle out of the truck, and—Lord, I don't know why!—threatened to shoot me. I grabbed the gun and we struggled. She wouldn't let it go. Suddenly, it went off and shot her. I did everything I could, but the wound was too bad. She died in my arms."

"Mama!" the girls screamed in horror. "Daddy, no!" they wailed.

"Lawd in heaven!" Etta cried. She clasped the girls to her bosom.

John Ed hugged his daughters, and felt their fragile frames trembling and shaking. They sobbed uncontrollably, shouting, "Mama's dead, mama's dead!" They were falling to pieces.

"It was a terrible accident. I'm so sorry!" he said; then dialed the Methodist minister's private phone number. "It's an emergency, preacher, we need you now."

The Reverend Henry Harris stayed well into the evening, until the exhausted, broken children finally fell asleep. John Ed told him the whole story, including the party and the car, which he knew would come out, anyway. "I don't know why any of it happened that way. But I just couldn't tell anybody. I was just crazy," he sobbed. Harris prayed with John Ed before leaving, then walked out into the cold night sorely troubled by what he had heard. Tragedies and trauma affect people differently, he knew, but this—the four-day delay and the well, in particular—was bizarre beyond belief.

With Etta remaining at the house to care for the children, John Ed went to Bill's office just before 5 P.M. "The judge is involved in a hearing, Mr. Tomlinson," his secretary said. "It may last into the evening." Then she left. In an empty office, he called Sarah at the fish camp but couldn't reach her. Next, he left a note for his brother to meet him at their mother's house as quickly as he could get there. "It's very urgent," he wrote.

Jo Dell's death and John Ed's arrest inflamed Henderson County like an unchecked prairie fire and gave the county's weekly, the *Henderson Ledger,* a bigger story than it could handle. But the four-person staff exulted in their sudden importance, and pursued the story for a few weeks with the tenacity of starving dogs; the sheriff their main source, but also interviewing practically anyone else who would stand still.

"Just get it right," their editor insisted. "Verify. No hearsay. Every word you write exposes us."

AT HIS PRELIMINARY HEARING in February, John Ed told his well-rehearsed story to a crowd estimated at seven hundred who packed the courthouse to standing room. Fourteen others testified, including the sheriff, Jo Dell's mother, the probate judge, Sarah's cousin, Barbara; and state medical examiner Sidney Nethery, who had performed the autopsy.

Circuit Solicitor Seth Yielding, who would prosecute, quickly labeled the case "first degree murder." Just as quickly, Presiding Judge James Etheridge agreed. He ruled, "In my opinion the evidence is clear and strong to support the charge of first degree murder," and bound John Ed over to the special grand jury that would be formed.

Yielding acted swiftly to organize the all-white, all-male grand jury. After hearing from several witnesses themselves, and asking questions, they voted to indict John Ed for murder in the first degree. The tightly-guarded grand jury met in the same courthouse room that a trial jury would use that spring.

John Ed was arraigned, returned to jail and pleaded innocent by reason of insanity. The family hired Franklin DeJarnette, a prominent Tuscaloosa trial lawyer, and Calhoun Cates, the county's best defense attorney. The trial was scheduled for March, to be presided over by Circuit Judge Walter Cargile, from neighboring Clarke County. To his surprise and concern, Cargile would quickly realize that he had never before conducted proceedings that had so many incendiary elements.

The Tomlinsons asked that John Ed be freed on bail, but the Alabama Court of Appeals denied the petition based on "such evidence and the governing legal principles."

The trial's scheduled beginning was delayed by defense claims that John Ed was ill and that public feeling would deny him a fair trial. Cargile had two doctors, one from each side, examine John Ed. Each said he was physically able to go on trial. The judge overruled both motions, and in April it finally started.

Every parking space on Butler's streets, and in any open field around town, was filled at least one hour before bailiff Shorty Talmadge stood at an open second floor window and bellowed to the countryside that court was in session. If the law had allowed, you could have sold tickets to the drama that unfolded in front of the polished oak pews at the historic courthouse that dated back some one hundred years. Nothing in the county's history touched it. Downtown Café and the fast food stops all stocked extra food; every bathroom had twice the usual amount of toilet paper; soft drink machines were fully loaded. The *Ledger* planned to double its press run, and knew it would sell every copy. Even the *Mobile Register* covered the story, but no other daily.

AND THREE WEEKS LATER, when a jury of his peers rejected John Ed's story, declared him guilty as charged, and gave him a life sentence, every corner of town talk said the same thing: he'll never serve a day. They were close to being right.

. . . .

Chapter 20

"Where is Henderson County?"

"Southwest Alabama. About two hours below Tuscaloosa."

"And this is a trial?"

"Yeah, but it's more than that. Powerful family, Tomlinson, runs the county. Mother and two sons, four young grandchildren. One of the sons' wives was shot to death in January 1959. Her husband, the youngest son, was charged with murder, convicted, and sentenced to life. But the state Supreme Court overturned the verdict, based in part on errors the judge made in his charge to the jury. A girlfriend was involved, too. We used wire, mostly AP out of Mobile, for the first trial. Now the second trial is scheduled. That's the gist of it."

"Pretty strong stuff!"

"A good story, that's for sure. You and Carter head on down this Wednesday, get us a good advance piece. Stay overnight, if you like, but you'll probably want to cross the state line to Meridian. It's only forty-five minutes west of Butler."

"What's Butler?"

"County seat. Where this trial will be held. First one was, too."

I WAS IN MY fourth year as a general assignment reporter for the *Birmingham Star*, and Stanley Meyer was in his tenth year as its city editor. We talked in March 1961, on a Monday afternoon, after the Red Streak final edition had gone to press. A few of the dozen news-side reporters still hung around, typing next day copy, and the bank of teletype machines in the Associated Press office, adjacent to the big news room, clacked continuously spitting out stories on thick rolls of paper for the morning news cycle. But our copy desk, and the sports and womens departments had emptied out, and the city desk's three phones, each with four lines, the hub of the news operation, weren't ringing constantly, all of which allowed another chaotic news day to slow down and cross the finish line.

We produced six editions—starting with the northwest Mississippi edition at nine-thirty every morning, followed quickly by the statewide Alabama edition with just a few replates, and ending sometime past 3 P.M. with the last of four Birmingham area editions. All were carrier-delivered except the Red Streak, which downtown street vendors sold by shouting that day's Wall Street numbers or a page one banner headline. Today it was about the United Mine Workers threatening to strike, a story of keen interest in this smoggy steel-making town, where skies stayed thick with residue blown out of the blast furnaces and smokestacks in the western suburbs, Ensley and Fairfield. Birmingham proper sat in Jones Valley, its low elevation the perfect geography to be draped by filthy and dangerous air.

Alabama's largest newspaper, the *Star* had a circulation approaching 350,000 and distribution in virtually all of the sixty-seven counties. It was locally owned and managed by its founder, the Clarke Ashworth family, one of Birmingham's most historic names. The *Star* lived downtown in a four-story red brick box—ranks of noisy, hot linotype machines on the fourth floor, presses in the basement, and everything else sandwiched between. The news departments occupied the entire second floor; ours and the morning competitor *Daily Herald,* which had less than half our circulation numbers.

My editors, Charlie Lake and Meyer, were seasoned journalists who had paid their dues by covering the full spectrum of beats, from politics to crime to generally boring civic dinners. Both kept their focus and concentration impressively well under the constant pressure of deadlines, phones, breaking stories, endless interruptions, and managing a staff of strong personalities, some of whom were a self-anointed prima donna. Meyer could stay calm if all hell was breaking loose, while the excitable Lake might slam down a phone, or yell to a reporter, above the newsroom clamor, "Get over here! Whaddya mean by this graf?" With their proven expertise and opposite personalities, they were perfect mentors.

Through high school and four years at Birmingham-Methodist, a liberal arts college, I had worked part-time, taking on increased responsibilities as a substitute for vacationing reporters, covering prep football, and had even won state recognition—my first reporting certificate—for a feature story about a hobo killed by lightning while passing through town. That all but assured me a job offer, and after graduation the *Star* had hired me for eighty-five dollars a week.

I would be general assignment, Stan decided, which meant learning to cover every kind of story, any beat, and familiarizing myself with every phase of the news side. In my first four full-time years I had page one bylines across the board, including Alabama's pivotal role in America's infant space program, gory murders, deadly weather and growing racial unrest. Stan said I got those assignments because I earned them through good technique and meeting deadlines. At twenty-three, I had begun to be seasoned.

Chapter 21

The day after my short discussion with Meyer, he isolated me in the morgue—or news room's library—to read the coverage of John Ed Tomlinson's first trial for his wife's death, and to fill a green, pocket-sized pad with notes. Audrey Simmons, the pleasant, business-like librarian, brought me envelopes of AP stories of the proceedings, and also clips from the *Mobile Register,* which had staffed the trial, start to finish. Lake told me he had ordered them so I would know what I'd be up against.

But I couldn't know. I had never even attended a trial, much less coverrd one, and this high-profile murder case seemed to promise baptism by immersion. The more I read about testimony and legal wrangling, the more I thought, "Crap, I'll be a lost ball in high weeds."

Carefully, I studied the *Register* reporter's style, his use of direct quotes and descriptive material; how he described the setting in court and the testimony of a procession of witnesses for both sides; thirty-two for the prosecution and ninety-two for the defense had been subpoenaed. Gradually, what to do and how to do it began to jell. But the trial itself—its personalities, taking notes rapid-fire, and producing a logical narrative on deadline—would prove to be a challenge like I had never known.

The clips reported an aggressive prosecution led by Circuit Solicitor Seth Yielding, chief prosecutor for several southwest Alabama counties, and his friend, Tom Bostick, the solicitor in the neighboring judicial district of three counties. The defense was presented by prominent Tuscaloosa attorney Franklin DeJarnette, with Calhoun Cates, described as Henderson County's best defense lawyer, in second chair.

Sarah Davis, identified as John Ed's other woman, didn't testify, but Robert Whatley, to whom she was supposedly engaged, did take the stand and confirmed their engagement. Also, the jury heard testimony of the doctor who administered their prenuptial blood test in Waynesboro, Mississippi. State Toxicologist Sidney Nethery said under oath that the fatal shot to Jo Dell was fired more than twelve inches away, and that she was standing or crouching when hit. Instant death, he said.

Barbara Evans, Sarah's cousin and longtime friend, testified she heard John Ed and Sarah talk of love and marriage at Woody's, a popular roadhouse down the main highway to Mobile.

Rose Tomlinson, John Ed and Bill's mother, told the jury she saw Jo Dell threaten John Ed with a shotgun in their living room. Even the Tomlinson's oldest of two daughters, Margaret, thirteen (Melissa was nine) was called to testify of what she heard when that happened. To the Tomlinsons, putting that child on the witness stand was the prosecution's most damnable decision.

And so it went for a week, offense and defense, gripping copy. Finally, on the sixth day, the witness everyone was waiting for. "I'll be damned, he did testify, after all," I muttered. John Ed had spent most of that day defending himself, describing his version of his wife's death, and swearing under oath, that so help me God, he had not planned to kill Jo Dell on that cold morning in the woods of south Henderson County.

Had I known Mr. DeJarnette, or even heard of him; had I known squat about high stakes criminal trial strategy, it would have been branch water clear that John Ed's legal team was rolling the dice in calling him to testify; gambling on his reputation among the locals and his family's power in the county and west Alabama; gambling that while the jury liked Jo Dell and hated what he did with her body, they would forgive this man who was one of them, except he was a *rich* good old boy. "I know these men, and they want to hear him," Cal Cates had said in one story. "On cross, Seth will go after him, but John Ed won't break."

The newspaper pictured John Ed wearing khakis shirt and pants, sitting straight in the witness box. The story said that Yielding pounded him on cross-examination, but that John Ed—in five hours in the witness chair—never flinched or backed off his sworn testimony about what happened.

Only once did his self-control waver, said the reporter. It happened when Yielding introduced as evidence an 8x10 black and white picture of the well that he had made a few weeks before the trial. Over defense objections, he gained the court's permission to let the jury see it because it was central to the investigation of Jo Dell's death. The gruesome image of a ragged hole and a crude wood ladder protruding out of the top passed slowly from juror to juror. As it did, John Ed closed his eyes and lowered his head.

His account of what happened was that he and Jo Dell had agreed on terms of a divorce the night before, but by morning she had changed her mind and refused to let him keep their two girls and twin boys. Originally, they were going to Butler that day, but instead he drove them south, into the woodlands to a tract of land where he was going to plant pine seedlings. "She was mad and upset, but I wanted her approval for the seedlings," he said.

"I stopped just beyond the well. I got out and walked a ways—just to let her get over being mad—and then came back. But when I came back, she was still mad. I asked her to get out of the truck and talk it over. But she wouldn't so I walked off again. I heard her get out and walk toward me. She said that I thought I was a big shot. Then I turned around and saw she had the gun, pointing it at me.

"We scuffled over it. I was having trouble getting it away from her. She was doubled over it. I finally pulled it away from her. I pushed her shoulder and that's when it went off. She fell away from me. I don't know if I set the rifle down, or threw it down. I grabbed her up. I thought she fainted at first, and started carrying her to the car. Then I saw some blood and saw that she was dead."

I continued to read, absorbed by John Ed's reaction to suddenly seeing his wife die; he didn't put her in the car and drive like hell for help; instead, he left her on the cold ground and drove—rather casually, it seemed—back to Silas; not to summon help, but to tell his mother, for God's sake, then remembered she had gone to Mobile for the day. So, he picked up a friend and drove to Butler without saying a word about what had happened. He tried to see his brother, the probate judge, but Bill was busy. Later that day he returned and was able to see him, but still didn't mention the shooting.

John Ed testified that the next day he went back to the site with a bulldozer and pushed his wife's body into a nearby abandoned well. He told the court, "I picked up the rifle. I don't know how I did it. I put the rifle on the tractor, came on back and covered her up."

That same night, John Ed and several friends gathered at his house to fry fish and drink whiskey. He told his mother-in-law that Jo Dell was down at Dauphin Island for a few days of rest.

ONCE MORE THAT WEEKEND, John Ed saw his brother, and told him, as well, Jo Dell was at Dauphin Island. Finally, late Monday, the fourth day after the shooting, after making a quick trip to Mobile to leave a car for Jo Dell to drive back in support of his story, John Ed finally admitted the truth to his brother at their mother's house in Silas.

DeJarnette closed the questioning of his witness by asking the key question as bluntly as a punch to the jaw: "John Ed Tomlinson, did you murder your wife?

"I did not. It was an accidental shooting as we fought over the rifle."

"Your witness," DeJarnette said.

. . . .

Chapter 22

The clippings described Seth Yielding standing soldier straight, as if awaiting inspection. Then, breathing in and exhaling, his eyes never leaving John Ed, walking the ten feet to the witness box. His time had come, after all the years of living in the shadow of the Tomlinsons.

He began routinely, but not repetitively, methodically leading John Ed toward the crux of his case against him, one question and one step at a time: his friendship with Sarah, noticed by many, including Jo Dell; his daybreak visits to Sarah in her bedroom, witnessed by the housekeeper; time spent with Sarah at her brother's fish camp; these among other building blocks in a relationship that John Ed denied was serious, but that other testimony would picture as a well-known affair.

"Mr. Tomlinson," said Seth, "you have testified that you spread a story that your wife went to Dauphin Island the weekend of January 29, 1959, to rest and to be alone, that she had been depressed and nervous during the holidays and needed to get away. Was that the gist of your testimony?"

"It was," he replied.

Seth continued. "You spread yet another story about that weekend that had to do with a motel in Citronelle. Is that right?"

"Yes."

"What did you say?"

"I said I had found her there with a doctor from Mobile that she had been seeing for depression."

"Now tell the court, Mr. Tomlinson, at any time that weekend was your wife at Dauphin Island, or was she with a doctor at a motel?"

"No."

"Those were lies, weren't they, Mr. Tomlinson? In fact—"

"Objection!" DeJarnette said.

"Overruled," Circuit Judge Walter Cargile replied.

"In fact," Seth continued, as intense now as if he was personally strapping John Ed in the electric chair, "Jo Dell was already dead. You had shot her dead—"

"Objection!"

"Overruled."

"—shot her dead for the love of another woman, Sarah Davis, and thrown away her body in an old well like a sack of garbage! Look at this picture again!" he shouted, taking it from the evidence table and holding it in John Ed's face. "That's what you did to the mother of your four little children, and this jury of good men will convict you for it!"

"Objection!"

"Withdrawn," Seth intoned, and returned to his chair. "Your witness," he said.

I closed the clip file and muttered, "Damn, what a moment! How could he think he could get away with such lies and deceit?"

. . . .

Chapter 23

Seven days after it began—including two Saturdays of court and eloquent summations that demanded conviction and death, and acquittal and freedom—the jury of twelve white men got the case. They appeared to listen intently to their charge by Judge Cargile, who spoke for one hour while each juror was said to squirm his butt in uncomfortable hardwood chairs. Finally, he dismissed them with a written summary of what he had said. The jury would not be sequestered, he had decided, but were never to mention the trial outside of the courthouse.

THE TWELVE, PLUS TWO alternates, ate supper at the Downtown Café, a block away, relaxed for a while longer, then decided not to quit for the night but to start work.

It was just past 9 P.M. on that humid April night when they had finally sat down together on the second floor, windows open, floor fan swishing back and forth, pitcher of ice water and paper cups on the table. To the man, they were irritable: tired of their straight-back wooden chairs; tired of listening to witnesses, lawyers, and the judge; just tired, period.

The eloquence of the closing statements given by the prosecution and defense rang in their brains. But the essence of the summations boiled down to a single key question: accident or murder?

On first ballot they elected their foreman, Ira Crockett, a forty-five-year-old truck driver, from Toxey, another of the county's lonesome crossroads. Then they settled down and began making progress quicker than they expected. First thing, a key point from the judge's long-winded charge came up: John Ed's confession, twice mentioned, right there in the written instructions.

"There ain't but one living witness to what happened," said juror Eddie Pope. "John Ed says it was accidental. Personally, I don't believe him, but he didn't confess to anything. Cargile shouldn't have said that."

"JUDGE, THEY'RE DELIBERATING," BAILIFF Shorty Talmadge reported at 10 P.M. "They don't want to quit, yet. They're saying they might be getting somewhere."

Judge Cargile, himself worn out, chewed his unlit cigar and tried to rest on a small, sagging sofa in an office a few steps away from the bench. "Lord, I hope so. I just want to go home, away from this mess," he said quietly. At 11:10 P.M. he got his wish.

Guilty of first degree murder, said foreman Puckett, as the late-night hangers-on gasped. He then delivered the jury's recommendation, life in prison. A reporter wrote of seeing John Ed glower at the twelve, not seeing them individually, but as a unit of men he knew by first name who had renounced him in judgment.

Judge Cargile polled the jury one at a time. "This is your verdict?" he asked solemnly, and each one answered, "It is, Your Honor." He then imposed the life sentence. The judge asked, "Mr. Tomlinson, is there anything you want to say?"

"Nothing, Your Honor," the words barely audible in the silence of the room.

Thanking the jury for its attentiveness over nine long days and for playing their part well in making America's system of justice work once again, the judge dismissed the men at 11:25 P.M., freeing them to go home to their beds. Duty done in full, retribution exacted, they would sleep well.

ROSE TOMLINSON SAT ON a front pew behind her son, staring ahead grimly; she didn't make a sound as a deputy led John Ed away, free of handcuffs, to a patrol car for the one-block ride back to his jail cell. Her other son, beside her, hung his head. She defiant, he crushed.

John Ed huddled under the blanket in his cell, but still had chills. He asked for more cover, and the night deputy gave him another scratchy thin blanket "Those bastards," he said, trying to get comfortable on his hard bunk. "They'll have to look at me one day, then they'll be sorry for what they did."

Sarah went home, drank three shots of straight vodka, and cried herself to sleep.

Mrs. Wilkes slept for the first night in weeks. "Thank you, Lord," she prayed. "Jo Dell, your soul is rested."

Chapter 24

In the grip of rage and humiliation, Rose stayed several minutes after the courtroom cleared. Bill finally stood and coaxed his mother to leave. "It's over for now, mama," he said.

"But it's not finished," she replied softly, not looking at him. "They'll pay in hell for what they did."

Henry, who cleaned the courthouse, came to the pew where the lone figure sat and asked hesitantly if he could turn out the lights and lock up soon.

"Yes, Henry," she answered; then stood and walked out into the warm midnight.

ON MAY 1, 1959, John Ed was driven to Kilby state penitentiary, knowing he would be ten years older before being eligible for parole. His defense team appealed the verdict in a 37-page motion filed within two weeks. It asked for a new trial and to have the verdict and sentence set aside. The motion was based on 171 grounds, most of them defense objections the judge had denied. But two points in particular were cited, one of which the jury had spotted right away.

Judge Cargile ruled on June 4 to allow the motion, and a month later heard a full day of arguments from both sides. Then he immediately ruled against a retrial, leaving the verdict and sentence intact.

The defense appealed again, this time to the Alabama Supreme Court, which didn't hear arguments for nine months, until March 1960. Eight more months passed; then, on December 1, 1960, the court ruled for the Tomlinsons and against Judge Cargile, reversing the conviction and returning the case to Henderson County. A second trial was scheduled for March 1961.

The Supreme Court grounded its ruling on two factors—first, what it called "hearsay testimony" by the state's medical examiner, Dr. Nethery, that described Jo Dell's likely defensive position when struck by the fatal bullet; second, Cargile's mistake in saying "confession" twice in his written charge, when John Ed had never confessed to anything.

Chapter 25

Folding the last few clips, I put them back in their envelope. "Full circle," I said aloud. "Here we go again." What I didn't read, however, what had not been written because reporters couldn't witness a jury's deliberations; what I couldn't do, lacking the experience to grasp the nuances in such an inflamed environment, was interpret the temperament and mindset of those men.

With no perspective shaped by prior trial coverage, I couldn't move beyond those printed words and see the jury as they were: ordinary, hard-working, God-fearing, churchgoing farmers, truck drivers, paper mill workers, merchants, day laborers; who almost daily, except Sunday, wore coveralls, denim shirts, and low-cut boots; who chewed Garrett snuff, smoked Camels, and drank moonshine or Bellows; every last one of whom knew of the Tomlinsons, some of whom had worked for Mr. John, or John Ed, or Rose, or the probate judge, and cashed a paycheck bearing one of their signatures.

There was no way I could know that this jury might have given John Ed the benefit of the doubt that it was as he swore to God, the worst possible accident. They might have dismissed the shaky testimony about him romancing another woman. They might have shown leniency of some kind to the man they knew well and liked. Instead, they wouldn't have any of it. No way in hell.

Yes, he had taken her out to the woods, where she was shot dead. Indisputable facts. But then John Ed screwed himself. In these parts a man respected his wife and treated her accordingly. Might hold an arm to cross the street, open the door for her, tease her playfully, generally speak of her kindly. And if he was still living when she died, dress her nicely for visitation at the church so friends could admire her one last time and say how pretty she looked while a woman played "What a Friend We Have in Jesus" and "Softly and Tenderly" on an untuned piano. At the funeral a little choir, or soloist, would sing "How Great Thou Art," and the deceased would be dignified as loving wife, perfect mother, a new angel in heaven, and another of God's sunbeams. At the cemetery, she would be prayed over lovingly and, surrounded by artificial grass and artificial flowers, finally lowered to her earthly rest as scripture assured her soul of an eternal heavenly home.

That was what a husband did, with little variation. One thing was certain: those women—faithful wives, caring mothers, good homemakers—would never be treated like trash, thrown into an abandoned well and buried in mud. Anyone who did that would not be forgiven. Which made what John Ed did to Jo Dell as lowdown as a man could be. And it was only right that she finally had a decent funeral, with friends and other admirers filling the church, but no thanks to him who had thrown her away and wouldn't even bring her out of the woods. God Almighty, they had seen the picture!

THOSE ACQUAINTANCES OF MR. and Mrs. John Ed Tomlinson, seated together around an oblong table, behind a locked door, came to quick agreement about all that. They agreed, as well, about John Ed's despicable behavior on the very night of the shooting, frying fish and drinking whiskey at his house like everything was normal, when Jo Dell was lying dead and covered with mud, where he had left her. And, then, God knows why, he even said he'd caught her screwing someone at a motel in Citronelle, when she was already dead, for God's sake. If her being killed wasn't awful enough, then he had to call her a whore. Damn him!

We can't let him get away with any of that, those husbands had said one to another. For Jo Dell's sake, and the honor of our own wives, we have to make it right by her. He has to pay. We'll see to it.

. . . .

Chapter 26

"I'll be going out of town for a few days," I told my wife, Claire, on Tuesday evening. "Ace Carter and I have to go down to Henderson County, southwest of here, for a Sunday piece on a big trial that starts there next week. We're going down tomorrow, and come back late Thursday or Friday.

"Anything special about it?" she asked.

"It's a pretty big deal—powerful family, a son gone bad, accused of killing his wife for another woman, and burying her in an abandoned well. He was tried and convicted in 1959, but the state Supreme Court reversed the verdict. Now he's being tried again."

"You covering the trial, too?"

"Yes. Starts next Monday. I was surprised to get the assignment, since I've never been near a courtroom. But it's a big story, statewide, so I'm glad to have it."

"Compliments to you, husband. Any idea how long?"

"First one was seven days. This one will go that long, I think."

Claire and our one-year-old son would be lonely, but she was proud of my standing at the paper, and had long since accustomed herself to the demands of the news business.

I MET ACE UP in photo early Wednesday and at 9 A.M. we left in a *Star* company station wagon; its bright orange paint and large black letters nothing short of a moving target, if anybody wanted to single us out.

"We might as well be riding in a bull's eye," Ace, the driver, said as we turned off U.S. 11 about ninety miles west of Birmingham and headed south toward Henderson County. Thirty-two years old, six years at the *Star,* Ace was the best young photographer on staff. He particularly liked breaking news and stories with a rough edge, like this one.

"One thing, everybody'll know who we are," he mused.

"That's what I'm afraid of," I muttered.

SLOWED BY EIGHTEEN-WHEELERS CARRYING tons of long pine logs on a two-lane road to the regional paper mill, we arrived in Butler at about 2 P.M. Right away, we made two swings around the courthouse square, the long orange vehicle predictably drawing stares. The news would spread fast: the *Star* was in town. Then we stopped at the sheriff's office for our first encounter with one of the locals.

"Welcome, boys," said Sheriff Lonnie Hutton. "What brings you to town?" He grinned, and spat an arc of tobacco juice into a spittoon two feet away. "As if I didn't know."

"Yes sir, we're here to get an advance story about the trial, and we'll be back for the trial, itself," I said politely but with an air of confidence. "Our first time here, and we're going to ride around this afternoon, just to get our bearings. Wanted to let you know that we'll be out and about."

"Ten-four," the sheriff replied. "Anything else?"

"Could you point us in the direction of John Ed Tomlinson's house? At least we'd like to ride by."

"Head south on the main road. It's six-seven miles out, on your left. Back off the road, gravel driveway. Big brick job. The kids live there now with their grandmother, Rose Tomlinson, and you know the rest, I guess."

"Yes sir."

"Be careful around here this evening. I'm not saying there'll be a problem, but not everybody will appreciate your company."

"We will, thank you."

ACE TOOK PICTURES OF the courthouse exterior and the town square. We found the house easily—nothing else so big nearby—and he shot from the driveway. Somewhat hidden by towering pines, the place looked peaceful but felt slightly ominous.

We went on to Silas, a few miles farther south, and pulled in at the feed store. A Negro, who looked middle-aged, sat on a stump near the door, whittling. "Looking for Leroy," I said.

"He done gone."

"Maybe so. I don't see him. Reckon he'll be here in the morning?"

"Could be."

I walked closer to the man and handed him a five dollar bill. "If you see him this evening, would you tell him that I'll be here tomorrow morning at seven, and would like to talk to him for a few minutes."

"I'll see 'bout it."

Chapter 27

We left a 5 A.M. wake up call at the City Motel in Meridian, had breakfast, and were back at the feed store before 7 A.M. Our man saw us coming and walked out to meet the car. A chunky man, wearing dirty coveralls and work shirt, he looked to be about thirty.

"You're Leroy?

"Yassuh."

"Got some identification, so I can be sure?"

"Yassuh." He pulled a Social Security card out of his shirt pocket. Rastus Leroy Simmons, it read.

All three of us felt eyes from somewhere, so I didn't ask Leroy to get in the car. "What we want to do is go out to the well," I said. "You went out there with John Ed, I believe. Is that right?

"Yassuh."

"Will you take us to it? There's ten bucks for you, if you'll do it."

"Yassuh, I will."

"We'll be back in twenty minutes, to the gas station across the road. I'll buy some gas. Meet us there. Okay?"

"Yassuh."

We pulled into the gas station at 7:30 A.M. and bought five gallons of regular. I paid the man inside, whose jaw bulged with Red Man, and who looked me over with an unwelcome gaze.

"Reckon you know you're not wanted down here," he said after taking my dollar-fifty. "Y'all oughta go on back to yore big city newspaper 'fore there's trouble. We can handle our bidness."

"We're not looking for trouble, sir, and won't be starting any," I replied. "We're just here doing our job, and won't stay any longer than necessary until the trial starts. It was nice talking with you."

Chapter 28

Leroy appeared out of nowhere and quickly got into the back seat. He slumped down, out of sight. In the gas station, Tom Owens dialed a local phone number. "Them reporters just bought gas here and headed off in the direction of the well. Got themselves a nigger as their guide. It's Leroy Simmons, I think. Kinda looked like him."

"They shouldn't done that," said the person Owens had called. "And Leroy fucked himself taking their money, if he did. We'll be talkin' to him 'bout that."

LEROY SAID, "TAKE THE main road south."

We drove about five miles. "Next turning, right." It was a rutted dirt road that wound into the grassy countryside. "Look for a hole in de fence. Left." The break in the barbed wire put us into a field. A few hundred yards ahead loomed the edge of the woods. "Go yonder to de trees. Dat's it."

Ace, Leroy, and I walked out of the sunny chill into tree-shaded shadows. "It's just ovah dere," said Leroy, "an' I'm stayin' here. Ain't going dar." He pointed, and the two of us went that way, and came upon it.

"Jesus!" Ace whispered, almost prayerfully, staring at the forbidding hole in the ground, whose ominous opening looked far too small to swallow an adult body. "What a awful place to be buried. If he came back the next day, and she was already stiff, he musta had to stand her on end to drop her in there. Jesus!" Instinctively, he stepped back and began shooting.

"No wonder the jury nailed him," I said. "This is a horrible end for anyone, and she was his wife!" Seeing the hole, and remembering John Ed's lame testimony about what happened here, turned my stomach, for I didn't yet have the inner fiber, which most reporters acquire, to shut off their emotions when looking at death in the raw.

No need to make notes. The scene burned into my brain and would smolder there for years. "You ready, Ace? Got what you need? Let's get the hell out of here."

Leroy was asleep in the station wagon, stretched out on the back seat. Doors slamming and the engine starting woke him. "Back out lak ya came in." I handed him his ten dollars, and let him out half a mile from the gas station, so nobody would see him leaving the orange news car.

"Thanks, Leroy. You'll be all right?" I said.

"Yassuh."

· · · · · · · · · · ·
Chapter 29

Driving back to Butler, we stopped again at the Tomlinson house, and getting our nerve up rang the doorbell. Rose answered the door, a tall, angular woman, her thin face framed by combed white hair, wearing a fashionable dress and glasses with tortoise shell frame. We introduced ourselves.

"We'll be here for the trial, and came down this week to get familiar with the places that I expect will come up," I said in a friendly voice. She looked me over—young stranger, intruder, must have run through her mind—with a stern and piercing expression. Nonetheless, we were invited in. Hospitality prevailed, but cold as a wedge.

"We'll sit in the living room," she said, and lost no time in small talk. She had already decided this would be a very short visit. "Don't prejudge based on the first trial. Jo Dell's death was a sad accident. My son didn't any more kill his wife than you did." Then she stood, her signal that we should leave.

"If there's a picture of Mr. and Mrs. Tomlinson, could we please borrow it for the paper?" I asked. She left the room and returned with a snapshot of Jo Dell and a wallet-sized head shot of John Ed. "Now you bring them back," she said.

"Yes ma'am. Next week. Thank you for seeing us, ma'am, it was nice to meet you," I said.

"Goodbye."

"Tough customer," said Ace as we turned back onto the main road. "She could make big trouble."

"And probably will," I replied. "She didn't appreciate us being there, and we'll need to be very careful."

WE HAD COFFEE IN Butler at the Downtown Café, and introduced ourselves to the few late morning customers. I asked what they thought about the upcoming trial.

"I don't reckon I want to say anythin' about that," a middle-aged man replied, toothpick in one corner of his mouth. "Hit's our bidness, anyway, not your'n."

"Could I have your name, sir?"

"No, mister, you cain't."

Our waitress wouldn't give her name, either, but said, as we paid our bill, "Lots of folks think that jury decided right, and that he should pay big time for what he did."

I tried to get a couple more quick interviews as we walked to the sheriff's office, but, not surprisingly, found people wary. Do they just resent us, or are they afraid to say anything, I wondered.

We called on Sheriff Hutton mainly to make sure he knew we'd be leaving soon. "Any problems, boys?" Everything went smoothly, we replied, without going into detail. "I'm glad it did, but folks might not be so gracious once the trial starts." Two warnings in two days, I thought.

"Mind if we make a picture of you?" Ace asked.

"I reckon it's okay. Whereabouts?" He tucked his shirt in, hitched up his holster, and smoothed his dark hair.

"Back at the cell where you held John Ed. Is that okay?" Hutton drew himself up into an unsmiling, professional pose at the cell door, and Ace did the best he could with little to work with.

"Thanks, sheriff. We'll see you next week."

Chapter 30

Ace shot a few street scenes around the square, and before leaving town we stopped at the courthouse where a trial was under way in the spacious room where we would work. A young black woman was testifying against a black defendant charged with raping her. She described the crime in colorful detail.

"Are you saying, then, Miss Daniel, that he held you down in the bed all night, as this was happening?" the prosecutor asked.

"Not exactly," she replied. "Once he let me up for a drink of water."

We decided to leave then before anyone heard us laughing.

Before we left town I called Sarah Davis's house, hoping she would see us, but no one answered. Then we started home, made the Full Plate in Bessemer for a late lunch, and were back at the *Star* by 4 p.m. Ace went up to run his film.

"Good trip," I told Stan Meyer, and summarized the highlights, including the sheriff's warnings.

"Pay attention to that," said Meyer.

"I'll write tomorrow, if it's okay," I said. "You're not going to believe that well when you see Ace's pictures."

"Make it sing, Anderson."

"Thanks for this assignment."

My two stories, four of Ace's photos, and the pictures of Jo Dell and John Ed dominated page one the next Sunday. The headline, "The Loud Silence at Silas," reflected the tone of the main story, which was that most people didn't want to talk about this unpleasantness, and the few who would refused to be identified.

One person had said, "I'm just as nervous as I can be over the renewal of this case. I think everyone else is, too." Another woman spoke of widespread fear in the county that the Tomlinsons would put economic pressure on anyone whom they knew talked.

My other story recapped the first trial and previewed the second. It said that ninety-four witnesses had been subpoenaed, and noted that an ex-convict had been arrested in Birmingham and accused of trying to intimidate a witness who was sure to testify in the second trial. The witness, Barbara Ann Evans, cousin and close friend of Sarah Davis, had testified at the first trial of seeing John Ed and Sarah together several times before Jo Dell's death, and that she had heard them talk of love and marriage.

It was decent work, sprinkled with quotes and color that gave the pieces depth and reality. Carter and I would cover the trial, the paper said.

In Henderson County that Sunday, extra papers sold, and the coverage was all the talk in church and on the benches around the square in Butler after lunch. People didn't like what they read; they felt under attack by an outsider, this big, upstate newspaper from a city whose steel mills and smoky air they didn't like either. They resented being dragged into the open statewide, their business exposed like this, which caused many of them to make an unspoken promise: they would be watching for the bright orange station wagon, and those it brought back into their community might be sorry they were stirring things up.

We arrived back in Meridian on Sunday night and checked into the City Motel. Once in our room, Ace said, "If you don't need the bathroom for a few minutes, I'm going to try something."

"Like what?"

"I'm gonna blacken the bathroom with masking tape around the door, plug in my dark room light, and see if I can run some film in the lavatory. It should work, which means that I can send negatives back every night, with the best ones clipped, instead of undeveloped rolls."

A Trailways bus left Meridian every night at 11:30 P.M., scheduled to arrive at the Birmingham terminal at 4 A.M., perfect for an early pickup of my copy and Ace's negatives. Stories and pictures would be on the city desk by 6 A.M. We would be busy every night making the plan work.

Chapter 31

The monthly singing at Bethel Holiness Church, a few miles out from Silas, featured the popular Heavenly Fliers Quartet, from Philadelphia, Mississippi, one hour away across the state line. Almost one hundred folks came out for the concert on a freezing February weeknight. The middle-aged men would do some of their signature songs—including their theme, "I'll Fly Away"—right after the offering was collected. They were already anticipating their fifty percent of the money dropped into the collection plate, this in addition to their two hundred dollar fee.

Tom Owens placed his five dollars into the plate, passed it to the next couple, and whispered to his wife, "I've got to slip out. I'll be back in a few minutes." Lou Anne Owens smiled at her husband. She knew not to ask. He walked through the front door and saw the car he was expecting stopped just off the blacktop, its parking lights on. Owens got in the front seat of the dirty Impala.

"We're ready," said the driver, who wore a white hood.

Glancing into the back seat, Owens saw Leroy Simmons squeezed between two more burly men, each of whom held a 4-10 shotgun between his knees. These men, too, were wearing white hoods. Owens put his on, covering his face and neck.

A loosely tied rope dangled from around Leroy's neck, and his wide eyes looked like black saucers with thin white rims. He was so pitifully afraid that he'd already peed his pants and was trying desperately to keep a shit from coming. Tears coursed down his sunken cheeks, but he dared not speak. Couldn't have if he'd wanted. He could only wait; only God knew for what, but he reckoned it would be bad.

The four who had "borrowed" Leroy for a little while drove him to a quarry close to the county line, down a lonely graveled road that nobody ever traveled unless they had business to be there. They parked near the quarry's edge and the Klansmen got out, except Leroy couldn't bring himself to move until he felt the rope tug at his neck. The men huddled around their prey, looking at him through the slits in their hoods.

His mind numb, terror raised up to narrate his end. They'll club me to the ground and I'll scream and beg, but they'll keep hittin' me till I'm quiet and dead. Then they'll trow me over the edge into whatever's down there. And when it rains I'll be covered with water and rot till there's nothin' but bones. This nigger'll be gone, like he was never heah, nevuh bawn. And nobody will neveh know nothin' 'bout what really happen.

A light in his face jerked Leroy back to the present. He squinted in the direction of the one who was speaking. "Leroy, around here you're a pretty good nigger. Work a little bit, mind your bidness, shoot some craps, drink too much on occasion, screw several women. Pretty good, 'cause we watch you, and we know 'bout you. But, you sorry excuse for a black bastard, you skinned your black ass the other day, gettin' sweet with those reporters from Birmingham. Showed 'em the well, you sonofabitch. Took a few bills; been spendin' them around. We know."

Frozen in place, trembling and sweating, Leroy watched the hood's mouth opening, his glazed eyes fixed on the sinister sounds it made. He shit his pants.

"You're ours, motherfucker. And we like you so much we're gonna let you live. You'll go back tonight, to wherever rats like you go. But listen good to what I'm saying. You step outa line again, have anything else at all to do with them reporters, and you'll see us again. We'll come after you, and we'll be the last people you ever see on this earth before you go to hell. And the same thing'll happen if you say one word about this little visit. We'll be watchin' and listenin'. Now git back in the car, *Mister* Simmons."

They put Leroy in the back seat again, where he sat on his load and caused the stink to rise. "Hot damn! We sure 'nuff scared this little nigger," one of the hoods chuckled. He rolled down a window for fresh, cold air as they moved back into the night.

Tom Owens slipped back into his pew during the last encore. Lou Anne smiled and squeezed his hand. "Sweet singin', ain't it," he whispered. They left with everybody else and drove home to Silas.

Leroy's kidnappers let him out down the road from his house, and he walked on home, smellin' and shakin'. But he gathered his wits together to say to himself defiantly, alone in the freezing darkness, "This darkie, he know a lot more 'bout that murder than they thinks I do. An' one day, it'll be Leroy's turn." He put the seat of his coveralls into a pail of soapy water, cleaned himself off and went to bed.

Chapter 32

"**G**entlemen, we have to get a handle on this situation, and I'm glad you've come. Together, we can do that. What we say here stays here, so we can be frank.

"Our problem is in the aftermath. If Mr. Tomlinson hadn't disposed of his wife's body like a sack of trash; if he hadn't lied to his brother three times that weekend; if he hadn't spread those stupid, flimsy lies to everyone else he saw; first, that she was off at the beach, and second, that he had caught her fucking a doctor at a motel down toward Mobile; if he hadn't had a party at his house the very night of the shooting, with his girlfriend swishing around, as if they both were celebrating her death.

"But John Ed Tomlinson, dumb ass that he is, did all of the above! And, added together, they make acquittal an almost impossible task! He couldn't have played into the prosecution's hands better if Seth Yielding had written a script for him to follow. He can't be that stupid; but maybe he really is."

On a bleak midwinter Monday morning, temperature unwilling to budge above freezing in downtown Birmingham, Strudwick Bowden spoke intently to five white men, all in their fifties, each wearing a dark suit, starched white shirt, gold cufflinks, and striped tie, as if dressed by central casting to be lawyers. They matched him perfectly, except that his ruggedly handsome face and thick, swept-back mane of white hair gave him a distinctive appearance that always set him apart from ordinary beings.

The five men occupied brown leather swivel chairs with padded arms, pulled close to a rectangular, polished teak table. Bowden hoped to see an

66   GRUESOME

eyebrow raise, a nose twitch, a mouth smile or grimace, a forehead furrow; anything to indicate a response to the opening of his presentation. But he saw nothing but expressionless faces. Then, one of the cookie-cutter figures spoke.

"No, Strudwick, John Ed isn't stupid. Anything but, I'd say. But his actions were more stupid than anyone I think I've ever seen." Thomas Calhoun Cates, second chair for the defense at the first trial, spoke up, seated just to Bowden's left. "His actions inflamed practically every man and woman in Henderson County, especially those chosen to judge him. When push came to shove, he didn't stand a chance of getting leniency of any kind."

Cal Cates lived in Butler, born there, made his living there, knew the people, young to old, by skin color, income level, church affiliation, social standing, and the habits they kept hidden. With the conviction of a preacher at an altar call—or one who had talked quietly to each juror after the first trial—he said, "John Ed violated the established standards of the community for plain ol' decency and the treatment of one's woman. The jury swore to one another, and would have taken a blood oath, that he was no better than a low-life son-of-a-bitch, and they would make him pay with hard time so he'd have to live every day with what he'd done."

Bowden addressed another dark suit. "Mr. DeJarnette, do you agree?"

"Absolutely. Cal said it very well," replied Franklin DeJarnette, the suave Tuscaloosan who was lead defense counsel at the first trial. "Anything I added would be repetitious."

The three others at the table, all members of the fifty-plus staff at Bowden and Associates, of Birmingham, remained silent, expressionless.

"Interesting," Bowden responded. "What I'm hearing confirms what I said earlier, that Jo Dell Tomlinson's death is almost incidental to this case. John Ed would not have been indicted for murder and we wouldn't be here today if he had just acted like any decent husband would whose wife had been shot to death accidentally, and not like a prick! Frank," he asked, "what was your strategy to countermand this strong community feeling against John Ed?"

"Cal can answer as well as me. The facts of the debacle were established and substantiated by witnesses, including Bill Tomlinson. So we tried to develop a picture of temporary insanity; John Ed falling apart, going to pieces, acting irrationally in ways totally foreign to his normal behavior."

"We debated about putting him on the stand," said Cates. "But the jury and everybody else needed to hear him say it. He was convincing and held up well under tough cross-examination from Seth."

"We also determined that the fatal shot could have been fired during a struggle, as he maintained it was," said DeJarnette. "But, as you say, Strudwick, these elements of doubt seemed to bear little consequence once the jury got the case. Let me add, too, that we knew we had a reversal in the bag when Judge Cargile misfired and referred to John Ed's 'confession.' There were many other sound grounds, but none so strong as that."

Bowden, whom the Tomlinsons had hired to lead a new defense team, and depose DeJarnette, saw no need to extend the conference any longer. "So, gentlemen, this is February, the trial is three months away, in April. We have our marching orders; but which way do we move? I suggest the following: one, leave the apparent, pending divorce of John Ed from Jo Dell in place, but erase the 'other woman' angle to the extent we can; two, play up the experts' opinion that the shot could have been accidental, which is critical to our chances; three, milk 'temporary insanity' for all we can get, and be sure to ask this new jury in our opening statement, 'Couldn't you, too, have lost your senses in the horror of such an accident?'; keep John Ed off the stand unless we have to have him, because he'll just inflame another jury and sure as hell won't help himself; when that damnable picture of the well goes into evidence, drill the jury with the fact that he isn't on trial for that.

"Whatever additional thoughts you have, please convey them to me, to Cal, or one of these other men from my firm; you have their cards. Thank you all for coming, and for the vital role you have played thus far, and will continue to play, in trying to free a man who damn sure screwed up royally, but nonetheless who is innocent of murder."

The room emptied quickly, leaving behind the large oil portraits of Anthony Bowden, the firm's founder, and Strudwick Bowden, Sr. An elaborate display of ornate national and state awards given the firm in its first hundred years filled a wall.

The son stood alone with the stern visage of his father, in his lifetime the most feared, respected, and often reviled lion of those accused in Alabama, and anywhere else his strategies were needed. The father's mantle had fallen upon his only son, and he wore it well. That son muttered the most dominant principle of his life with the firmness of addressing a jury. "Gentlemen, Cicero defined a man's philosophy as his life's guide. My guide in life, in a word, is win. Whatever it takes, win."

Chapter 33

On another day in February 1961, Seth Yielding thought about Harry Gilmer, the All-American halfback for the University of Alabama in the mid-forties, Seth, a 1952 graduate of the Capstone, hadn't seen Gilmer's startling offensive daring, but had read and heard enough about Alabama football to know full well that he was already sculpted as a Crimson Tide legend.

"He came right at 'em, I'll bet," Seth said, seated at his desk, alone in his office. "Passed and ran right down their throats. Never let up. Well, Mr. Bowden, get yourself ready. Harry Gilmer style, I'm coming after you. For all your swagger and reputation, you're coming to my county and my courtroom. My home field. I'll be prepared and waiting. There won't be a reversal this time."

The mistake made in April 1959 still gnawed at Seth. He had beaten John Ed and the Tomlinsons soundly, a crushing defeat for Rose and Bill, and all the family's power. The misstatement made in his closing argument had led Judge Cargile to make the one reference in charging the jury that, on appeal, would ricochet and nullify the prosecution's success. Seth had relived it countless times: "For him to say 'confession,' and mention it twice, reflects more on me than him. That won't happen again, Mr. Bowden. I'll nail John Ed beyond reasonable doubt this time, just as I did before."

THIRTY-TWO, HAPPILY MARRIED, THE father of a son and daughter, churchgoing Baptist, of high stature in his environs, Seth still proclaimed himself a country boy from Silas. If the occasion called for it, he could slip into faded jeans and a denim shirt, then soften his speech, warm it with diphthongs, and bend the cadence. He could tell crusty jokes about farmers and city slickers, and he savored fried chicken and peach cobbler wherever and whenever they were served. All of which kept him connected with the juries, sheriffs, and police who measured his skills. In the way he talked, ate, and dressed, he could become one of them.

But just beneath the homespun surface lay a crafty and sophisticated prosecutor, a coat-and-tie circuit solicitor who possessed the winner's toughness of a Harry Gilmer. Those accused of a felony knew they would stand eye to eye with an experienced attorney who gave no quarter in seeking justice. Defenders knew he would mount his case aggressively. The presiding judge saw him as thorough and usually at the top of his game. "Strudwick Bowden, you will, too. I'm about to kick your ass," Seth said to himself.

For John Ed to be Seth's most important case, and by far the region's biggest trial ever, he thought it wouldn't be that hard to win a second time. His game plan was sound: philandering husband who talked openly about love and marriage with his mistress; loyal wife, embarrassed and betrayed until she could no longer take it and demanded a divorce; the final showdown in the lonely woods, where John Ed decided he would kill her so he could have the children; a fine, respected woman thrown away in a well; the lies he told until he finally had to own the truth.

With unrelenting tenacity Seth, in opening remarks at the first trial, had borne down on the well he had once visited, on John Ed's lies, and had never let up. "It was pure, unbridled premeditated murder," he snarled at the jury; and could see in their eyes, as they watched him and listened, that no man should treat his wife that way. Nothing that John Ed said in his own defense, or any other doubts that DeJarnette and Cates developed made a dime's worth of difference to those men. DeJarnette was too soft, anyway, wanting sympathy for John Ed. Cal, as second chair, had to take his cues from Frank. Between the two of them, they had misread the jury. Hell, guilt or innocence wasn't the question once they got the case. It was the punishment. If Cargile hadn't screwed up—! He banged his fist on the desk.

Chapter 34

John Ed's life sentence had devastated the Tomlinsons. Rose hardened as she watched her boy taken back to jail, then sat awhile before leaving the empty courtroom and going into the night, eyes rivets of molten steel, face white as cotton. No tears or outward fury. But over and over she muttered, "I don't know where I failed in raising my son."

Seth and Bill Tomlinson had met each other's gaze as the courtroom emptied that night. Visibly pale and shaken, Bill spoke from his place at the defense table. "You hounded him too hard, Seth. My brother isn't a murderer and you've known that all along. This was personal between you and my family, the culmination of years of your jealousy and envy over what we had and you didn't. You used Jo Dell's tragic death in a spiteful way. And calling their child to testify was unconscionable. We won't forget it."

"The jury decided this case, Bill, I didn't," Seth replied, choosing not to carry it further, except to tell a lie: "Your family and its business are of no concern to me."

It was midnight when Seth unlocked his office, went inside to his desk, set his briefcase down, poured himself half a chaser glass of Early Times, and proposed a crude toast. "Here's to the Tomlinsons, bastards all. Now I guess you won't stand so tall."

The bourbon warmed and relaxed him. Putting the glass down, he sat on the edge of the desk and made one more comment into the surrounding darkness: "Well done, Seth." Then he went home. His desk calendar read April 16, 1959.

BUT NOW IT WAS February 1961. Alone with his thoughts once again, he pulled himself away from the game won, then lost, and back to what lay ahead. "That was then. This is now. The score is zero-zero. Come on, Mr. Bowden. Let's get it on."

Chapter 35

Minutes after the verdict and sentence the two defense attorneys each assured the Tomlinsons of the certainty of winning on appeal and the result being overturned. DeJarnette and Cates would prepare the appeal immediately.

Bill Tomlinson slept five hours, came to his office the next morning at 8 A.M., and called the private number of newly inaugurated governor Morris Sullivan. Joey Hickman, the governor's executive assistant, answered.

"Joey, this is Bill Tomlinson, probate judge over in Butler, Henderson County."

"Good morning, Bill! What can the State of Alabama do for you today?"

"Check the governor's calendar. I need to see him for about thirty minutes."

"Get here by 10 A.M., and we'll work you in."

"I'm on my way. Thanks." Bill hung up.

"Mrs. Dixon," he called. His secretary walked briskly into his office, stenographer's notebook in hand. "Cancel all my appointments for the day. I have to go to Montgomery, leaving now. I should be back by mid-afternoon."

The probate judge drove the eighty miles to the state capital steadily, never faster than the sixty-five-mile-per-hour speed limit, but he was shaking inside. He must get the governor's sympathetic attention, he thought. Fuck John Ed, that stupid pissant; this is our family's honor at stake.

Bill was ushered into the executive office, a gaudy display of welcoming gifts and just-hung plaques and photographs. Wearing a pinstripe suit, the governor sat at a desk that held several carefully stacked sets of papers, waiting for his friend of the years going back to law school. He stood and they shook hands. "Bill, it's good to see you. How are you and the family?"

"Again, Morris, the congratulations of all your supporters in Henderson County. With what seems to lie ahead of us, the outsiders and all, our state is very fortunate to have your leadership.

"But to your question. Been better, Morris. You probably haven't heard, but my brother, John Ed, was convicted of murder last night in the accidental shooting of his wife. That sounds contradictory, I know, but it was an accident. The jury gave him life, and Judge Walter Cargile imposed sentence. We will, of course, appeal to the Supreme Court, and I've come to ask you—plead with you—to help us any way that you can."

"I'm terribly sorry, Bill. It's deeply troubling. I have no better friends anywhere than your family. And now, you and Rose, your families, and JoDell's family have my profound sympathy. I was aware of the case, but haven't seen much about in the papers."

"Mobile was the only daily to cover the trial. The Associated Press got its coverage from them."

"Keep me informed about the appeal, Bill. Call my private number. When the time comes, I'll do what I can."

"That means everything to us, governor. Thank you."

"My regards to Nancy and Rose. Take care of yourself, and tell John Ed I'm thinking about him," said the governor, who personally knew each member of the eight-man Alabama Supreme Court.

The meeting lasted no more than five minutes, but Bill Tomlinson left having gotten what he came for.

. . . .

Chapter 36

Rose slept at John Ed's house; Etta, the housekeeper, had kept the children. Together, they got them dressed and fed, and the girls caught the 7:30 A.M. school bus, as usual. Rose told Etta about the verdict and instructed her to stay over until school was out, then she could go home.

"I'm so sorry, Mrs. Tomlinson," she said tearfully. "It ain't right."

Rose cooked lunch for John Ed, a ritual she had begun the day after his arrest in February. At noon on the dot, she entered Sheriff Hutton's office. Nodding to the deputy on duty, she walked past him and into the cell block carrying a cloth-covered tray containing two fried pork chops, boiled cabbage, corn sticks, sweet tea, and apple cobbler.

"Don't you worry, son," she said. "The whole trial was so messed up that the outcome is sure to be overturned. Bill is in Montgomery right now talking to the governor."

"Thank you, mama. I know y'all are doing all you can. Don't worry about me, neither." His voice was strong, but he was pale, and for the first time in his life looked frail.

Sarah hurried to the jail that morning, arriving at 9 A.M., soon after she got her oldest off to school. She looked attractive in a skirt, blouse, and cardigan. The deputy allowed her five minutes, She and John Ed whispered and held hands through the bars.

"It can't be over. It can't end like this," she sobbed, tears pooling in her brown eyes. "I don't want to live without you."

"It looks bad right now, baby, I know that. Fuckin' jury got carried away, and they are my friends, or were. But good things are going to happen for us. It will take time, but they will."

"What's going to happen?"

"We'll get this verdict reversed. The governor is gonna help us at the Supreme Court. Then I'll have a new trial, and, by God, we'll have a better jury. We'll see to that. They might even turn me loose.

"What about now?"

"I'll be going off to prison soon, down to Kilby. That's the law. But there's weekly visitation, and y'all can come to see me."

"God, I can't stand it!" she sobbed, then caught herself with steely inner will. He needed her strength now. "We will, baby, we'll be there. We'll be dressed up like it was Sunday, so you'll be proud to see us. But could we ever be alone, just us? I need you right now. How can I exist without your embrace, your kisses, and loving?"

"I know, honey, I feel the same way. I'll try to swing it. Maybe I can."

"Time's up!" the jailer intoned. They clasped hands tightly. "Bye, darlin', I'll be back tomorrow."

Chapter 37

Two weeks later, on a sunny day in May 1959, Sheriff Hutton, serving only his first year of office in Henderson County, turned his official car east out of Butler and drove his friend of several years to prison. They left at mid-morning, after a procession of visitors had come to say goodbye. Rose arrived first, bringing her boy two fresh biscuits and a promise: "We will free you, son." She brought his daughters, as well, whom she had gotten excused from school. The girls chorused cheerfully, "We love you, daddy!"

John Ed almost broke down. "I love you, too, my darlings; don't forget, and come to see me."

Next came Sarah, looking especially pretty, who clutched at him through the bars and said she would be down to visit the next Sunday. Last to come was Bill Tomlinson, who said, as they shook hands, "We'll keep fighting. And the governor is on our side. Don't give up."

As THEY DROVE TOWARD Montgomery, John Ed said firmly, "Lonnie, honest to God, I didn't kill Jo Dell. It was an awful accident, as God is my witness. They wouldn't believe me, damn them to hell."

From Montgomery they turned south on U.S. 31 for twenty miles and soon approached Kilby state penitentiary, sitting in the middle of ten cleared acres, its forbidding stone walls surrounded by super strength chain link fencing twelve feet high, topped by two feet of razor wire that glistened in the midday sun. Towers with sirens and searchlights stood guard at the corners.

Hutton decided he'd be honest with John Ed as they neared the gate. "I shouldn't be saying this, after the jury's decision, but I'll say it anyway, as your friend and as a husband myself. You wouldn't be sitting here, or going to prison, if you'd just brought her out of the woods and to a hospital like any caring man would do. The well and all, the jury wouldn't let that go. Why did you do that, why?"

John Ed stared at Kilby's dreaded gray concrete walls as they grew closer. He didn't answer.

ROSE DIDN'T GO BACK to the jail after her younger boy was taken away, or for the nearly two years it took for the appeal to meander through the legal maze of motions, delays, hearings and rulings. Once every month or so she would visit John Ed, but the experience depressed her terribly, and she would write him regularly instead, sending news especially about the children. Bill was good about bringing Margaret and Melissa to see their father. Occasionally, if Nancy or Rose could ride with him, they would bring the twin boys, Jacob and Jessie, as well.

Sarah and the girls, always wearing their Sunday clothes, visited faithfully and did their best—with candy, cigarettes, school pictures and cards—to make every trip a special occasion for John Ed. Sometimes, he was able to trade with the guards who supervised visitation; cigarettes for a few minutes alone with Sarah. Between visits to the prison, she helped her brother at the fish camp and found enough other temporary work to keep the days from dragging too badly and to keep herself steady financially.

John Ed quickly became a model inmate: stayed away from trouble, worked in the laundry, exercised regularly, read books from the prison library and any magazine he was allowed. He could take care of himself if it became necessary, but the bullies left him alone. He also grew to like Charles Allen, who had been sent up for forgery from Birmingham. One day in the yard, John Ed began telling him about the trial, going easy on the bit about the well, but talking in detail about Barbara Evans's testimony that linked him with Sarah romantically.

"She didn't do me any good," John Ed said.

"Sure as hell didn't," his new friend replied. "Tell you what, ol' buddy. I'm outa here in a few months. Maybe I'll just have a little visit with Miss Barbara Evans and let her know you didn't appreciate what she said."

"Just don't say anything that could backfire on me."

"Don't worry about it."

Chapter 38

Finally, in December 1960, with Governor Sullivan watching closely from a respectful distance, the Supreme Court justices heeded his subtle influence—nothing in writing that could be traced, one meeting with his friend of ten years, Chief Justice Ronald Edge. Issued on a Friday afternoon, the opinion focused primarily on reversible errors made by the trial judge twice in citing John Ed's "confession," while charging the jury.

The court said:

"We see no escape from reversing the judgment of conviction because of the giving of written charge {two} at the request of the state. That charge reads, 'There is no rule of law requiring you, gentlemen of the jury, to give equal credence to every part of the confessions made by the defendant and introduced as evidence before you, unless it is clearly disproved. All of the confessions must be weighed in the light of the surrounding circumstances, the motives which may have induced [them], and [their] consistency with other evidence; and you, gentlemen, without capriciously accepting or rejecting any portion, should credit such parts as you find reason for believing, and reject that part for which you find reason for disbelieving.' No confession from the defendant was introduced as evidence. The defendant at all times professed his innocence. His testimony, as well as the statements made by him which were introduced by the state, show that he claimed the shooting was an accident. . . . We may use the word 'confession' for admission. But to sum up mere exculpatory admissions and designate them a confession implies they amount to a confession of guilt."

The court also dissented from the testimony of state medical examiner Sidney Nethery about Jo Dell's position when she was shot. The justices ruled as hearsay Nethery's opinion that she could have been on the ground, arms raised, begging for her life, when shot.

The justices' action sent the case back to Henderson County. After another arraignment, the second trial was docketed for spring 1961.

CHRISTMAS WAS THE HAPPIEST in years in the Tomlinson family; hope burned as brightly as the candles arranged on the mantle that in the new year John Ed would be a free man again and piece a life back together with Sarah and their children. Rose didn't make merry, however, as she despised Sarah Davis even more than she had Jo Dell.

At the end of January, Sheriff Hutton brought John Ed home to a familiar routine. Rose began cooking his lunch again, Sarah saw him daily, and he gave minimal help in plotting his defense. Strudwick Bowden and his scheming style intimidated John Ed, but nonetheless he trusted him. Unwillingly, he agreed not to testify.

"The jury needs to hear me, not just sitting there all day!" John Ed protested. "They need to hear me say—to swear before God—that it was an accident!"

"You said that last time, and they didn't buy it," Bill Tomlinson countered sternly. "They turned against you when Seth pounded you about the well, and lies you told about Jo Dell. This jury doesn't need to hear that. This time we're going to hammer home the points we want to make. Plant our own seeds of doubt about murder. This is going to be a different trial."

WHEN CHARLES ALLEN WAS paroled out of Kilby, he returned to Birmingham and made good on his word to John Ed. By asking around and using certain contacts suggested by John Ed, he learned that Barbara Evans now lived in Birmingham and had recently married. So he called the newly wedded Mrs. Walker and, without threatening her directly, suggested with unmistakable meaning that she shouldn't testify against his friend a second time, but if she did he would produce three men who would damage her reputation by testifying that she had shacked up with them.

But Allen wasn't smart. Barbara Walker, incensed and frightened by the threat, instinctively had the call traced, got a number and gave it to Seth, who followed the tip and had Allen arrested and charged with witness intimidation. In short order Allen was convicted, had his parole revoked, was sentenced to six months, and fined five hundred dollars.

Strudwick Bowden quickly devised a statement denying involvement by any of the Tomlinsons, himself, or Calhoun Cates. "We will meet the testimony of this or any other witness at the coming trial with the shield of innocence," he said.

Chapter 39

Trixie Hart, a good cook, who learned it well from her mama, had supper five minutes from ready. She was dishing up the chopped steak and gravy, pole beans, potatoes, and fried okra from the garden, and the corn bread was out of the oven. Her kitchen had a secondhand, four burner electric stove, secondhand refrigerator with a small compartment for two ice trays, a chipped porcelain sink and an eating table covered with a red-and-white checkered oil cloth that wiped off easily. The floor was rolled linoleum, worn and cracked. A rusting water heater stood in a corner, next to the stove. The kitchen reflected the rest of the basic frame house; living room with wood-burning heater, two small bedrooms, bathroom, covered front porch. The roof leaked in one bedroom, and the floors were drafty because the crawl space beneath them was open.

"Y'all come to the table!" As Trixie called out, the telephone jangled three times, the party line signal that it was their ring. Her husband, Ernest, answered.

"Ernest Hart?" The speaker, a man, spoke quietly. It was a local voice.

"Speaking."

"Yore brother's on the Tomlinson jury."

"Lester?"

"Right. And we want you to get a message to him."

"Who is this?"

"That ain't important. Listen close, now. Tell him to go light on John Ed and we'll take good care of him and you after it's all over."

Ernest lowered his voice to a near whisper and looked around to make sure no one else had come into the living room. "Naw, I can't do that. Nobody'll be able to talk to any man on the jury about the trial till hit's all over."

"Figure out how, Ernest. This ain't askin'. We're telling you, do it; just don't get caught."

"I'm telling you, I won't. Hit's against the law."

"There's more'n one well out in those woods, Ernest. Don't be stupid. I'll be callin' you back." Then he hung up.

Ernest went to the bathroom and splashed cold water on his face to recover his composure. Then he joined Trixie and their daughter, Amy, eight, at the table, looking solemn and pale.

"Who was it, hon? Are you all right?"

"Somebody to tell me that Lester's been put on the new Tomlinson jury. Didn't give his name. Nothing important."

"Lord, I'm glad it's not you."

"Supper looks good. I'm hungry." They held hands, and together intoned, "God is great, God is good, let us thank Him for our food. By His hands we must be fed. Thank you, Lord, for our daily bread. Amen."

· · · · · · · · · · ·
Chapter 40

On a sunny, mid-April morning in 1961, Circuit Judge Walter Cargile— who deplored being back on this bench and in Henderson County— administered the oath to fourteen men who raised their right hands at their hard, wooden seats, each a virtual cut-out copy of the first jury to sit there. All white, hard-working, with regular jobs, late thirties to mid-fifties, acquainted with the Tomlinsons in one way or another. Like the judge, they didn't want this job, either, but had sworn not to be swayed by the first trial or its verdict, and to base their decision on the evidence, and not on friendship or emotion. They would see John Ed as the law did—presumed innocent unless determined to be guilty beyond a reasonable doubt.

THE EXPECTED CROWDS WERE one thing, but press coverage was another, and the judge wanted to know who would be writing his name. So he had a sign-in sheet put at a podium out in the hall, which reminded me of a registry at a funeral. Dutifully, the local weekly, the *Mobile Register*, the one local radio station, and Ace Carter and I did as told.

I tried to read the jury from my place on the bench reserved for reporters, down front and close to the witness box. But my first impression saw nothing but a grouping of tanned faces, combed hair, and long-sleeve sport shirts. Their rough-cut lifestyles—that figured to include moonshine, Red Man, and a piece on the side occasionally—allowed them to identify with the man they would judge. They would never have his money or power, but otherwise defendant and jury stood on level ground.

"Darned if they don't look alike," said Ace, sitting beside me. "Could they all be related? Surely not." Actually, two were; the Campbell brothers, Jerry and Ron. Something else, too, which wouldn't have caught my or Ace's attention, anyway—Lester Hart had taken an end seat on the second row. Juror number twelve. The two alternates sat at the other end.

Instinctively, from his uncomfortable wooden chair at the defense table, Strudwick Bowden eyed the jury he had partially picked. As always, no matter the courtroom, he was dressed to impress—navy blue suit, blue striped tie, starched white shirt, cufflinks, shined black shoes—and was the most conspicuous person at this assemblage in downtrodden west Alabama. His wavy white hair was swept back smoothly, and with his high forehead, Roman nose and piercing brown eyes he looked exactly as he had planned.

Bowden studied those men, searching them for differences, mannerisms, anything to individualize them. They were his only concern. With his alternating tones of calm and rage, his catlike quickness to object and pounce, his commanding presence, and a style that he alone brought into a courtroom, he would control this jury. There was no difference in this one and the hundreds of others he had claimed by a proven combination. Control and win.

Seth Yielding, suit rumpled but shirt starched, approached the defense table. His voice cordial, and with an inbred courtesy toward strangers, he said, "Good morning, Mr. Bowden. Welcome to Henderson County. I hope your stay will be hospitable."

"And to you, Mr. Yielding. I'm sure it will be." They shook hands.

Seth greeted his friend Cal Cates, who, as usual, was chewing the stub of an unlit cigar, and Bill Tomlinson, both of them also seated at the table. He nodded to John Ed, now thirty-eight, two years older than when Jo Dell died. Once again, he had entered a plea of not guilty by reason of insanity, as he had two years earlier. Wearing his trademark khaki work clothes, the defendant didn't acknowledge Seth's gesture but looked hard at his adversary as thoughts crossed his mind: You sonofabitch, you'll pay for slandering my daddy's good family name, and for dragging my girls into this. You'll pay!

Turning away, Seth muttered to himself, "I just met the best defense lawyer this court will ever see. The game is on."

. . . .

Chapter 41

In the prosecution's opening statement, Yielding struck hard. "Premeditated murder!" were his first words. "Nothing but premeditated murder—because John Ed Tomlinson loved another woman and wanted out of his marriage, but desperately wanted custody of his four children and knew that his affair would make for a messy fight with his wife, Jo Dell, and inevitably would drag his family into it. So he devised a plan to lure her out to the Tom Everett tract, where he said he wanted to plant pine seedlings, there to kill her and bury the body in a ghastly grave, an old well. Then to lie to us, friends and family alike, that it had happened accidentally during an argument after he had discovered her and a Mobile doctor in bed together at a Citronelle motel.

"But, gentlemen of the jury, John Ed couldn't make the story work. Couldn't put all the pieces together. So he had to backtrack and concoct another lie, that she had threatened him with a rifle, they had wrestled over the gun and it went off, killing her. Then, having lost all self-control, he took a bulldozer back out there the next day, dropped her into an old well and buried her under a cover of thick mud, intending that to be her hidden grave. To cover himself, he conceived yet another lie that she was at the beach for the weekend. And he had a drinking party at his house the night of the same day he killed her, for God's sake! On and on, until he couldn't devise any more excuses and finally had to admit to the killing, and the well, and the lies to his brother, the respected William Tomlinson, our probate judge, and to the sheriff and his mother."

Standing at the defense table, near the defendant, who looked at him with burning hatred, Yielding concluded his remarks. "None of John Ed's stories worked because they didn't happen! He had to be rid of his wife, once and for all, because it was the only way he could be assured of having his new woman and also his children.

"We will prove this case for exactly what it is," he said with intensity. "Premeditated murder!"

Strudwick Bowden retaliated with an opening statement made calmly and with clear emphasis that this was a horrible accident but not a horrendous crime. Despite Seth's bluster, he saw no need for fireworks yet. The girlfriend, if there was one, was still just hearsay.

"She had pointed a rifle at him during a bitter argument over a divorce. He grabbed it. As they fought it went off. She fell and he could see she was dead on the ground. This husband panicked and ran away. He hid the horrible news overnight, then the next morning went back out there and made a terrible decision that has become the crux of this case. He placed her body in a well. Gentlemen of the jury, you are husbands, and in your God-given common sense you know John Ed shouldn't have made such a mistake. But it is possible that in a similar set of circumstances, you, too, would have lost control of your judgment."

Bowden walked to the jury box and stood no more than eight feet from Lester Hart, in his end seat, who watched him with a glazed look, as if he might be dropping off. "And, gentlemen, please remember from this moment forward that John Ed Tomlinson is not being tried before you for what happened at that well. He is on trial for his life for what happened during a sudden struggle that ensued when he thought his wife would kill him. The rifle she held went off, and, instead of him, she was killed.

"There were only two witnesses to that awful moment, One is John Ed, who has sworn to this court once before that what happened was a tragic accident. The other is Jo Dell Tomlinson . . . and she is not here.

"Gentlemen, the evidence will show, and we will prove, that Jo Dell Tomlinson died not from a heinous murder plot, but from a terrible accident, and that John Ed is innocent of the charge made wrongfully against him.

"Thank you," Bowden said softly, and returned to his seat.

As CIRCUIT SOLICITOR THOMAS Bostick, there at Seth's invitation, listened carefully to Bowden's approach, it reminded him of the case he had prosecuted a few months before in Sumter County, next door west of Henderson County. It had a spooky similarity to this one, that Yielding had pointed out when he asked Bostick to be a special prosecutor.

Two carnival workers, on a crime spree across east Mississippi and west Alabama, had broken into a farmhouse in Sumter County. They shot the husband and wife who lived there, and dropped them into the well. But the woman was still alive and to keep her head above water she climbed on the submerged body of her husband, and stood there screaming until someone heard her the next day.

The killers were caught, and Bostick never doubted that the wounded woman's ghastly experience in the well weighed heavily with the jury who convicted them both, sending one to the electric chair and the other to life in prison.

"Say what you will, Mr. Bowden," Bostick thought, seated beside Yielding. "But you'll never separate out the well from this jury's mind."

· · · · · · · · · ·

Chapter 42

"**N**ow, just a minute. We're going to object to that because . . ." If Strudwick Bowden bombarded the courtroom with that ringing statement once during the prosecution's presentation, he did it fifty times. He challenged every foothold that Seth and Tom tried to establish against John Ed. Judge

Cargile sustained and overruled his objections about evenly, but a strategy became evident: disrupt the prosecutors' strategy at every turn, make them back up and go another way, speak indirectly to the jury by this plan.

He displayed his prowess at the trial's first crucial testimony, on the third day.

Twice, the defense disrupted a state's witness and Seth's attempts to have the jury hear that Jo Dell could have been shot while on the ground and cringing from her killer. On the stand again was state toxicologist Nethery, the first to examine the body. Seth had introduced that possibility in questioning the witness.

On cross-examination, however, Bowden asked, "Is it your opinion that the evidence you found is consistent with a wound that may be inflicted during a struggle over a rifle?"

"It's possible that it could happen during a struggle over a rifle," Nethery answered.

The crafty Bowden—winning Judge Cargile's approval to do so—even let Nethery use him to demonstrate what might have been Jo Dell's position when shot, not on the ground, but bent over slightly, her right arm at a sixty-degree angle. The bullet missed her spinal column by one-sixteenth of an inch, Nethery said, which indicated it didn't pass through her body in a straight line.

Seth then tried to rescue the testimony on cross-examination: "Is it not true that Mrs. Tomlinson could have been in a cringing position, turning away?"

"Objection, Your Honor."

"Sustained."

"From your findings, and based on the evidence you have given to this court and the jury, could this bullet have been fired from a number of feet away while she was in a cringing position and in no contact with the person who held the gun?"

"We're going to object to that, too, Your Honor. Use of the word, 'cringing' calls for an illegal opinion and conclusion."

"Sustained."

The best finish Seth could get from Nethery was his opinion that the rifle probably was twelve inches or more from Jo Dell when fired. But ending three hours of give and take, every move carefully made, Bowden countered by getting Nethery to assert that if she had been shot from a normal shooting position, the bullet would have ranged downward, not upward, as his examination found. Seth objected: overruled.

The point-counterpoint drama between the lead attorneys fascinated me. I took notes and quotes as fast as I could write.

More crucial testimony followed the lunch recess when the state called Barbara Evans Walker to the witness chair. A small diamond gleamed on her left ring finger, and the slender twenty-three year old looked especially smart in a fitted print dress, pastel blue sweater over her shoulders and cream pumps. She wasn't Henderson County gossip anymore, but now a respectable Birmingham resident, and she wanted every person in court to know it and have a good look at a woman changed.

Those drinking nights and carousing with John Ed and Sarah had receded deeply into her earlier life, as one seeks to allay discretion of the moment, but—Charles Allen be damned—under oath she would remember them again, and tell what she had seen and heard, what she was party to, one last time. For you, Sarah, she whispered, who loved a bad man. John Ed, you can go to hell for what you did to poor Jo Dell.

With specifics and in sharp detail, Mrs. Walker reconstructed several instances in early 1959 when the three of them drove an hour down the highway to neighboring Washington County to Nathan's Roadhouse, played music, and had several drinks; went to another honky-tonk at nearby Millry, where they laughed and drank; to Mobile on that weekend so he could leave a car ostensibly for Jo Dell to drive back from Dauphin Island, stopping for whiskey on the way back. They also had gone to Meridian in summer 1958 for John Ed to tend to business.

At Nathan's: "I went over to play the jukebox, and when I came back they were talking about where they would live, and said it would be at Sarah's house." He kissed her on the cheek as we drove home later that night, she said.

She testified of other occasions hearing John Ed and Sarah talk of love and marriage, not trying to hide it from her. But that wasn't the mood on the trip to Mobile. Coming back, said Mrs. Walker, "He was extremely nervous."

Driving from Mobile, the three in one car, she said John Ed stopped to make a phone call, and as he and the women got close to home, Bill Tomlinson appeared in his car and pulled up behind them. The brothers talked privately for several minutes, and afterward John Ed told Sarah and Barbara that Jo Dell was putting him under a two thousand dollar peace bond and charging him with cruelty to their children.

"He told us he didn't have the money," Barbara said. "Sarah signed a check for one thousand dollars and said, 'John, you know this is going to court.' He replied, 'Yes, but you'll be out of it.'"

Barbara testified that she attended a party and fish fry at John Ed's house on January 27, and heard him say he was celebrating his freedom; he was getting a divorce and giving Jo Dell three thousand dollars and a car, among other things.

As I heard these declarations, speed-writing in my own shorthand, I also tried to watch the jury. The men seemed to listen intently, their eyes on the attractive witness whose composure didn't falter throughout her testimony. But Bowden hasn't pounced yet, I thought.

· · · · · · · · · ·

Chapter 43

Gently starting his cross-examination, as if holding her hand along a slippery path, Bowden established that Barbara Walker had known Sarah casually for ten years or more, but had come to know John Ed only after he began seeing Sarah in early 1958. The women became close and talked about things, she said.

"Miss Evans, I'm sorry, Mrs. Walker," he addressed her with subtle cattiness, getting a ripple of chuckles from the courtroom, whose every hard bench was filled, "Mrs. Walker, do you know Robert Whatley?"

"Yes."

"Who is he?"

"A local logger. He worked for John Ed."

"The defendant."

"Yes."

"Do you have firsthand knowledge that Mr. Whatley knows Sarah Davis?"

"Yes, I do."

"Tell the court what you know."

"Objection, Your Honor," Seth interjected.

"Overruled."

"They had been dating for several months."

"And this was in what time period?"

"Most of 1958."

"From your firsthand knowledge, was this a casual friendship, or more?"

"More. They had become engaged toward the end of that year." An audible buzz swept across the courtroom, and I put an exclamation point by that note.

"Well, then, they didn't just want to go to church together, did they? Their relationship had gotten serious, had it not?" Bowden drove home his obvious point. "Let's see, now, Mrs. Walker. If Sarah was Robert Whatley's fiancé she wouldn't have any reason to be talking marriage with John Ed, would she?"

"No sir. But that's what I heard."

"Or what you thought you heard, Mrs. Walker, with the whiskey flowing, the music playing, and loud talk all around," said Bowden, his tone suddenly carrying the edge of a butcher knife.

"Objection!" cried Seth, on his feet.

"I'll allow it," said Cargile.

"No more questions," Bowden said. "But, Your Honor, I'd like to reserve the right to recall this witness."

Seth decided to counter Bowden's last statement, and stood again. "Redirect, Your Honor."

"Proceed."

"Mrs. Walker, there may have been alcohol, music and crowd noise, but you have testified under oath that what you heard and saw between John Ed Tomlinson and Sarah Davis on numerous occasions is the truth. Is that still your testimony?"

"It is."

"Thank you. No further questions at this time."

Cargile glanced at the clock hanging on the wall and then at the jury. Some of the men sat slumped; they all looked tired.

"That's enough for today; we'll begin again tomorrow at nine. Court is adjourned," he said firmly.

"All rise!" said Bailiff Talmadge as Cargile left the bench.

Smiling and unruffled, as if days like this invigorated him, Bowden stopped in the hallway with reporters for a few minutes. His strategy required it at the close of each session. He cultivated reporters as assets—a long-standing practice now perfected because they were so gullible as to swallow every comment, and to him it was child's play.

"We've just begun, but I'd say we had a good day," he said. "The defendant is presumed innocent, and nothing that was said altered that presumption. No, Mrs. Walker's testimony didn't hurt us at all. In fact, she just established the fact that Sarah Davis was engaged to another man at the time. Thank you, that's all. Good night, gentlemen."

. . . .

Chapter 44

She stood in a small cluster of twenty or so people who had sat in court for several hours and now wanted to end the day by edging close enough to Bowden to catch some of his comments to the press. But she had no interest in what the attorney was saying. Lindsey Rush was watching the reporters ask questions and take notes, eying one in particular. She was no closer now than when she had sat two rows behind him all day, where she had come to feel inexplicably possessed by curiosity and emotions; even drawn to this young man with coat-and-tie appearance, professional conduct, and appealing looks. During the afternoon she had made, for her, a bold and impetuous decision, totally foreign to her nature, to not just wonder about him from afar, but to make his acquaintance. She had even chuckled about it, thinking nothing ventured, nothing gained.

Casually dressed for early spring in a high-neck scarlet sweater and matching cardigan, oxford gray skirt, socks and black penny loafers, Lindsey was not inconspicuous surrounded by the gathering of mostly men. A well-proportioned body displayed her nicely. Her softly shaped face was highlighted by friendly blue eyes, inviting lips, and framed by hair the golden hue of freshly cut wheat that fell to her shoulders. The total look erased any mistaken impression that she was a high school girl.

BOWDEN ENDED THE INTERVIEW after a few minutes. I closed my notebook and glanced back at the people to see someone smiling at me. They scattered, but she lingered, hesitantly, I thought.

Walking over, I said, "That's a rare sight around here—a pretty smile such as yours."

"Most everybody I know says you're not welcome here, they don't like what you write, or you, and wish you'd leave," she replied pleasantly.

"Won't be soon enough for me," I said. "Quick as the trial ends. So, what persuaded you to go against the grain? And what's your name?"

"Lindsey. Well, I just think somebody ought to recognize that you're just doing your job, nothing personal against any of us."

"You're a brave lady," I said as we walked together out the massive double doors, past the stately columns, and down the steps. "Is your car close by?" It was almost dark and getting chilly.

"No, my aunt dropped me off. I'm staying with her this week."

"So you don't live here?"

"No, Mobile."

"Well, if you don't mind being seen with the enemy, or riding in his car, I'll take you home. But you know the rumors about you will spread." Ace, in the Star car, had gone on ahead to Meridian. This would be his last week here unless Stan Meyer changed the plan. I was driving another company car, less obvious, a fifty-eight Chevy two-door,

"I'm not worried," Lindsey said. "Go west on State Street, it's just out of town."

I had to ask, seeing that she wore a narrow gold band: "What does your husband do?"

"Construction work, drywall and all. Does your wife work? Take the next left, it's the third house." She had noticed my ring.

"She does, mostly at home, raising our son; he's two. She's also a fine musician." I stopped at her direction at a two-story frame house, with a wide, welcoming front porch, and the light on by the door.

"Nice meeting you, Mr. Anderson. I'll be there tomorrow." Smiling again, she brushed my hand lightly and said, "My instincts were right."

"How's that?"

"A reporter can be a gentleman, too."

I smiled back. "Well, it never hurts to try."

I pulled away and headed toward Meridian, with a short night's worth of hard writing ahead, thinking about a story line as I drove. But more than that, I thought about this attractive new someone who looked lady-like, but seemed tough enough to dismiss the prospect of ugly gossip and rumor, who had appeared out of nowhere to say, let's be friends, when, for damn sure, nobody else did.

For reasons I wouldn't question right now, she had come to my door at this place where—for the first time on any story—I felt little else but cold resentment. And if she was asking to come in, I would be cautious, for I knew nothing about her, and that could be foolish, dangerous, or both. But what the hell. I would say yes.

. . . .

Chapter 45

I didn't have to look far to find Lindsey the next day; she had seated herself on the end of a bench two rows behind me. "Good morning," I said cheerfully, walking up the aisle and seeing that her golden hair was pulled back into a saucy ponytail. "Nice to see you."

She smiled warmly as a couple sitting beside her frowned disapprovingly.

"If you're free at lunch I've brought a picnic. We could find a spot outside. It won't be too cool."

"That's a great alternative to another burger. Let's do it," I replied.

"Oyez! Oyez! Honorable Circuit Court of Henderson County is now in session. Come into court!" Bailiff Talmadge, in bellowing good voice, shouted over the town square from a second story window promptly at 9 A.M., as he did every spring and fall, when court was convened. With perfect timing the call also ushered in Judge Cargile, who walked briskly from chambers.

Immediately, he said, "Will the lead attorneys please approach." Yielding and Bowden walked forward to stand side by side before the bench. He spoke to them softly: "If Sarah Davis was to be a witness during this trial, at any time, strike her from the list. I have learned that she has left the state and cannot be located. I strongly doubt that she will appear to testify."

Neither man's expressions gave away their feelings as they returned to their chairs, but Bowden was exuberant. "They've just lost a key part of their puzzle," he thought. Yielding felt sucker-punched in the stomach. "Sonofabitch!" he muttered.

"Mr. Yielding, call your first witness," Cargile instructed.

"The state calls Annie Wilkes." She walked sedately to the witness box, wearing glasses, a white hat, black dress and minimal makeup. She clutched a handkerchief.

"Mrs. Wilkes, please state your age."

"Fifty-eight."

"Your daughter was Jo Dell Tomlinson, is that correct?"

Bowden interrupted. "Objection. Stating the obvious."

"I'll allow it, Mr. Bowden," Cargile responded.

"Yes, she is . . ." Then Annie Wilkes stopped in mid-sentence, breathed deeply, and looked at the jury. "She was my daughter. She is dead."

"Objection."

"Overruled."

Methodically and gently, Seth established the family history of this woman, whom he had known and admired for years. Jo Dell was her only child, honor graduate of County High and, at the time of her death, president of the elementary school PTA, a high school band mother, and a member of the Women's Missionary Union at First Methodist Church. Mrs. Wilkes's husband, Albert, had died only six months earlier, and now, except for part time-help, she alone ran the neighborly Wilkes General Store on the square, just across the street. Important facts to underscore the family's proud standing among local citizens, Seth reasoned.

"This is not a toy lawyer," Bowden thought as he watched and wrote on his yellow legal pad. "This is a formidable foe; a poised, smooth lawyer whose questions are encouraging, leading, persuasive and suggestive. But I'll prevail. I always do."

As Seth was ending, according to plan he suddenly pitched a hard ball. "Mrs. Wilkes, when were you convinced that Jo Dell might be dead?"

"Now just a minute, we're going to object to that because the question calls for guesswork," Bowden said, suddenly on his feet.

"I'll allow it, but Mr. Yielding, stay on point."

Speaking softly, but with notable emphasis, she answered. "I was spending part of the weekend at Jo Dell's house and had asked John Ed where she was. It seemed like he was angry. He called me a crazy old fool and said she was at their beach house at Dauphin Island for the weekend, resting. He said he was going to meet her at the Battle House in Mobile. I didn't believe him."

"The Battle House. That's a hotel?" he said.

"Yes," she replied.

"And when did you learn Jo Dell was dead?"

"Monday night, at Jo Dell's house. Sheriff Hutton told me. He had me brought over."

Shifting back to a gentle approach, Seth brought out several more qualities and facts about Jo Dell—she had had health problems after the twins' birth three years earlier; had undergone a hysterectomy at the Mobile Infirmary in fall 1958, but now was in good health; she cooked, kept the house, and for a long time had kept the books for John Ed and paid the men who worked for him.

Mrs. Wilkes also testified that she was at the Tomlinson house when John Ed had the party on the night of January 29, and stayed in a bedroom as he asked her to do. His oldest daughter, Margaret, spent time in the kitchen with her father and his guests, and brought her grandmother a plate of fish.

"Your witness," Seth finally said, moving toward his chair.

Strudwick Bowden, anything but gentle and caring, on cross-examination tried to establish that John Ed had given "innumerable checks" as gifts to his mother-in-law and her husband. He cited checks payable to Mr. Wilkes in life, plus four hundred dollars to help pay his funeral expenses.

"Do you remember John Ed giving your husband one thousand dollars?" he asked.

"I do not," she replied emphatically.

"And the four hundred dollar check?"

"I do not."

Prosecution objection prompted an exchange between the two sides in which the suggestion was made to put John Ed on the stand and let him explain the checks. Bowden replied to that sarcastically. "We'll handle our case the way we see it unless Your Honor objects. Then we'll handle it your way."

The judge ended the argument by saying, "It's almost 10:30. Let's recess until 11.

I hurried to a vacant office I had spotted earlier to call the Star collect. This dramatic testimony needed to get into the home editions. As I dictated the highlights, four teenage boys with long sideburns and duck tails came in, wearing jeans and T-shirts. They gathered at the desk to listen and tried to look threatening.

When I was finished they crowded me a little more. "Mr. Reporter," said their spokesman, who didn't give his name, "this is a warning. Stay away from our girls. We catch you with one and we'll whip your Birmingham ass. And don't think we won't." Then they left. I passed off the comments as tough guy bluster. My mistake.

Cargile was gaveling order in the court when I slipped into my seat. Seth then called Gary Reynolds, of Mobile, Jo Dell's first cousin. He testified of going to the beach house on January 31 and finding it empty. "I came back and called Mrs. Annie Wilkes, but talked to Mrs. Rose, who answered. I told her that Jo Dell wasn't there. I asked for Annie, but she never came on the line."

"By Rose, you mean John Ed's mother, Rose Tomlinson"

"Yes sir." Reynolds said.

"Your witness."

Bowden replied, "No questions."

The last witness of the morning was Jane Douglas, postmistress at Silas, who disclosed that John Ed and Jo Dell once lived in her house, and that their first child, Margaret, was born there. She described Jo Dell as "the perfect mother" and a cheerful person who said good things about John Ed. She visited in their home the late afternoon of January 29, but said Jo Dell wasn't there.

During Bowden's cross-examination, Douglas said Jo Dell was "nervous" following her hysterectomy and because her mother couldn't adjust after Mr. Wilkes's death. But on redirect, the witness said Jo Dell "was on the road to recovery," and went with the school band to Governor Sullivan's inauguration, and also was planning to accompany the band to Mardi Gras in Mobile.

Seth finished his redirect at 11:45 A.M. and Cargile recessed for lunch until 1 P.M.

This testimony didn't merit another hurried phone call to the City Desk, and I was glad to see Lindsey waiting for me in the hall, holding a shopping bag. "I'm in your hands," I said. "Where to?"

She replied, "You drive, I'll navigate."

· · · · · · · · · · ·

Chapter 46

A few blocks east of the town square, we stopped at Memorial Cemetery, the smaller of the two cemeteries in Butler. A low rock wall enclosed it, and majestic old water oaks offered shade even at midday. We walked through the open gate and over to a rectangular plot, big enough for three graves, its centerpiece a large marble monument engraved "Wilkes." Two headstones were set in a surface of crushed rock. A few tufts of grass poked through, reaching for sunlight.

Lindsey said quietly, "Jo Dell is here, and her father, with space for her mother. You need to see it."

"Why here?" I questioned. "They were married when she died. Why isn't she in a Tomlinson plot?"

"Mrs. Wilkes wouldn't have it. From the outset she believed John Ed killed her daughter."

I went to her gray marble headstone and read the inscription:

JO DELL WILKES TOMLINSON

JUNE 27, 1925–JAN. 29, 1959

"The feelings run deeper than I imagined," I said.

"They would be hard to measure," Lindsey said. "More like hatred, I think."

We spread a tarp from my car under a tree, outside the cemetery wall, and sat on it. From a cooler she offered ham sandwiches, soft drinks and peanut butter cookies, which tasted delectable, considering the peaceful April setting, and especially the company.

"You've brought a bit of pleasure to a tough assignment," I ventured. "And you'll grow on me, if you're not careful."

"Don't let it," she replied, looking at me intently, not smiling, close enough that I could smell her perfume. "Dan," she said, "my family is in the Tomlinson camp. My father worked for John Ed's father some years ago, and the aunt I'm staying with is on the defense's list as a character witness. Some of our people, who really don't like your newspaper, or you either, have pressed me to cozy up to you, and before this trial ends to compromise you, and in the process discredit your work down here and back at your paper. In short, get you in trouble. Yesterday, with that on my mind, I sat close enough to get a good look at you. And last night, for various reasons, I decided that I wanted no part of causing you trouble. I will tell my people that it's not like me to do this, and that I'll not do it. They won't like it, but so what? I can control that."

She continued, "What I don't seem to be able to control, for now, at least, are undeniable feelings I've suddenly developed. We're at the center of an explosive situation, but it will end soon, one way or another, and you'll be gone—I know all that—and maybe that's pushing me forward. But in the time we have, I want to know you better, become your friend, and," her voice trailing off, "whatever else. Wow, this isn't like me; I'm normally reserved, even shy, and I can't believe I'm saying this, or that I feel this way."

I had listened silently, caught unaware. I reached for her hand and pressed it tightly for a moment. "Lindsey," I said, "in some ways I think we are like two searching people who happened to meet and are glad we did. It seems that these circumstances have us reaching toward each other, knowing that time is short and we can't be hesitant, whatever the outcome. I'm drawn to you because you're lovely and I'm very vulnerable down here. I'm sure you could have entrapped me. Lucky for me you changed your mind. I don't know where any of this could lead, but odds are we'll find out."

"So be it," she replied solemnly, then suddenly beamed. "Well, I'm glad that's out of the way." We both laughed.

Cleaning up our picnic, we headed back to the courthouse. As we did I thought, we hadn't even mentioned our spouses, making this a totally self-serving circumstance. We entered court just as Judge Cargile stepped up to his desk.

AFTERNOON TESTIMONY WAS BLAND and slow, consisting first of a Silas man who said that John Ed's Chevrolet was parked at Sarah's house "on occasion," usually early morning, but then offered that John Ed was cutting timber nearby. Yielding's next witness was a lifelong woodsman who produced the only real nugget of testimony, a sketch of the Everett land that he said he knew well, and was 120 acres. He showed the court the well site, an old road, and a place where tree stumps had been bulldozed over. The well was fenced with net wire and barbed wire, he said. Also, he claimed, no seedlings had been planted around where the bulldozer had worked, before or after the killing.

Bowden let these witnesses pass quietly, and they turned out to be the state's last volley of testimony against John Ed. The judge, himself tired, didn't want to absorb anyone else's words and adjourned proceedings.

Combatants sparred with the press in the hall, Yielding saying, "We're stronger than before, more complete in that we're proving motive, plan, and design. After he killed her, his actions of concealing her show the degree of the crime. We've proved a connection to Sarah Davis that is unimpeachable. How can they prove Jo Dell wasn't a good wife?"

I missed Bowden's comments. He was leaving as Seth finished. I would read them in the *Mobile Register*. But I had enough cross-examination to write a balanced story.

THE JURY WALKED TOGETHER, with deputy escort, to Downtown Café, a few blocks away, glad to be outside and stretching their legs. They ate supper leisurely, got refills of sweet tea and banana pudding, and shared conversation about most everything except the trial.

The twelfth man, Lester, got a little something extra with his meal. Tucked inside his folded paper napkin was a piece of small note paper. He pulled it out in his lap and read the large printing inconspicuously—"Do right. We're watching."

By 7:30 P.M., the jury had disbanded for the night, going home, taking with them the judge's strict instructions not to discuss the trial in any way, to disassociate from anyone who mentioned it, and not to read or hear any news about it.

· · · · · · · · · ·

Chapter 47

Lindsey and I had supper together, but bypassed the café and the jury. We went to Joe Nabors's Social Club, the roadhouse south of town that offered a limited menu along with its alcohol. Arriving about 6:30 P.M., we found the place crowded with early boozers and ringing with juke box tunes. A couple was leaving, so we claimed their booth and quickly disappeared unnoticed behind a screen of cigarette smoke and noisy people—just what we wanted.

Right away, I got myself a beer and Lindsey a soft drink, and ordered two fish plates from the bar. Then I returned to slide in, press close, and put my arm around her. She turned slightly, looked into my eyes with anticipation, and parted her lips lightly. I kissed her gently, but she pressed her lips tightly against mine. My arm pulled her closer still. We broke the awkward embrace, but kissed again. And a third time, softly.

"My God," she whispered, breathing heavily. "I knew it would be like this."

"And you are really something," I responded.

Suddenly her blue eyes sparkled, and for the second time that day she said, "Well, I'm glad that's out of the way." I got our food and we chatted easily as we ate, smiling at what we had done, not noticing that three young men at a nearby table had taken it all in.

SHE HAD BEEN BORN in Mobile, grew up there, and went to Murphy High School; fell in love her senior year and married the summer after graduation. Worked as a legal aide at a Mobile law firm, while her husband, also a graduate, attended trade school to learn construction skills. They had an apartment, no children, and would celebrate their second anniversary in August. Her family's connection to the Tomlinsons, and the reversed conviction, prompted her to take a week of vacation during a lull in the legal season, and come up to Butler for the second trial. She had to go home this weekend and back to work.

Lindsey learned that I was born in Florida but moved to Birmingham at age twelve to live with my mother and her second husband. Began journalism at my high school paper and as a Saturday copy boy at the *Star*. Worked my way through Birmingham-Methodist College and married when my wife and I were in our junior year. Started full time at the newspaper after graduation. One son, Sam, born in January 1960. I play around on the guitar and enjoy singing. I didn't volunteer any more background. Don't, my wall advised.

"Better go," I said, after we ate. "I'm getting worried abut my deadline. My copy has to make the midnight bus to Birmingham."

"Only if you insist," she said playfully.

It was 8 P.M. when we headed back, stopping briefly at her aunt's. I kissed her goodnight and drove on to Meridian with barely two hours to write and get the story to the bus station. I shouldn't have cut the deadline so close because she was already making it hard to concentrate. You've started something, I said to myself. Now what are you going to do with it?

Chapter 48

Seth worked late that Thursday night, sipping bourbon, feeling its mellow warmth and reviewing pages of notes, hearing in his head certain witnesses again, and evaluating the strength of his case. A comment he had made to the reporters came to mind: "We have as strong a case as we've ever had."

"Damn right we do," he said, turning out the light at midnight and going home.

STUDYING THE PROSECUTION'S WITNESS list, underlining several names, adding up his strengths, Strudwick Bowden also worked late. "We have the upper hand," he concluded. "They don't have anywhere else to go." He sharpened his plan just before going to bed, so was fully prepared when, at 9:16 on the morning of the sixth day, Yielding stood and declared, "Your Honor, the state rests."

Bowden struck instantly with notice of a motion that surprised Judge Cargile and caused him to excuse the jury from hearing it. "We ask the court to issue a directed verdict of innocent," Bowden said. "Judge, the prosecution's testimony is wholly insufficient to make out a prima facia case. There is no evidence introduced in the record to authorize this case to go to a jury—not of first degree murder, second degree murder, manslaughter in the first degree, or manslaughter in the second degree."

This end run to stop the trial didn't catch Yielding off guard; he had awakened at 5 A.M. with the thought that it was not beyond Bowden to try it. He responded with a just-completed statement that summarized the state's key points, and noted that the judge—himself fresh and alert—was listening intently. He ended saying, "We are making a complete case, Your Honor, even stronger than before."

Cargile's response to both men was to call a twenty-minute recess. "I'll have my ruling at that time," he said.

Bowden's ploy stirred the early spectators, who filled about half of the seats, to full voice. I looked around for Lindsey, who was in her usual place, and who smiled and winked. I was also spotting Bill Tomlinson and Rose for reaction in case Bowden won his motion.

Judge Cargile returned to the bench at ten and summoned Bowden and Yielding to approach. He spoke directly to them, but his voice carried into the front pews, including where I sat. "With all due respect, Mr. Bowden—and it is substantial, to be sure—the testimony presented thus far merits this trial continuing to a just conclusion. Motion denied. Mr. Bowden, call your first witness."

That witness was the president of Henderson National Bank, Albert Hawkins, with known connections to the Tomlinsons. During his testimony, Bowden entered into evidence two checks showing payment of utility bills for the Wilkes, bearing John Ed's signature, from Jo Dell's and John Ed's joint account.

"Good," Yielding breathed to himself. "Bowden has just stumbled."

On cross-examination, Yielding presented a letter signed by J. E. Tomlinson, whose envelope was addressed to "Mrs. Sarah Tomlinson."

Bowden erupted as if the envelope might contain an expression of incendiary love, which would prove John Ed's clear intent. Harshly, he protested that the letter could not be introduced as rebuttal to the previous testimony, that it should have surfaced during the state's case, and if it were allowed he would ask for a mistrial.

"You opened that door, Mr. Bowden, I'll allow it," Judge Cargile said calmly. Over defense objections, that letter and two others were allowed as state's evidence. Yielding did not attempt to disclose their content. Bowden dropped the mistrial threat.

A procession of eighteen character witnesses—men, women, white, black—accounted for the rest of the morning and half of the afternoon. All said they knew John Ed well, some had worked for him for years, and each one said he had a good reputation. "I've never heard anything against his good name," said one man. Another, a former circuit judge and long acquainted with the Tomlinsons, said a man's reputation "was something that spoke out. If his reputation had been bad, I'd have known it."

Bowden's final witness of the day was Cyrus Bonner, who told the court he had had 46,000 pine seedlings planted on the Everett tract in November

1958, but that none were set out around the well site.

The judge then adjourned the sixth day, with Bowden saying afterward that he should be finished early the next week. He added with an intended air of mystery, "I'm unsure of whether Mr. Tomlinson or Ms. Davis's fiancé, Mr. Whatley, will take the stand."

He answered my obvious question: "No, I don't rule it out."

Lindsey had told me at lunch that she had to return to Mobile for the weekend. "I go back to work on Monday," she said, "but I'll be back if I can get the time off. I'll miss you." She would leave the courthouse with her aunt that evening without being able to say goodbye. Two men who stood unnoticed in the hall watched them go.

I had checked out of the Meridian motel that morning, so was ready to roll, too, and figured to be home by 9 P.M. I mapped out Sunday stories as I drove, Lindsey and the improbable week strong on my mind. My weekend boiled down to a short Sunday, but it was good to have it with Claire and Sam.

. . . .

Chapter 49

Bill Tomlinson and four others—Strudwick Bowden, Cal Cates, Rose Tomlinson, and a Bowden firm neophyte summoned from Birmingham to take notes—clustered around the probate judge's conference table late Saturday afternoon. They talked strategy for two hours.

"Here's where are," said Bowden. "We've raised irrefutable doubt about the angle of the fatal bullet. We've cast a shadow of doubt upon the alleged romance between John Ed and Sarah Davis. We know beyond a doubt that John Ed helped the Wilkes pay their bills. We've established that John Ed was known generally as a man of good reputation. We've planted the thought with the jury that any one of them conceivably could have gone over the edge in a comparable way, as we're saying John Ed did in suffering temporary insanity."

Bill Tomlinson interjected, "And don't forget that John Ed has always maintained that the shooting was accidental."

"Which brings up the issue of John Ed taking the stand," Bowden responded. "It backfired last time because, although he didn't crack or lose composure under Yielding's barrage, the jury would not let go of the well. And that's why we don't need to open that volatile subject this time. The record clearly shows John Ed's earlier testimony—and he has never wavered—that Jo Dell died accidentally and that he is innocent of murder. And the only other witness is dead. Now, he might have been screwing Sarah Davis, but she isn't here to testify, either, making that a relatively moot issue. And the letters from him to her bear little importance at this time."

Knowing full well the force of his reasoning, Bowden nonetheless polled the meeting, asking, "Do we need John Ed?" They were unanimous: "No." Final parts of the defense were put in place, and the group adjourned to Bill and Nancy Tomlinson's house for drinks, dinner, and less serious conversation.

MONDAY MORNING, BOWDEN CALLED five more witnesses, one of whom was Peter Harrell, administrative officer of the county agricultural conservation program. Harrell disclosed that Rose Tomlinson herself had an interest in the Everett tract of land, owning two contracts and planning to set out pine seedlings, which was done in fall 1959, but not near the abandoned well. Another witness testified of seeing John Ed at his brother's office at midday on January 29, 1959, pacing the floor and looking nervous. Testimony of the other three seemed of minimal consequence.

At 11 A.M., according to his plan, Bowden announced, "Your Honor, the defense rests." Judge Cargile then recessed the court until 1 P.M.

I looked for Lindsey and didn't see her, but hoped that she would come back this week. She had stayed very near the surface of my emotions all weekend. I wanted to know she was there, stoking the flickering feelings between us.

Yielding questioned two rebuttal witnesses once court reconvened. One was Annie Wilkes, who testified mostly about money. She said Jo Dell had paid a few of her utility bills and had written her husband a check for timber he sold and John Ed cut, but that she didn't know of any other monetary gifts or business transactions between the Tomlinson and Wilkes families. Sitting beside her son at the defense table, Rose watched Mrs. Wilkes with a stern expression as she stepped down from the stand and left the room.

Yielding's other witness was Warren Roach, a county agricultural official, who spoke of visits made to the Everett tract from October 1958 to April 1961. Under meticulous questioning, Roach confirmed the point that no pine seedlings had been planted in the vicinity of the old well or in the area that had been bulldozed. Hearing that, John Ed looked grim and shook his head.

The state rested again shortly before 2 P.M. and Judge Cargile summoned the attorneys into his chambers for a conference about closing arguments. The jurors were led away to relax for a while in the jury room. All of us left in the crowded, hot courtroom—the main floor being nearly full—grew restless as we waited on the hard pews, stood to stretch, drifted into the hall, or went to pee.

MRS. WILKES HAD RETURNED and sat quietly in the middle of the front row. Bill Tomlinson, his coat off, came forward to speak briefly to John Ed and Rose.

The attorneys and the judge reappeared after about thirty minutes. "We will begin closing arguments, after which I will charge the jury," said Cargile. "The attorneys and I estimate this process will take some five hours." At that comment, the jury openly exchanged oh-no glances and spectators murmured noisily. Sharp raps of the judge's gavel restored decorum.

· · · · · · · · · ·
Chapter 50

Up first was Tom Bostick, the veteran circuit solicitor from Marengo County. He knew several on the jury by name, and others in the room as well. He said, "The state has presented one of the strongest cases of first degree murder ever heard in Henderson County, and I will give you, the jury, five major points in support of that statement.

"First, John Ed and his girlfriend, Sarah Davis, were openly running all over the place together—to Laurel, Meridian, Jackson, Mobile, and honky tonks down the highway, to name just a few. You've heard the sworn testimony of people who either went with them or saw them. Plus, he wrote to her as Mrs. Sarah Tomlinson!

"Second, John Ed and Jo Dell did not go to the Tom Everett tract to talk about planting pine trees. There is no evidence of any pine trees planted closer than 130 yards to the old well where he buried her.

"Third, where are the powder burns that would have resulted from a bullet fired at close range, as John Ed says happened. Yes, men of the jury, it is possible that this was an accident, but if that was the case, and it was you and your wife out there, you would have placed her back in the truck and driven like a mad man getting her to a doctor. That's human nature! But what did John Ed do? He started covering up this crime in less than thirty minutes, and proceeded to build a story based solely on lies.

"Fourth, by God, he had a party that same night at his house with Sarah, his lover, and friends. Fried fish, drank whiskey, told Jo Dell's mother—who was there to keep the children— to stay in her room. And called her an old fool for worrying about her daughter's whereabouts.

"Fifth, he took a car to Mobile as part of the ruse that she was down there resting and would drive it back. All part of a brazen plan!

"Gentlemen, you have not heard a single fact that would cause you to believe that Jo Dell met her death by accident. To the contrary, there is not but one verdict you can reach. That is, guilty of first degree murder."

SETH BIDED HIS TIME, listening carefully as Bostick worked the plan and step by step covered all the ground his side had gained. Seth was ready for this moment, so energized he could have sprinted a mile in the day's humid heat. Suit coat off, shirt sleeves turned up, this was all business and he didn't want to be on show.

Moving away from the prosecution table to the open space in front of the judge, he stopped a few feet from the jury box and made a half turn back to the defense chairs. Pointing at John Ed, he said, with all the meaning his opening could carry, "You, the jury, are judges of the fact. And the fact is, none of John Ed Tomlinson's stories, explanations, and lies tell us anything but premeditated murder. And another fact is that he has not testified in his own behalf to tell you men that he didn't do it.

"Instead, in his sworn statement to our good sheriff, he called this Christian woman, his wife of fourteen years, the mother of his four children, a prominent member of our community—a whore! Said he found her in bed with a doctor from Mobile at a Citronelle motel. Lie!

"Next, he said they went out to the Everett tract to look over an area for planting pine trees. With the evidence you've heard it doesn't add up. Lie!" Picking up the rifle from the evidence table, he held it against his body and fanned the hammer. "It couldn't have just gone off! Any way she may have turned, she'd have been facing him. You can see her, almost hear her, begging for life, not to die, but to go back to her two daughters and twin sons. But John Ed wasn't listening. He would not be stopped from carrying out his devious and gruesome plan to destroy his wife for the passion of another woman."

Slamming the defense's strategy to show John Ed as a caring husband who helped out his in-laws financially, Seth asked the jury to consider, "Is a dollar value going to be placed on Jo Dell's head? Four hundred dollar funeral bill, eight dollar phone bill, twenty dollar light bill?"

Rose Tomlinson kept her head erect and watched Seth intently as he proceeded. Once she cleaned her glasses and once, when he invoked the Bible, she mouthed something to herself that no one could hear. John Ed folded and unfolded his arms, fidgeted with his hands, and listened with a calm expression.

An hour passed before Seth finished, saying in conclusion, "We have here a man guilty of first degree murder, and the people of this county won't stand for it. I challenge this jury not to let the State of Alabama, not to let the intervening two years since the first trial—when your friends and neighbors judged him guilty as charged—not to let those years wash away the crime that's been done." Placing the death weapon back on the defense table, Seth took his seat, and the courtroom crowd, as one, exhaled. Judge Cargile called a recess of twenty minutes.

Chapter 51

Unwinding, the jury relaxed in its guarded room, some smoking, others drinking from the pitcher of ice water or cold soft drinks placed on the table. Several took a leak.

"Mighty strong," said one lean, leathery member. "Him concocting that lie that Jo Dell was a whore. Damn him!" Murmured agreement followed from a few of the others. Lester Hart listened silently, wanting no one to pay him any attention. Minutes later, a deputy led them back to their places.

"Mr. Bowden, Mr. Cates, you may proceed," the judge said after gaveling court back to business. Cates stood and a well-rehearsed plan went into play. He walked halfway to the jury, then stopped to slowly survey these men whom he knew, including their good habits and bad habits. They knew that he knew.

"You are members of our community in good standing and respect, chosen carefully to make a difficult judgment of someone else whom you know—as you have heard numerous witnesses say—is respected and liked as husband, father, woodsman and friend on our streets. That man there," he said, gesturing toward John Ed, "who, we have shown, helps others. Doesn't hurt them.

"You have only heard one of the charges made against John Ed Tomlinson. But remember that the indictment also embraces second degree murder and manslaughter in the first degree. Remember, too, that he wears a shield of innocence that the framers of our nation's Constitution gave to each citizen. So," said Cates, stepping toward the jury, hands outstretched in an obvious gesture for sympathy, "it is up to the state to prove willful, malicious, deliberate, premeditated guilt.

"And, I will tell you," he said forcefully, voice rising, "that the state has failed miserably by its evidence to prove any case against this defendant. By its chief and star witnesses, the state, in fact, has made a perfect defense for the charges against the defendant. That, members of the jury, is the third thing you must remember. And the following points tell you why.

"No eyewitness testimony has been presented. And John Ed has never wavered—not once!—in saying that Jo Dell's death was accidental. The state's expert witness, toxicologist Sidney Nethery, said himself that a wound of this nature was similar to one made accidentally, during a struggle. He was the defense's best witness!"

Cates then moved to the other-woman allegation, saying Barbara Evans Walker's testimony was riddled with "many conflicting statements" and that the defense had been "shackled" in trying to talk to her. "It was the circuit solicitor's duty to keep the truth from coming out." Twice Yielding objected to Cates's pointed references, but twice Cargile overruled.

Continuing that line of thought, Cates acknowledged the kinship between Sarah Davis and Jo Dell, noting that they had visited each other's houses. And, noting John Ed's role, he said, "Is it a crime to hold hands with a lovely girl and to have your picture made? Is being a friend to a woman, associating and speaking to her, a motive for murder? If so, there wouldn't be many wives left." The last comment drew muted chuckles from the crowd. He then downplayed the divorce angle, saying it was a natural step to take if a husband and wife were "having trouble."

Standing now at the jury box, Cates appeared to measure each man, then fired point-blank: "The state's only witnesses have given enough testimony to create reasonable doubt in your minds about guilt. Where's the motive, for goodness sake? You've got to turn him loose."

Nearing his conclusion, Cates walked away from the jury, got the rifle from the evidence table, and demonstrated how it could have fired accidentally. To that point he added—knowing it was already embedded in the minds of these husbands—"What happened afterward were acts of a man who panicked. He went crazy. The well was the unfortunate act of a crazy man. And please bear in mind, because it is crucial, that John Ed wasn't indicted for that, but after two long years behind prison bars don't you think he's paid for that? And also being seen with Sarah Davis, and maybe holding her hand?

"Your 'not guilty' verdict will not erase the suffering and pain this boy has endured," Cates said. "So I plead with you, based on the testimony of the state's own witnesses, to turn this boy loose. He's paid for burying her."

ANTICIPATING A LONG SUMMATION by Strudwick Bowden, Judge Cargile called a fifteen-minute recess to ease the tension of the day, as much as anything. But the bleary-eyed jury—shouted at, preached to about what it must do and not do for nearly three hours—sent the judge a note, asking him to please adjourn; they had had enough. "The jury is tired, we're all tired," he told the court. "We'll have the final summation tomorrow, beginning at 9:30 A.M. This court is adjourned."

"Sonofabitch!" Seth Yielding whispered, but didn't change expression. His thought turned quickly to framing a rebuttal. He wanted, needed, the last word.

· · · · · · · · · · ·

Chapter 52

My most reliable overnight companion, the City Motel, awaited me in Meridian. A few more nights, that's all, I thought. It's almost over. But the fact of Lindsey being gone suddenly loomed large.

"Evenin' Mr. Anderson," John, the cordial night clerk greeted me. "You'll be stayin' all week?"

"A few nights, anyway. The jury will get the case tomorrow," I replied.

"Your key, suh. Oh, yeah, some mail come for you, too." He handed me a small envelope addressed by hand. I knew it was from her.

Dear Dan,

You will never know how hard it was for me to walk out of that courtroom Friday evening without being able to say goodbye. I tried to think of an excuse to go back after my aunt and I got downstairs, but none of them panned out. I was really surprised when you called Saturday evening, but I just wish you had called about thirty minutes before you did. My husband had just been there a few minutes and I couldn't talk. I had been thinking about you all morning and wishing there was some way I could go to Butler when the telephone rang and it was you. I haven't been able to get my mind on anything but us since I came home. How did you know where to call? And please answer this letter. Send it to me, General Delivery, Prichard, Ala.

Yours very truly, Lindsey

I HAD GONE TO work on the previous Saturday knowing I would make the call; knowing it could prove to be a risky mistake, but willing to take the chance, even to put her at risk, to make contact and hear the voice I missed badly. Quickly she had covered, then later found the moment and had answered, writing somewhat tentatively, but with definite meaning that I fully understood. To her we were real.

Again, however, the reality of circumstances rose in me, a sharp signal to stop here and now, to let our small flame flicker out before we fueled it any further. But the pull of us, one to the other, was too strong. She had needs and in me saw someone she had quickly decided could meet the deepest of them. Experience told me that one of us surely would go at some point. Or both. But I answered the letter that night.

· · · · · · · · · ·

Chapter 53

Strudwick Bowden looked impressive, and knew it, in a two-hundred-dollar gray suit, patterned navy tie and starched white shirt with French cuffs. He ambled into court on the eighth morning feeling as fully prepared to close and secure his client's acquittal as he had ever been at trial.

Strategy was fixed in place in the form of sixty-one written charges he presented to Judge Cargile at 9:31 A.M., one minute after bailiff Talmadge had bellowed out the window that this court was now in session.

"Your Honor," Bowden said, "we respectfully request you to rule on each of these motions before we proceed this morning. Those you allow will be delivered to the jury, along with the evidence, for their consideration."

"Court will recess until 10:45 A.M.," Cargile replied, accepting the typed pages.

The probate judge, sitting in the first pew behind the defense table, didn't leave immediately, so I walked over and asked his thoughts. "I'm prayerfully confident that my brother will be acquitted," Bill Tomlinson said. "We feel that the weaknesses of the state's own witnesses have made a strong case for the defense. That's why we didn't proceed to present much of the same testimony back to the jury for a second time. It would only have magnified some of what they heard unnecessarily. That's all I want to say now."

The jury reappeared just before 11 A.M. and Judge Cargile summoned Bowden to the bench. "The items checked are allowed, and no others," he said, handing Bowden the pages. The attorney looked at them carefully at the defense table, thinking.

To the jury, the judge said, "This will be the final summation." To Bowden, "You may proceed."

The proven champion of courtroom battles rose authoritatively. With one hand he swept through his thick mane of white hair with a practiced flair; with the other he picked up a yellow legal pad. The main floor, filled now to capacity; the balcony filled with blacks and interspersed with whites; those without seats lining the back wall—these several hundred spectators hushed to expectant silence, awaiting the one whose reputation preceded him, even in a river's backwater, Henderson County. "Properly respectful," Bowden thought to himself.

Remaining where he stood, he turned around, back to the judge, and opened by playing the crowd with homespun sincerity perfected by the skills of a veteran performer.

"If it wasn't for the tragedy of this matter, the lingering sadness still felt by so many of you, and even the many others not here, this has been a happy occasion for me to be here," now gesturing, "amid old friends and to make new friends. From the first day, I have felt an absence of ill will and irritability, which someone of my experience would quickly pick up."

Now he left John Ed and Cal at their table and moved to face the jury, standing about ten feet from them. "I'm here because it's necessary for this defendant to have representatives before this tribunal. Collectively, you must see this matter as one that demands of you to think not hurriedly but calmly, not in a frenzied way but in a deliberate way. You can't guess a man into the penitentiary. You wouldn't. You're not that kind of people."

Time now to address the very justice system he believed in with his whole being, but which, when necessary, he could maneuver and manipulate with no second thoughts of conscience. "A presumption of innocence accompanies this man's every movement, until the evidence presented by the State of Alabama overcomes that innocence, and the testimony you hear releases your every possible doubt."

Confronting the jury again with pointed forefinger and voice trembling. "We're not trying John Ed for what he did when his mind was aflame; when every part of his makeup was stirring as it never had before! Mr. Yielding said, if he had been in the woods with a loved one and this had happened, he would have gone crazy. That's what happened to John Ed—he went crazy! He saw the face of his mother, of Judge Tomlinson and thought of his political life. He knew death when he saw it, so headed back to tell the awful truth to his brother, but couldn't do it; to his children, but couldn't do it; to a gathering of friends, but couldn't do it. His mind had almost snapped, leaving him to wander around in a virtual daze over a long weekend. What had happened, gentlemen of the jury, was an accident, a terrible and tragic accident, beyond any question of doubt."

Shuffling back and forth now, left hand in coat pocket, right hand gesturing, lock of white hair lying on his sweaty brow. "And now we come here with two pictures. One, presented by the state, describes this man as the devil incarnate, and you have seen that disturbing photograph. The other picture—and testimony justifies this belief—depicts a man that loved his family, loves his children, and made every provision for them. A man who loved the woods, and who snaked logs from early morning until after dark. I ask you, is there a thing about him characteristic of a hardened criminal? Why did he go to the woods? Because he loved the woods."

Timbre of voice varies from shout to whisper. "Is there anyone in the world who can say there was ever any intention on the part of this boy to murder his wife? Who said he didn't? The testimony said he didn't. Dr. Nethery's inferences are that it was an accident. You saw the position he

put me in, then, as an expert, he said it appeared to him to be an accident."
("Objection!" Yielding shouts. "Mr. Bowden is misstating the evidence."
Judge Cargile overrules.) "How can we differ with that when we take into
consideration the posture of the body?"

Shouting with fury. "They want you to convict him for what he did after
the lady was shot! They want you to convict him because he went crazy!
Death was instant. What happened to him, he went crazy, and didn't have
the intestinal fortitude to tell his brother, so he went away!"

Calmer, as if explaining. "Self-preservation is the first law of nature,
no matter whom you're struggling with. He didn't want to kill his wife, he
wanted to take that instrument of death away from his wife. Certainly, in
the process, there was talk of divorce. There isn't any question that a casual
observer could have known there was trouble in that house, that affection
had cooled on one side or another. Jo Dell became panicky after the birth of
their twins. She wanted no more of him, became afraid, moved to another
room. They talk about a party, but John Ed wasn't dancing or eating fish.
He was trying to make up his mind to talk to his brother about this thing.
And was there any testimony to indicate monkey business at this fish fry?"

The unseen witness (a Bowden trademark). "Listen to what Old Man
Physical Facts has to say to us—he says it was an accident because her posture
says so, her arm upraised says so, the fact that her spine wasn't destroyed says
so. John Ed has always said—has never wavered—that it was an accident.
There was only one other witness . . . and she is not here."

Giving Seth Yielding his own medicine. "Even the state said yesterday
it probably could have been an accident, but it could have happened in
one thousand ways. It is incumbent upon the state to prove *the* way it happened. If they don't, it's your privilege to exculpate this man and let him go.
Their case is built upon a rock-bed of circumstantial evidence—a dangerous
thing—when all of the testimony says it was an accident!"

Lastly. "Be true to thy own self, and thou canst not then be false to
anyone. . . . Bear well in mind your experiences in life, and if the State of
Alabama hasn't proven their case, stand on your hind legs and say so!"

Strudwick Bowden took his seat and stared at the wall behind Judge
Cargile. The effect developed to perfection over a storied career settled on

the overflow crowd. As if struck mute, no one moved, no one coughed, no one said a word.

Chapter 54

All the air had been sucked from the room, or so it seemed. If anyone breathed, it was inaudible. We just sat there, having never before witnessed the likes of such forceful eloquence. I had written furiously and just hoped that I could convey it properly to my readers.

Even special prosecutor Bostick termed Bowden's soliloquy "splendid." Then, reasserting his own role, he rebutted the assumptions and conclusions the jury had heard.

"Who says his mind is diseased? There is no evidence of insanity! This court would do well to say you cannot consider a defense of insanity. You have no insanity. His mind was inflamed with lust for a woman down on the river, and with wanting to remove his wife without giving up the children or making a property settlement. He never shed a tear for his children or Mrs. Wilkes. Perhaps he was concerned only for his brother's political future and for his mother's feelings.

"The killing of someone with a weapon raises the presumption of malice, and shifts the proof that it wasn't malice to the defense. What about this case disproves the malice? He planned it deliberately because of what he did before and afterward. All the time he was carrying out a careful plan. First, killing her; second, putting out the word that she had gone to Mobile; third, burying her body, never to be recovered, then letting it appear she had vanished of her own accord; fourth, deliberately not telling anyone; fifth, finally, relating his version of the killing only when his wall of lies crumbled down, and making that cowardly, dastardly claim about Jo Dell at a motel.

"Why are you being asked to turn this man loose? Because his walls are crumbling? Because he gets scared and tells the sheriff a malicious lie? I have never seen a case like that, where you would ask a jury to believe a statement like that!

"There is only one living eyewitness, and he will not testify. But I don't need an eyewitness to reenact what took place. He told her he wanted a divorce, and they were arguing. He takes her out there and she doesn't pacify him. She will not give up her children or let Sarah come into her home. The gun was raised, but not by Jo Dell. She threw up her arms to ward it off. Look at John Ed. Big and strong. Do you think for a minute that he couldn't take a rifle away from any woman in this courtroom? He swears it fired accidentally, and I don't say it can't be done, but it wouldn't be easy. Dr. Nethery says the same thing, and you heard it.

"If you will just use your common sense, you can return only one verdict: guilty of first degree murder, life in prison.

· · · · · · · · · · ·

Chapter 55

Judge Cargile recessed court for lunch just past 11:30 A.M. and sent bailiff Talmadge out to bring him back a cheeseburger and large sweet tea. As he ate, he thought hard about this trial and the one before it, finally muttering to himself, "Goddammit, I'm the cause of all this—me and my screw-up the first time. The jury was right, John Ed got what he deserved for what he did, and ought to be serving his time. Would be, too, if I hadn't let Seth Yielding lead me into saying, 'confession.' What a fuckin' law school mistake. Shit!"

Finishing his burger, he stopped beating himself up over something two years in his past. Instead, he promised himself an error-free charge to this jury. Court reconvened at one-thirty, and the fourteen jurors, rested and fed, walked in with a spring in their steps, eager to get their instructions and start work. With exacting care, judge Cargile described four degrees of homicide the jury could consider:

First degree murder, an unlawful, willful, deliberate, premeditated killing, with malice. Penalty: life in prison or death by electrocution.

Second degree murder, an unlawful and willful killing, with malice. Minimum sentence of ten years, no maximum.

First degree manslaughter, an unlawful, intentional killing, sentence of one to ten years.

Second degree manslaughter, an unlawful, accidental killing committed while doing an unlawful act. Sentence, one day to twelve months in the county jail, fine not to exceed five hundred dollars.

"You may find the defendant not guilty," the judge continued. "Not guilty also embraces self-defense. The law defines self-defense as the right to use reasonable force to protect oneself or members of the family from bodily harm.

"But insanity is a special plea, which is not embraced by a plea of not guilty. Every man over fourteen years of age is presumed to be sane, and the burden of proving insanity is on the accused.

"An accident," he said, "is that which happens without one's design. It is a sudden event. Excusable. If a person fires a shot accidentally, he cannot be convicted.

"Good character must be proved, and may entitle a defendant to be acquitted; although without such proof the jury may convict.

"Finally, you may fall back on your own experience. Gentlemen, you may retire to begin your deliberation."

· · · · · · · · · · ·
Chapter 56

Judge Cargile's instructions, and the less specific comments he made, lasted fifty-five minutes. As the big wall clock read 3:10 P.M., he sent the twelve and two alternates away to more hard chairs in their nearby room whose big windows overlooked the square; a floor fan circulated air and rustled the papers on the eight-foot wood table.

"I nominate Norm Pickett to be our foreman," said Albert Hall, pouring himself a paper cup of water. Murmurs of conversation had begun as the eight smokers lit up. But the talk stopped as the two exchanged glances and Pickett nodded. In the quiet, no one mentioned another name, and a unanimous voice vote sealed it. Norman Pickett, a forty-two-year-old cotton grower who farmed fifty leased acres, would direct the deliberations and ultimately speak for these men.

"I'm just so glad we don't have to hear any more evidence," said Jimmy Johnson, emphasizing the *dence*. "I'm tired of being talked at."

A chorus followed, "That's for damn sure."

Pickett spoke. "Look here, my friends; ain't no use in us wasting time. Let's see where we're at. Secret ballot." He took two pages from a legal tablet and tore each page into six pieces. "You alternates, now you don't vote," he said to Gary Dixon and Wilbur Smith. "That's the decision of the judge."

"Vote yes for guilty, no for not guilty." Folded votes were passed to Pickett, who opened four, then another four, and looked back at the faces watching him. "Eight yeses," he said. He unfolded the last four. "Eleven guilty. One no."

"I ain't surprised," responded George Pierce, a paper mill worker. "He's definitely guilty."

Others nodded and said firmly, "Yes," and "damn right." But Pickett cut them off, saying, "One of you doesn't feel that way. And I expect you all know that this vote is the easiest one we'll take until we're done.

"Guilty of what? That's the question," Pickett said.

"Murder," answered Jimmy Johnson.

"What degree?" Pickett asked.

Johnson sat silent, lips tight.

Carl Fleming spoke up. "Naw, I say manslaughter." He ran a gas station up close to U.S. 11, and his brother Chris had once cut timber for John Ed. "I don't think he planned to kill Jo Dell."

"You're sayin' first degree murder?" Pickett asked, turning back to Johnson, who replied, "I just ain't sure."

"Y'all raise your hands if you think John Ed committed first degree murder," said Pickett. Six hands went up, including his. He sighed and looked out across the table. "We got a long way to go."

For two more hours the jury debated various key points of the trial—the amount of circumstantial evidence, angle of the rifle when fired, the other woman, John Ed's lies about the beach house and the motel, and that Jo Dell had been dead for four days before he told his version of what had happened.

"I know he ain't charged with what happened at the well. I know we're not supposed to let that influence us," said Tom Harper, a timber man. "But I just can't forget it. My God! It's the worst thing I've ever heard!"

The jury voted informally again, at about 6 P.M. Following Pickett's instruction, they indicated murder, manslaughter or not guilty. Six voted murder, five manslaughter, the one holdout, not guilty. Resignation seemed to permeate the room; an overtone of fixed minds.

Pickett requested a long supper break, which Judge Cargile granted. His announcement emptied the court, which had remained about half full. John Ed, his brother, and his mother went back to the jail to eat. Bill Tomlinson brought three plates from the Downtown Café.

I called the *Star,* reaching Stan at home. "No verdict yet. They've been at it since about three and have just taken a long supper break. If they go too late, I'd better phone in, because I'll probably miss the Meridian bus."

"I'll put someone on standby. Call as soon as you know something," Meyer said.

THE JURY RECONVENED AT 8 P.M., and right away Pickett got personal. He had thought about it over supper and made his decision. "This is not the time for any of us to be coy. We're holding John Ed's life in our hands, and we need to let our positions be known.

"First degree murder. Show of hands. Hall, Harper, Pickett. Second degree murder. Hands, please. Johnson, Pierce, Dunn, Brown, Avery. Manslaughter, first degree. Hands up. Fleming, Woolsey, Hill. Manslaughter, second degree. Hands. None. Not guilty. Raise your hand. Hart.

"Thank you," Pickett said. "We seem to favor second degree right now. And I could change if it would help us reach a verdict. Does anyone else think he could? Hill raised his hand. "That's seven," Pickett said. Then he looked at the holdout. "Lester, what makes you think John Ed is not guilty of the charge?"

"Because, over two trials now, he has never wavered in saying Jo Dell's death was a terrible accident; that he loved his family and was a man of good reputation. I don't believe that John Ed is a killer. He's paid over two years for putting her in the well, and I just think it should be over. Let him get back to his life."

Voices rose in protest. "Bullshit! He killed Jo Dell!" exclaimed Fleming. "Guilty as hell," said Woolsey. "I'd never vote to turn him loose!"

Pickett let the raw feelings run for thirty minutes and finally play out. There won't be a verdict tonight, anyway, he thought. Maybe we'll all sleep better having said what we think.

· · · · · · · · · · ·
Chapter 57

At 10 P.M. Judge Cargile summoned the men back into court for a report. Pickett reported a verdict was doubtful. It was not what the judge wanted to hear and he would not accept it. "We're adjourned for the night," he said. "Get a good rest and try again tomorrow." Sullen and bone-tired, the jury filed out, their expressions reflecting the discord they felt.

The courtroom had been full throughout the evening, "like an election night," someone had said. It was hot, with two window fans on high. But people were packed tight, wearing everything from flowery dresses to dingy coveralls to shirt-and-tie. Rose Tomlinson and Bill had remained almost the whole time. Mrs. Wilkes, her sister and the sister's husband waited quietly on the front row.

John Ed had waited calmly, too, looking relaxed and talking at times with his sister-in-law Nancy, the sheriff, and the mayor. Strudwick Bowden was accustomed to waiting, but he gradually began to feel a nagging anxiety in his chest, akin to a spell of indigestion coming on, which was not the way his trials usually ended. Still, he looked comfortable as he flipped through a news magazine, and then, more carefully, read that day's Birmingham paper. That boy, Anderson, he's doing a pretty fair job, he thought. The prosecution chairs were empty, Seth and Bostick having gone to supper when the jury did. They didn't expect to return to court until after the jury resumed its deliberation.

I hurried to find a phone and again called Stan at home. "I'll be ready to dictate shortly," I said.

Stan replied, "Wait ten minutes, then call the City Desk."

I did, and dictated my story of no verdict after five hours for the next day's early editions. Dog tired, I somehow drove to Meridian and, thankfully, went to bed.

NORM PICKETT WAS UP by six the next morning. Drinking coffee, he wondered how in hell he could steer this jury into a unanimous agreement of some kind. Or if it was possible. He didn't want to let the court down, or the county. He reckoned that Hall and Harper could accept second degree murder, with a hefty sentence. If that happened, he thought he could then persuade Fleming and Woolsey to get on board. That left just Hart, whose rationale for not guilty showed that he was adamant.

There's more than what he's sayin', Pickett said to himself. He's a poor sharecropper with a family to feed. I wonder if they got to him.

Lester had lain awake thinking into the early morning hours. "I cain't hold out for no time, hit ain't right, no matter what I say. I gotta give 'em somethin', but I know what else I hafta do, too."

RESTED AND EACH MAN ready to get this over with, the jury gathered at 9 A.M., some sitting, some standing, most drinking coffee from the café and chatting idly about work, weather, and family.

"Will all of you please sit down," said Pickett, who arrived ready to act on his plan. "My friends, we worked five hard hours yesterday, getting to know each other better, expressing our feelings about this trial, and discussing a possible penalty. It was obvious when we left that we were a good bit divided on a verdict, but also that seven of us had said we could accept second degree murder.

"I sense that could be where we're going. So, in the interest of serving justice—which we are accountable to do—I'd like for Mr. Hall and Mr. Harper to get together in a corner for ten minutes and decide what penalty you'd agree to for a second-degree murder verdict. And, Mr. Fleming and Mr. Woolsey, y'all do the same. The rest of us, we'll relax while we wait."

Hart approached Pickett during the break. "Whadda I do?" he asked. Pickett replied, "Think hard about your position, Lester, and if eleven of us agree on second degree murder and a penalty, think about whether, in good conscience, you could force us to be a hung jury. And whether you'd want to live with that."

"Thirty years, for me and Woolsey," said Fleming, when they gathered again. "But . . . .oh hell, nothing."

"Fifty years, or we don't budge off first degree," said Harper.

"Maybe now we're getting somewhere," said Pickett, appreciation showing in his voice.

Woolsey would have none of it. "We ain't nowhere less'n Hart steps up!" he retorted bitterly.

Before Hart could respond, Pickett interrupted. "Leave that alone for now. Just to confirm where we're at, show of hands on second degree murder, just the conviction, not the penalty."

Hands went up, some still hesitant. "Eleven.

"All right," said Pickett. Then he tore two legal pages from a tablet and made them into twelve smaller pieces. Passing them out, he said, "Write the number of years you'd give John Ed. But before you do that, anybody who wants to say something, say it."

For a long sixty seconds, no one spoke. Three poured water, two lit up, the rest sat still, heads down. Pierce broke the silence. "Look at the evidence. He wanted that woman, Sarah, bad; went to her bedroom every early mornin' he could, talked in public of marryin' her, sent that letter, didn't care who saw 'em together. But wanted to keep his kids, too, and there wasn't but one way to do that. Get Jo Dell out of the way for good. He may or may not have carried her to the woods to kill her, but she ended up dead just the same, and he was all but free to have what he wanted. Then what he did with her! Lord, ah cain't get that picture outa my mind!"

Brown followed. "If he'd just brought her back to the hospital, dead or not, like any of us woulda done! And if he hadn't smeared her with that god-awful lie about her being shacked up at that motel. She was his wife of fourteen years, for Christ's sake, gave him four children, and that's what he did to her! Tried to ruin her, and her already dead!"

Pickett waited. "Other comments?" he asked. No one spoke. "Then write down your number and pass it down." He read out the results. "Sixty years, four. Fifty years, two. Thirty years, two. Twenty-five, three. Five, one."

"Fuck you, Lester!" Fleming shouted. "Five fuckin' years, and you heard the same testimony we did. How could you?"

Lester shouted back, "'Cause I think it's right!"

"Naw, you don't," Avery countered. "Them Tomlinsons got to you! Admit it!"

"I'll whip yore ass for sayin' that!" Hart yelled, coming around the table.

Pickett stopped him. "Sit back down, Lester. We've got more to handle than your five years."

Gotta be patient, Pickett thought, can't push nobody. "We're not that far apart," he said. "And if the eleven of us can settle on a number, I believe Lester'll come around." He hoped to God he was right. "So let's break for an early lunch. It's 11:30. Think some more where you're at. We all believe John Ed's got to be punished, it's just how much. Then let's sit back down at 1:30, finish this up, and go home knowin' that we've done right by Jo Dell."

Judge Cargile wasn't about to question the jury's request. The bailiff stationed at the jury room door had told the judge, from what he could hear, they seemed to be working hard to come to agreement.

I phoned in a short update at noon, as an outwardly relaxed John Ed went back to his cell for lunch. I thought my copy would make the last home delivery and the Red Streak street edition.

After lunch the foreman had the jury vote again—three wanting thirty years, six fifty years and two sixty years. "We're circling around fifty years," said Pickett. "If some of you will move, we can reach that solid number, and then it'll be up to Lester to join us."

"I ain't movin' no more till I know what he'll do," Brown said.

"I ain't either," a few others choroused.

Pickett looked intently at the holdout, and said firmly, "Lester, it's time for you to be a part of this jury."

Lester looked around the table and met the eyes of the men he had sat with for ten days. "I am a part of this here jury," he said, "and I've got my convictions same as you've got yours. I've moved, too, from not guilty to where I'm at, and that's where I'm gonna stay."

The eleven gazed back at him, each face bearing a hard expression of anger and resignation. But no one cussed or shouted their disgust.

Pickett stood up. "There's no point in prolonging this deliberation. I don't think we'll gain any more ground, no matter how long we might stay. So, we have to take a final vote to report to the judge. He passed out pieces of paper, then read the final tally aloud—nine of us, sixty years, two of us a life sentence, and one, five years. Are you ready to make this report?" All heads nodded.

Bailiff Talmadge knocked on the judge's door. Cargile put down that day's *Mobile Register*. "Jury's ready," Talmadge said.

The judge replied, "Tell them to wait fifteen minutes, until everybody who needs to be in court is here."

Talmadge delivered the message, as calls were made to those not already present. The jury waited quietly, smoking, drinking water, visiting the bathroom. When all key players were in the room, the jurors walked in slowly, not looking at anyone, and sat down. It was 4:20 P.M. Bad sign, Strudwick Bowden thought.

The judge asked, "Has the jury reached a verdict?"

Norman Pickett stood. "Judge, I think we've arrived at the only verdict we'll have—no verdict."

· · · · · · · · · · ·

Chapter 58

Gasps and loud murmurs gripped the half-full courtroom. "Order! Order, please," Cargile said firmly, rapping his gavel. He asked Pickett, "If I kept you together awhile longer, do you think you could reach a decision?"

"Judge," Picket answered, head erect, voice steady, "this jury is of the opinion we would never be able to reach a unanimous verdict in this case."

I saw John Ed smile and look back to where his mother and daughters were sitting. Bill Tomlinson put his arm around his brother.

The judge polled the jury: "Is it your opinion you're hopelessly dead-locked?"

Each man replied, "we are" or "at this time."

"Then, as much as I hate to declare a mistrial, I won't require you to stay together as long as you feel that way. This court thanks you for the attempt you made to reach a decision. You are dismissed. As the indictment against the defendant still stands, he remains in custody. No bond is allowed." John Ed would go back to jail.

Quickly, I cornered Pickett and asked him to please give me all the details that led to this hung jury, that readers everywhere would want to know. He summarized 11 hours and 45 minutes in that small jury room—several ballots being taken, sharp differences of opinion surfacing, occasional strong feelings, and ultimately a verdict of any kind becoming out of reach. Then he was willing to say something else to reflect the jury's final thinking, and perhaps send a message to both prosecution and defense. "We were close, except for one." He wouldn't give me that name, but I'd get it.

Looking around the room, I saw nothing but the stunned expressions of men with hands on hips, and women clutching purses, who couldn't believe what they had heard. Approaching a small group who hadn't moved yet, I asked for their reaction. They shook their heads, but one middle-aged man said forcefully, "We knew from the day the jury was struck, this one would be a mistrial."

"What? How was that?" I pressed him.

He would say no more, and began moving away. The lawyers, however, didn't hesitate. Yielding was adamant. "I still feel the same way, he should be convicted. He's still charged with first degree murder, and I'm going to ask for a special term of this court as soon as possible. Justice will never be served until that man is convicted."

"One more thing," I said to him. "You didn't call several people with close connections to this case to testify. Specifically, Bill and Nancy Tomlinson, Robert Whatley, Rose Tomlinson. Why?"

"We didn't want character witnesses for the defendant. Our case, as presented, was strong enough for conviction," he replied, which left my question dangling for the time being. I would try again when feelings settled a bit.

Somewhat subdued, Bowden spoke to me. "We're terribly disappointed. We'd hoped the jury could see its way clear to acquit the defendant. We felt the testimony, in its final analysis, was consistent with his innocence, and if the jury had acquitted the defendant, no sincere man could have criticized the verdict. This apparently was a fine group of men who, I'm convinced, made an honest effort to get together."

Bowden also indicated that all the lawyers might meet, at his request, to discuss the next steps that might be taken, including bail for John Ed and a special term of circuit court, just for this case. The next regular term was six months away, in October.

Bill Tomlinson was predictable: "We wanted an acquittal, and were close to getting it. But I feel that twelve very good, sound men wrestled with the problem and accepted that they couldn't reach a solution." I thought it odd that he would call his sister-in-law's violent death a "problem."

Judge Cargile appeared under control, but seethed with frustration inside. "Sonofabitch! They got to a juror! I knew it when Pickett told me the final count—eleven for conviction and heavy years, but one holding out for a fuckin' five years. That bastard! Wonder how much payoff he'll get?"

As HE HEADED HOME to Mobile in his black Buick Road Master, glad as hell to put Butler behind him, the honorable Walter Cargile needed a drink. He stopped at a roadhouse in the next county, had a double Jack-on-the-rocks standing unnoticed at the bar, and drank it too fast, feeling the always-pleasant sizzle in his stomach when the bourbon hit bottom. Then he ordered a cheese burger and Coke to go, to quickly get the alcohol off his breath.

It was after 6 p.m. when I left the quiet courthouse, and I wasn't about to drive home. I'd stay one last night in Meridian, have a few drinks and supper, and compose this very big story for the midnight bus. Then head to Birmingham come morning.

Tomlinson two, justice zero, came to mind as I drove the lonely road west. Lonely except for a car that stayed several lengths behind me, its brights on, choosing not to pass. Being escorted across the line, I thought, too tired to be nervous. It turned off as I neared Meridian.

Hearing the Butler radio bulletin announcing the outcome, I wondered aloud, "Where in the hell does this whole thing go from here?" I wondered why so many key figures didn't testify, and if Seth had evaded my question because he was hacked at being asked, frustrated by the no-verdict, or was there a deeper reason? I also remembered something else Bill had said to me, "We were very close to acquittal." Did he really know that, or was it just wishful bull shit?

My story, with Pickett's "very close" quote, nullified Bill's comment. He had made himself look bad in saying it, but why did he seem so sure?

· · · · · · · · · ·
Chapter 59

"Evenin', Mr. Anderson," said John, as I collected my key. "Big news outa da trial."

"Helluva day," I replied. He could see I was weary.

"Try Wideman's, downtown. Mighty fine food. It'll make ya feel better. And, oh, a letter came for ya."

Dear Dan,

A letter didn't come and didn't come, so it was like a prayer answered when I went to the Post Office today and asked for the mail. I felt like shouting when he handed me a letter postmarked Butler. I knew it was from you. I read it right there, and it was the most wonderful letter I have ever received, the way you can write what is in your heart so clearly.

You said that we hardly know each other; well, some way to me that doesn't seem right because I feel like I do know you. I was so happy last Wednesday evening when I went downtown and bought a paper. They had printed your picture with the story, so I cut it out to keep, at least that way I have something of you.

I didn't think it was possible to feel about anyone the way I feel about you. Isn't it funny how I haven't seen you but these few times in my life, yet I feel this way. How do you explain something like this?

Is there any way in the world you could ever come to Mobile, and I could see you while you were here? It would be something wonderful to look forward to. I will close thinking of you as always.

Lindsey

OVER TWO BOURBONS AND a shrimp platter at Wideman's, I reviewed the day's notes, the ending drama, began constructing the story in my head, and started thinking about follow-up stuff I'd need to get before leaving. I would answer Lindsey, but that would have to wait.

"WHAT'S FOR SUNDAY?" STAN Meyer asked on the day after my mistrial story led page one. Two pieces, I replied. One recapping trial highlights, with new stuff; the other, more reaction of the locals to the no-verdict, and to yet another trial.

"Go get 'em," he said, then added, "By the way, damn fine job down there." It was the highest praise this tough editor could dole out.

Bolstered by Ace's pictures that nailed the trial's aftermath, Sunday's presentation was strong. I hadn't known Ace was coming, but was mighty glad to see him show up that last morning. "Stan told me to get my butt down here," he said. "You don't want to know how fast I drove."

THAT WAS MY LAST Tomlinson copy until the third trial date was announced in July, and I was relieved to let it go. I badly needed the break from Jo Dell and John Ed. Number three would begin on November 20, 1961. I thought so: Thanksgiving week. Bowden and Bill Tomlinson said the insanity plea would be made again.

Back at the office a long, typed letter came to my mail box; onionskin copy, actually, from a north Alabama reader who unloaded on jury foreman Pickett, and the other eleven. With hammer-like emphasis this reader said, among other things:

"IT WOULD SEEM THAT the American Jurisprudence has reached a low ebb when 12 intelligent men can't arrive at a decision that was as clear cut as this one. . . . If any kind of woman had stated that someone attempted to rape her you would have probably given that man life just on her word. But when it's murder you have to decide whether or not he killed his wife and dumped her in the well, or pushed her in and then shot her, which is a great decision to make. If I'm ever tried for murder I hope it's in Henderson County. Did the Great Rich Man and his brother, the probate judge, scare you boys so much that you couldn't make an honest decision for fear of reprisal?"

During the summer of 1961, Birmingham endured a different kind of trial, this one by the world. The sworn segregated lifestyle of the Klan, White Citizen's Council, National States Rights Party and other extremists was juxtaposed against moderation and concessions proposed by reasonable community leaders, excluding the politicians.

The terrible pipe-and-bat beatings of Freedom Riders and newsmen on Mother's Day at the Trailways bus station would mark the city forever as a major battleground in "the movement," which now was engulfing the entire South. Based on what the world read, heard and saw, my hometown symbolized a fortress to preserve segregation, and we who lived there were America's worst racists. A front page editorial in my own newspaper on the Monday after the attacks, in fact, bore the headline, "Where Were the Police?" Eugene "Bull" Connor, police commissioner, had instructed his officers to stand by at the bus station and give the attackers ample time to do their bloody work.

Along with every other reporter—some much more involved than I was—I caught my share of bombings, church meetings, street protests, beatings, Klan rallies and the poisonous National States Rights Party. Of one state reporting award I received, my managing editor wrote:

"Nine miles away, the sound was just a small boom, lasting an instant. But seasoned by a summer of racial turmoil, the reporter knew it to be another bombing. Minutes later, the jangling home telephone of *Birmingham Star* staff writer Dan Anderson summoned him out of bed and into the night, across town to infamous 'Dynamite Hill.'

"The handsome brick home of the Negro attorney Arthur Shores had been attacked for a second time in sixteen days. Negroes were rioting, police were struggling to prevent worse violence, and no man was safe. Cars were stopped by the mobs, stoned, and windows smashed. Whites and Negroes were hit with bricks. Some were shot.

"Alone, unarmed, Anderson drove into the area a back way; looked, listened, interviewed, remained two hours, then left, driving with lights out, stopping for nothing. This is his account of the night."

My story accompanied the nomination letter.

So I WOULD GO back to Butler that fall a seasoned reporter, who no longer often slid by on the seat of his pants. I'd go carrying a proven reputation of producing under fire and bringing back the story. My bosses knew I could deliver. It's what we're paid for, but, trust me, not every reporter can do it.

Sometime that summer I finally answered Lindsey's letter.

> Dear Lindsey:
>
> Don't think I've forgotten you; I haven't. Far from it, I miss you and think of you a lot. I called once, but a man answered and I hung up. I didn't try that again. I don't want to put you under any suspicion. With all that's happening racially here, and throughout Alabama and the South, it won't be possible to get to Mobile before the next trial. We're all on call seven days a week.
>
> I wish that I had a better answer to your question in your last letter about us. The way I see it, we were vulnerable for different reasons. Then, we found ourselves brought together in a hostile environment and quickly realized that despite the differences, each of us could comfort the other in ways that came to mean a lot, and that we both want to continue, even under risky conditions. I won't go any further than that right now. I will when I see you again.
>
> Dan

SAYING HOW EXPLOSIVE THE summer was was like trying to describe August heat in Alabama. Sit-ins, marches, mass arrests, beatings, bombings, and dynamite explosions seemed to occur daily and dominated national news.

Extremist organizations and violent individuals fought the inevitable with resolve, weapons and rhetoric. They saluted their brazen standard bearers, Governors George Wallace and Ross Barnett of Mississippi.

Damning the national coverage, many southern publishers, including some in Alabama and Mississippi, shamefully buried this worldwide story with bare bones reporting and played it on inside pages with innocuous headlines. A significant out-of-state story might not run at all.

· · · · · · · · · · ·

Chapter 60

Small, isolated Henderson County was unimportant compared to some of its nearest neighbors like Montgomery, Mobile and Jackson. But it wasn't oblivious to the human rights struggle surrounding it and pressing closer. The Klan paraded boldly and bareheaded around the courthouse square on the Fourth of July and on Labor Day as a robed reminder that everyone should just keep their accustomed place in the local business-civic-social structure.

Inconspicuous among the Confederate flag-wavers, Leroy Simmons looked hard at the marchers each time, trying to identify a particular build, or swagger, or look in the eyes, and thought he spotted one or more of his captors from that cold night at the quarry, but he couldn't be sure. The Kluxers brought both holidays to a fiery climax, lighting up a ten-foot cross in an empty lot two blocks from the square.

Outwardly, everyday life didn't change, but unrest smoldered in the black churches beyond watchful eyes, as preachers in dry-cleaned finery tried to match the fevered eloquence of Dr. King, and walls reverberated with freedom songs shouted by sweaty choirs and fanning throngs. As the scriptures said, when the appointed time came, these of God's children must be ready.

In Tuscaloosa, eighty miles east, and the region's biggest city, a prominent and eloquent Methodist minister, J. H. Chitwood, lived by example and didn't fear to preach law, order and moderation to his congregation at First

Methodist Church, while knowing that many members resented hearing it. On a summer Sunday, in a sermon entitled "One Nation under God," he admonished his congregation.

"WE MUST MAKE UP our minds soon whether we are southerners first and owe our highest allegiance to the confederate flag; or whether we are Americans first and owe our highest allegiance to the stars and stripes. . . . Those who fly a confederate flag are free to do so only because Old Glory protects them.

"Christians do not terrorize a community by organizing a Ku Klux Klan, White Citizens Council, or any other group that would destroy the rights and freedoms of other human beings. Christians know one law, love. They know one freedom, freedom for everybody. No man is safe and free until every man is safe and free. . . . There is no time when a Christian is called on to thwart the law by lawless means. This is licensed anarchy."

Most clergy of the day weren't so bold from the pulpit, choosing instead to placate the majority in the pews by continuing to preach separate but equal or by just ignoring the revolution around them until literally it knocked down their door.

ABOUT ONCE A MONTH the Henderson County weekly, eying a profitable fourth quarter, served notice—by rehashing old news and occasionally finding a new nugget—that the trial was getting closer. It would be toward the end of football season and on the cusp of the holidays, but assuredly big news.

Or would it? Editor Leonard Bassett wasn't sure any more. At the café where he and his buddies always drank coffee, at the Civitan weekly lunch, at the benches around the square, at the Baptist church where Bassett was a deacon, even at home, almost nobody was talking about it yet. Peaceful demonstrations, violent retaliations and the Wallace-Barnett partnership were the big news, and they showed no signs of easing up. His small circulation area was enduring a too-quiet summer, giving Bassett the same wish every editor has when coverage is that soft—that something big should happen, and, Lord, I'm sorry, make it bad. But what else could happen with John Ed and Jo Dell? It was all out there. In the record. Twice.

Leroy would have thought differently. "Not all. No damn way. I know what I seen that day at John Ed's house," he'd mutter, but didn't dare breathe it to anyone. He'd kept it quiet for two years, afraid to speak up, but this time would be different. Fuck 'em. He'd bide his time, working odd jobs for the county and at people's houses, as he had been doing that January day. "It's Leroy what's got the bombshell," he'd say softly, going about his business for now, his nose clean of reporters and the Klan.

SETH YIELDING FIGURED THAT he knew the score. He drove his judicial circuit regularly and knew what he wasn't hearing in the neighboring counties. Except for the occasional, "Gonna git him this time?" he wasn't hearing anything about John Ed or the trial. "My folks are tired of it. To them it's done. Over. They've moved on. I think they'd as soon John Ed be released," Seth told his wife. From what she heard in her book club and church circle, she agreed.

But Yielding remained obsessed. Two years had passed, but he wouldn't allow indifference to weaken his resolve. This was still personal, although he didn't flaunt the fact. Twice he had proved murder beyond a reasonable doubt, only to be screwed by himself and the judge the first time, and a bought juror the second time. Hell, everybody knew about Lester, didn't they? Better house, nicer clothes, newer truck. Same fuckin' farmer. Gossip continued to taint his family.

"I'm not gonna let our people forget," Seth vowed quietly. "Not the murder, not the well, not the cover up, not his mistress. He's goin' down this time. Strike three"

"I DIDN'T LOSE, BUT I didn't win, either," groused Strudwick Bowden. "I don't count the no-verdict. It's not clear-cut enough. Anyway, most of those men were for a conviction. And that won't happen again." He would change strategy this time, push harder on the prevailing sentiment of the people—sympathy for the children, mother dead, father in prison, and, after two years, feelings strong to just end the whole messy situation. Would John Ed testify? Undecided. Sarah Davis? No way in hell. "But count on this," he said. "This defense won't be by committee. This time I'll call the shots. Period."

Chapter 61

"They took John Ed back to prison after the April mistrial," Sarah told me as our visit on her porch eased into a late afternoon pattern of dappled sunshine and longer shadows. The lemonade was gone, replaced by water.

"I saw him here in jail before he went away, then me and the girls visited him regularly," she said. "He began having back trouble, I think from those awful beds. Couldn't exercise enough. Started looking pale. I worried about his health."

"Where had you been during the trial? I asked.

"Just away," she replied. "At a cousin's." She was lying and knew that I could tell.

"You can do better than that," I said.

She looked at me and smiled. "Another time."

It was Walter Cargile's duty to preside once more, and he hated the thought. Wished to hell it wasn't his judicial circuit. Hated that he had fucked up the first trial and negated a deserved life sentence. Hated that peckerwood juror, Lester, who let himself be bought the second time, the single holdout against a conviction of a lot of years in prison. It was so damn obvious. The Tomlinsons were the only reason he wasn't run out of town.

"Same testimony, same circumstances, same faces one more time," he said. "I can recite it all from memory. Hope I can stay awake," he said sarcastically. "And it's Thanksgiving, too. Damn it all!" Then he poured himself a stiff bourbon and checked his stash of vodka for the pitcher he would keep on the dais.

My Sunday package of preview stories was scheduled, and on the Thursday before trial I returned to Butler, this time confident and composed. People I talked to— despite two years passing—still wouldn't give their names out of fear of Tomlinson retaliation.

"I'm just as nervous as I can be over the renewal of this case," said one.

"I think everyone else is, too." Another, speaking of John Ed's alleged affair with Sarah and his reputation for womanizing, said, "You didn't have to be told or shown what was going on to know." I tried to find Sarah, went to her house in Bladon Springs. She didn't answer the door. Unlisted phone.

But Yielding was eager and forthcoming. He told me, "We're ready. The state still has the evidence to prove first degree murder." As if anticipating my question dangling from trial two, he added with a smile, "There could be some surprise witnesses. We'll have to wait and see." Bowden didn't return my calls.

Thursday night, I reminded Claire that Ace and I would be going down on that Sunday. Court would open at nine Monday morning, I said.

"You'll be coming home on Wednesday night, I hope," she said, then reminded me, "the Thanksgiving gathering is at Mama and Daddy's, and maybe we can go shopping on Friday. I'll get our Christmas Club savings out, if you like."

"One person will control our holiday," I replied, probably too abruptly. "Judge Cargile. Surely he'll want to go home, and if the first days go to his satisfaction, it should not be a problem. But it's his call."

She didn't answer, but looked into my thoughts with resignation and began to cry, her body trembling and tears coursing down her soft cheeks. The pull of my work over a long summer of stressful conflict, now with the trial piled on, had finally crumbled her usually solid demeanor. I pulled her close and held her gently, as if she were fragile. Typically, she was a strong woman, but at this moment she needed soft comfort and the warmth of arms. I kissed the tears away. Her composure returned in a few minutes, and no more was said.

. . . .

Chapter 62

Monday morning wasn't cold, but the air had an edge and autumn was steadily coloring the hardwoods and roadside bushes between my motel in Meridian and Butler. How I loved this time of year.

The routine was so familiar by now that circuit court seemed to progress by the numbers, starting with bailiff Talmadge calling us all to stand for the judge's arrival.

Walter Cargile entered looking sternly at the usual players for the prosecution and defense, at us newsmen, this time not required to sign in, and at the fifty or so spectators, mostly men, scattered among the hard pews. John Ed wore his usual khakis and sat stiffly in a straight back chair, joined by his daughters and his mother at the defense table. He didn't look well.

He was rolling the dice with a third plea of innocent and innocent by reason of insanity considering what the Alabama Code said about it: "The burden is on him to establish the issue of legal sanity, raised by his plea, by a preponderance of the evidence. He must establish . . . to the satisfaction of the jury that he was affected with a mental condition when the crime was committed which either prevented a knowledge of right or wrong, as applied to this case, or which destroyed his power of choice."

"Good morning, everyone," the judge said with no cheerfulness in his voice. "Let's get to it."

Yielding and Bowden proceeded to narrow down the large jury pool of white men, culling primarily from the responses they gave to questions about dealings with the Tomlinsons, their feelings about capital punishment, and their ability to render judgment solely from facts and evidence. Forty prospective jurors were disqualified or excused; twenty-two others were struck over the five hours that ended at about 4:30 p.m. The judge earlier had prepared all of us for the reality that we could be there for two weeks.

The process of elimination left a jury in place that consisted of six farmers, and one each accountant, sawmill owner, field superintendent, industrial engineer, railroad superintendent, and truck driver. More intelligence and position than the second jury, I thought. These men, as had their predecessors, sat close enough to the dais to almost hear the judge breathe and notice him sip from the pitcher by his gavel.

"They look a lot like the last jury," I whispered to Ace.

"What did you expect?" he replied sardonically.

SETH YIELDING ENTERED COURT on the second day thinking he knew the story behind John Ed's obvious discomfort and had determined not to be sidetracked. The defendant reportedly had just had surgery in Mobile, and two ruptured discs had been removed from his spine. Clearly, he was hurting, and Seth was thinking, damned if I'm going to risk another mistrial.

Special prosecutor Tom Bostick, again assisting Yielding, in one breath told the judge, "the state is ready," and in the next breath suggested that the trial not begin as scheduled.

John Ed, the state reasoned, had not been released from the hospital, was still under a doctor's care, and required sedation periodically. Bostick said, "We don't want to try the man in pain who might come into court in a wheelchair." Then he added that he did not think the Alabama Supreme Court "would or should permit the verdict to stand, whether he wants to go on trial or not."

Bowden growled a reply with the authority of an aroused lion. "We announce ready. The jury is here, and the defendant is here. There is nothing before the court to justify continuance of this case."

Cargile quickly had heard enough. Exasperated already, he summoned everyone to a conference in his chambers and adjourned court until after lunch. The group included Dr. George Newton, of Butler, John Ed's physician.

When court reconvened, the judge announced what he had hoped he would be able to say, the trial would proceed. He quoted Dr. Newton as saying that only exploratory surgery was performed, and an "arthritic spur" was found, not ruptured discs.

"The doctor in charge has said to the court the defendant is physically able to stand trial, and he is being discharged from the hospital, as of now," Cargile said emphatically. Feeling protected, he said, "Let's get to it."

Chapter 63

Before adjourning court that day, the judge had heard his first replay in opening statements—Yielding asking the jury to find John Ed guilty of "a cold-blooded, malicious, premeditated murder" and to sentence him to death; Bowden countering that Jo Dell's death was "an unfortunate accident" and that the aftermath of burying her in a well was the result of a sudden fit of insanity and panic.

Sheriff Hutton, the first person outside of the Tomlinson family to learn of the killing, was sworn as a witness on day three, which immediately gave Wednesday promise of news that the first two days didn't deliver in plodding along. Despite my best efforts, our readers learned that the trial early-on smacked of rerun testimony in a story not worthy of page one.

The jury, too, had been squirmy and not fully attentive, but now, to the man, it leaned forward, its attention on the lawman who testified in vivid detail.

In a clear, chronological narrative, Hutton led the jury through his part in the story, starting with, "Mr. Bill Tomlinson called me to Mrs. Rose Tomlinson's house on the afternoon of January 29, 1959." He recounted what John Ed had told him about the shooting. His description of recovering Jo Dell's body was as chilling as the night when it was found. John Ed, he said, "used a shovel to point out the center of the well where he had pushed his wife's body and buried it. He had said, "'She's in there.'" Many in the crowded courtroom murmured, and I saw four of the jurors lower their eyes and shake their heads.

Hutton also testified that in John Ed's first statement the defendant had not mentioned several things that he did after the shooting. "He didn't say he had stopped at his mother's house, or that he had stopped at the county garage and arranged to take a bulldozer out to the shooting scene the next day. He didn't say he had driven to Butler with a friend, Woodrow Keene, or that he had taken Jo Dell's car to Mobile over the weekend to back up his claim that she was at the beach. One thing he did say, though, was that the shooting occurred a few hours after he caught her at a Citronelle motel with a doctor."

Yielding said to his witness, "Which proved not true, but another one of his lies."

"Objection!" Bowden thundered.

"Withdrawn," Yielding replied. "Your witness." Point made, he thought.

"Just one question, sheriff," Bowden said. "Did Mr. Tomlinson look like or sound like his normal self as he told you what happened?"

Hutton answered, "No, he didn't. He was trembling and his voice broke as he talked."

Cargile said the expected at day's end, when the last of ten witnesses had testified. "This court will reconvene tomorrow at 9 A.M. It is Thanksgiving, I know, and this building has never—even in old-timers' memory—held court on a national holiday. But it is our duty to continue moving this case along to its end, and not to be deterred by anything within our control. So we will. Court is adjourned."

The Thanksgiving angle and Bowden's comment to me—"My real work starts tomorrow; they put on their best witnesses"—were the best I had for my story. That, plus the lion's holiday message, made rather jovially: "I know of no law against working on a holiday. I know one thing: I'll write receipts on a holiday anytime anybody wants to pay me."

My story and Ace's routine pictures made it to the bus station in plenty of time. "I'll stay until the lunch recess tomorrow, then I'm heading back," Ace told me over supper. "Wish you were comin', too."

Claire wasn't happy and said so when I called. "It isn't often that I'm not proud of what you do, or that I don't like the paper. But, darn it, that's how I feel," she said. "Thanksgiving won't be the same. "

"No, it won't, and I'll really miss you and Sam, and everybody," I replied. "But give thanks that I can do this, that I've got a secure job, and that you know I'll be home as soon as I can. And save me some pumpkin pie."

"Gotcha," she said, adding softly, "Call me Thursday night. I love you."

"No slack from Cargile. We're all here tomorrow," I told city editor Stan Meyer in a call Wednesday night. He replied, "Unusual, all right, but not surprising. Tough duty. But at least you won't have to update. We're rolling at ten, one edition. What's your turkey day looking like?"

"No turkey and nothin' open that I know of. Funny thing, but no invitations to dinner, either. Looks like a couple of strong witnesses, the state investigator who led the original investigation, and the guy who did the autopsy. Friday copy should be meaty, for a change."

"You're doing okay, Anderson," he said. "Keep up your spirit."

I wasn't home. Ace was gone. No word from Lindsey. No afternoon football on a full stomach. But a good start of eggs, sausage, grits, and biscuits at 7 A.M. at a place the desk clerk promised would be open, Meridian's all-night Gravy Boat.

And as I drove toward Butler on a cold, colorless morning, flanked by bare trees and frost-bitten foliage, a favorite little Thanksgiving ditty came to mind, so I sang it to lift my spirits: *Over the river and through the woods to grandmother's house we go. The horse knows the way to carry the sleigh through white and drifting snow. Over the river and through the woods, oh how the wind does blow. It stings the nose and bites the toes as over the hills we go.*

. . . .

Chapter 64

Folks all over Henderson County were already busy cooking their feast, I thought, judged by the twelve locals who were scattered around the courtroom at 9 A.M. The warm, open space, its balcony empty, felt surreal with everybody who mattered knotted in a cluster inside the railing, facing Judge Cargile.

As the morning wore on the small audience found itself hearing the best testimony of the week, sharp question-answer exchanges between Bostick and Bowden, interspersed, as expected, with Bowden's objections.

Bostick said for the first time, I thought, taking notes, that after John Ed had told him of finding his wife at the motel in Citronelle, he then changed his story to say they were there in a trailer. This conversation had occurred on February 5, 1959, the morning after he admitted that his wife was dead. On cross-examination Bowden tried putting words in the witness's mouth: "Didn't Mr. Tomlinson unquestionably say she was shot accidentally when the rifle went off?"

But Bostick wouldn't budge. "To the best of my recollection, Mr. Strudwick, the word 'accidentally' was not used. I will not say it was not used because I don't remember."

Cargile broke for lunch after this lengthy testimony, allowing an extra hour for the jury to go home to eat. He instructed each man not to even mention the trial and to call the sheriff if anyone urged him to talk about it.

In an empty clerk's office I ate fried baloney on white bread and chips that I had bought at breakfast at the Gravy Boat, with a cold drink from a machine in the basement. My family, I knew, was just now blessing the bounty that filled their table—roast turkey and baked ham, cornbread dressing and giblet gravy, an array of garden vegetables that was sure to include mashed sweet potatoes topped with little golden marshmallows, buttery squash casserole, fatback-seasoned green beans, creamy mashed Irish potatoes, pickled beets for added color, spicy tomato relish, cranberry Jello salad, coffee and sweet tea. Plus wine for those who would. And finally, my mother's special coconut layer cake and Claire's mom's pumpkin and mincemeat pies. I could see it all, taste it all and feel the love that everyone would share as generously as the food. I finished my sandwich with a brief hunger pang of self-pity that passed quickly, and returned to court.

. . . .

Chapter 65

Seth's lunch was black coffee from a thermos and a wedge of his wife's cinnamon coffee cake; dinner would be that night, to celebrate not only the holiday but what he believed would be a winning work day, as well. The morning had gone good, he thought.

Strudwick Bowden dined with the Tomlinsons at Bill and Nancy Tomlinson's picturesque antebellum home, first enjoying two glasses of full-bodied merlot, served in Austrian crystal, a crackling fire enhancing the wine. Table talk excluded the trial, instead politely covering such pleasantries as family, football, and the drift toward winter. Afterward, Rose took two plates to John Ed. Bowden, too, was jovial and told stories about his previous cases that stretched into two and three trials. "Few and far between!" he said, laughing heartily. Bowden didn't say this, but felt it—a growing feeling that this jury was his.

SURPRISINGLY, A CROWD BEGAN gathering in the early afternoon, bellies full from their holiday feast. They had skipped football, would nap later, and welcomed a break from the same family conversations they had engaged in the previous Thanksgiving. They kept drifting in, by 3 P.M. filling the downstairs and most of the balcony. They barely stirred during two hours of testimony given by state toxicologist Nethery, who performed the autopsy on Jo Dell. They watched Nethery and Bowden, repeating a scene from trial two, reenact the shooting. Bowden portrayed Jo Dell, crouching with left arm raised to about a sixty-degree angle, as Nethery believed she was when struck by the 30-30 bullet. They heard Nethery say she was at least twelve inches away from John Ed, her left side toward the rifle, and she died instantly.

Finally, the full house heard a loud argument that centered on one word: struggle. At least twice, as Bowden cross-examined Nethery, he led him craftily toward saying the fatal wound could have occurred "during a struggle over a rifle."

"Objection!" shouted Yielding and Bostick, each time.

"Sustained," replied Cargile, his voice tense.

Bowden then rephrased: "Was the shooting an accident?"

Yielding objected too quickly, then withdrew it as Cargile sustained and Bowden also withdrew the question. Officially, then, the heavyweights' brief flurry was stricken from the court proceedings, meaning that the jury could not consider it in its deliberations. But it energized the crowd into prolonged murmuring until the judge rapped his gavel sharply and ordered quiet.

Nethery's testimony ended the day, and post-court comments were predictable. Yielding: "He left himself in a hole by not permitting Nethery's opinion on whether Jo Dell was shot accidentally." Bowden: "The testimony clearly showed she was shot during a struggle; the answer was the same without yes or no. I think our case is stronger."

Cheeseburger, fries, coffee, and apple pie were my supper back at the reliable Gravy Boat, whose pledge of available-when-needed endeared them to me forever. I went back to the motel, called home for a recap of the day, and had another pang of self-pity when Claire said it was wonderful except for my absence, and that everyone sent their love.

"Missed you so much," she said. "Can't wait for you to get home."

"Tomorrow night; I'll call when I leave," I said, avoiding what I knew very well could happen: Saturday court. "I love you. Hug Sam for me." Then I began writing, expecting to finish by ten. About nine the phone rang. The voice said softly and seductively, "Dan, I'm here. Can I come over?"

My reply was genuine, but caught by surprise it probably bore all the warmth of distant cousins saying hello again: "Lindsey! It's so good to hear your voice. Of course, come over. Room 110. Where are you?"

I had just finished my story when she knocked. And there she stood, a presence I had wanted to see since April, that had lived in my thoughts no matter where I was or what I was doing. She looked tantalizing—hair tucked beneath a Crimson Tide cap, bulky dark green fisherman's sweater, tight jeans, short casual boots, sparkling eyes and full lips that sent an invitation. She stepped out of the cold and into my arms as I pushed the door shut. "So long, too long," she whispered against my neck. "I've missed you so much, you have no idea." We kissed and the intensity rekindled a fire that we instantly realized had never burned out. We clutched each other in a heart-pounding embrace.

"I'm off from work tomorrow, and told him I was coming back to the trial. He was going hunting, thank God. So I left at dark and drove straight here, 'cause I knew where you'd be. He thinks I'm at my aunt's. She'll cover for me."

I said, "I hadn't given up on your being here; I had just stopped hoping, to ease the reality that you weren't there."

She replied, "I'll be there," leaving the assurance in mid-sentence for a second, as if she was about to expand the thought, but didn't.

"Tomorrow's story is done, and I should get it down to the bus station," I said. "Want to go, or can I bring you food, drink, anything?"

"No, thanks, I stopped earlier. Just you," she said with a flirtatious smile. "I'll wash the road off me and relax. Be long?"

"Typically, thirty minutes." A kiss and I was gone. I pulled out, and so did a second car several doors down. Quickly it blocked my exit. Two men got out and approached, coat collars turned up, caps pulled down to the dark glasses over their eyes.

Rolling down my window, I asked sharply, "What's going on?"

"Better not be nothin' goin' on, motherfucker," one replied. He held a tire iron in a gloved hand. "We warned you once, at the courthouse, to stay away from our women. But you didn't hear too good. We seen y'all at the roadhouse, and on your sweet, fuckin' little picnics; followed you the other night to see where you're stayin', and just now seen her go inta your room. If she's one of our women, we'll see you again, and beat your ass." He raised the tire iron.

"Get outa my way, you bastards!" I shouted, looking at the one holding the weapon. "You touch me and even your local cops won't protect you. Now move!"

The threatening voice responded. "Somethin' else, too, Mr. Reporter. We're callin' your office and tellin' your boss just how you been representin' your paper down here, trying to fuck our women. Your ass'll be grass. So you listen to what we say, smart boy, 'cause there ain't gonna be no more talkin'. Next time we're just gonna knock the shit outa you. Understand?"

He and the companion who hadn't spoken turned then, got back in their car and moved away. I got the tag number. They followed me to the bus station, but when I came out, they were gone.

The penny dropped as I drove back. We would have slept together, made love, without a doubt. Not now. But why not? Afraid for Lindsey? Afraid for myself? Afraid for my marriage, my job, my reputation? Hell, I didn't know. Maybe all the above.

Chapter 66

Lindsey has propped herself against the bed head with pillows, and swathed herself in my robe. She looks marvelous, with just her fresh-washed face and damp golden hair showing. Her fragrance permeates the room and stops me on my first step inside.

"You are a feast for all the senses," I say, sitting on the bed beside her. "Wait till you see what's underneath—or isn't," she replies, smiling. I take a deep breath and break the news. "But you can't stay. You have to go." She is sure I'm teasing.

"If I go outside like this, my places that shouldn't will freeze, and you won't like that."

"Lindsey, I've just gotten a second warning from Henderson hoods that your husband, my wife, my boss, and most of the county will find out if we continue this relationship. We can't let that happen. They tried once at the courthouse to scare me off, and they've been following us. To the roadhouse, the cemetery, followed me back here the other night, and now this." I am sure I sound cowardly and intimidated. Perhaps I am both.

"No," she answers, suddenly drawn, lips pursed, eyes filling with tears. "That can't happen, It's too dangerous with the situation down here. I know these people. Some would hurt you, and maybe me. We'll have to pretend. Be friends. My god!"

"We just have to know we're being watched, and not take chances," I say.
"Are they still outside?"
"They're gone."
"Then I'll go. I know the risk, but it doesn't change how I feel."
"Nor I."

She dresses in the bathroom at my urging, we hold tight at the door, and she says defiantly, "I'll be there tomorrow." Then she is out the door, into the cold midnight, driving away.

Seth Yielding got the phone call at home on the Tuesday night before Thanksgiving. "Go to Pensacola," a woman's voice said, one he didn't recognize. "That's where they got the marriage license."

"What are you talking about?" he said, thinking that he knew, but wanting to prolong the conversation. "Who is this?"

"It's there in the courthouse. I know. Pensacola." Then she hung up.

He called Bostick. "I've just gotten an anonymous call from a woman who said that John Ed and Sarah got a marriage license in Pensacola. First thing tomorrow, I need you to go to the Escambia County Courthouse and check it out. If they did, get a copy. This could seal the deal."

"Hot damn!" Bostick exclaimed. "I'll leave early and call your office with whatever I find."

The courthouse opened at eight and Bostick was there waiting. At the circuit clerk's office he showed identification and asked to see the list of marriage licenses issued since January 1, 1961. He was shown to a vacant conference room to scan the large, heavy volume that contained all the details.

In February, there it was. February 27 and 28. The application had been signed by Sarah Loraine Robertson at the clerk's office, and by John Ed Tomlinson in the Henderson County Jail. A different notary public had notarized each signature. Circuit Clerk Laura Drew, who made two copies for Bostick, said she remembered Sarah because she was from out of state. She added, "If it's needed at trial, good thing you came today. We're closed over the Thanksgiving weekend. Reopen Monday morning."

Bostick called Yielding's office and told the secretary, "Tell him it happened in February this year, and that I'm on the way back with two copies. Hot damn!"

"WHY THEN?" I ASKED Sarah as we sat talking on her porch.

She answered, not curtly, but matter-of-factly, which reporters like because it produces usable quotes. "We were afraid of a conviction at the second trial; and knew, too, that as his wife I couldn't be forced to testify against him. It made sense for those reasons, plus, we wanted our love formalized and legalized."

"So you hoped to be married during the second trial?" I asked.

"Yes," she replied. "I went back to Pensacola and got the license, and—"

"But you couldn't marry in Alabama with an out-of-state license. Did you think—"

She interrupted, "We hoped to pull some strings through the Tomlinsons and have the sheriff take us across the state line."

"Highly unlikely," I said.

Sarah nodded. "They decided it would be too risky for everybody, so we kept it our secret for all those months until it came out at trial three. We knew, too, there was no way to get an application anywhere in Alabama and keep it quiet."

"So why did you leave town during the trial, and where did you go?"

"If our plan was discovered and made public, I didn't want to be around, to be the target of more hostility and gossip. I went to stay with a friend in Montgomery. Frankly, I was amazed, with all the talk about us, that nothing leaked before Seth found out. Secrets are impossible to keep around here."

· · · · · · · · · ·

Chapter 68

Seth Yielding read and reread the document, carefully assessing its importance to his case. Potentially it was decisive, but without proof of a wedding it was nothing more than proof of commitment. John Ed was in jail at the time, so he would start with a call to the sheriff, who would be home on Thanksgiving night.

"Lonnie, this is Seth," he said. "A development has occurred in the trial. Could I run by and talk to you for a few minutes?"

They sipped coffee in Hutton's den. Yielding said, "I've found out about the application for a marriage license that John Ed and Sarah got in February of this year. He signed it while in your jail. What do you know about it?"

"Didn't know anything, right away," Hutton answered. "Sarah came to see him almost every day, and we didn't eavesdrop on her visits, except to monitor the time allowed. So I didn't know they had done anything like that until John Ed asked if I'd let them be married there in the jail. I knew it'd mean a lot to the Tomlinsons if I agreed, so I did. Then I learned that Sarah had got the application in Pensacola, and knew they couldn't be married in Alabama unless they got a license in-state."

"And you kept silent about all this during the second trial," Yielding said. "Why was that?"

Hutton replied, "It didn't look like neither John Ed or Sarah would testify, they weren't on the witness list, so I figured it wouldn't have a bearing."

"Poor judgment on your part. I don't see how you could think that, when it might have turned the case," Yielding said, controlling an urge to call his friend a dumb ass, also fully aware of Hutton's ties to Tomlinson power. "But that's not the issue now. I'm going to put the application into evidence tomorrow, and call you to testify about what you knew. Everything."

"How'd you find out?" Hutton asked, as Yielding stood to leave.

"That's not for you to know right now. Or anyone else. Bostick and you are all that know I have it. And it stays that way until tomorrow, understand? By the way, did they ever get a license?"

"Not that I know of. First off, they knew the marriage would have to performed in Florida, and I'd have to escort John Ed across the Florida line to a justice of the peace. I said that wouldn't be possible. As far as I know they never tried to get an application in Alabama."

"Son of a bitch!" Yielding exclaimed softly. "Thanks for the coffee."

. . . .

Chapter 69

On a day the courthouse was otherwise silent, Friday's first witness was Barbara Evans Walker, who still lived in Birmingham and who gave a morning-long recap of trial two testimony.

Bostick's questioning led her to tell, among other things, of John Ed's invitation to fry fish, drink whiskey, and dance at his house on January 30, 1959. She also recalled traveling to Mobile with John Ed and Sarah to leave a car for Jo Dell to drive home from the beach. She then recounted Bill Tomlinson meeting them on the way back and telling John Ed that Jo Dell had hired an attorney, put him under two thousand dollar bond, and was accusing him of cruelty to their children.

Cross-examining her, Bowden was direct and tough, his hard voice varying from softly sinister to shouting. With rapid-fire questions and comments, he pressed to get an admission that she and Yielding conspired about her testimony, and alleged that her father and the prosecutor had guided her in what to say and not say.

"Did you testify in April that your father had told you that Yielding had said that when lawyers came to see you that you didn't have to talk?"

"I don't remember whether that question was asked or not."

"But you did refuse to talk to lawyers."

"I did."

Barbara Walker vividly remembered the first time she faced this man and that his nasty badgering didn't break her then. It wouldn't now, either.

"Judge, he's brow-beating Mrs. Walker," Bostick said.

Cargile told Bowden, "Just proceed without any side remarks. The court is not going to put up with this, I'm warning you, Mr. Bowden.

Bowden countered with the rejoinder that the state was "cheating the defendant's rights." Then he changed tactics to focus on the man he wanted the jury to believe Sarah was to have married, and it wasn't John Ed.

"You knew Robert Whatley and Sarah Davis were engaged."

"They said they were."

"You knew it, didn't you."

"I didn't know."

"Don't you know you testified positively and definitely that Robert and Sarah were engaged, and that you testified under the sanctity of an oath on that witness chair. Didn't you testify to that—"

"That's been two years ago, my gosh."

"—and that they had announced their engagement, and that John Ed was to be his best man, and he was going to lend them his car for their honeymoon?"

"I don't know about the car."

Cargile felt irritable and gaveled a thirty-minute recess. Barbara Evans Walker went to the bathroom, drank a cup of water, and spoke to no one in the witness waiting room. He's vicious, but I'll control my composure and my nerves, she kept telling herself.

She was seated in the witness chair again when Bowden and Yielding clustered around her. Bowden read her testimony from both the second and first trials. Asked if she had heard Sarah say that she and Robert Whatley were going to be married, one of the transcripts recorded her answer: "Yes sir." A transcript also quoted her as saying she knew, in a general sense, when the wedding would be, but now was saying she didn't recall any of that previous testimony. Bowden asked to have her earlier statements admitted into this trial record. Cargile agreed.

On redirect from Yielding, Walker said she didn't know if Sarah and Robert had ever gotten married. Cargile dismissed her just before noon and set lunch until 1:30 P.M.

LINDSEY LINGERED OUTSIDE AND we walked to the Downtown Café, just off the square. No one seemed to pay us any attention.

"Bowden's a bulldog, but that woman wasn't intimidated a bit," she said as we ate the blue plate special that included turkey and cornbread dressing, plus mashed sweet potatoes.

"What does your intuition say about this Whatley angle?" I asked.

"Darned if I can figure it out," she replied. "If Sarah and Barbara were really close, Sarah would tell her the truth. But maybe it all was changing as she and John Ed began to get serious. Love can happen fast and change one's perspective. It has for me."

"Wonder what the jury is believing?" I said.

"Closing arguments will be very important," she said.

We got a few curious looks sitting there, but nothing we thought ominous. Others noticed as we walked a few blocks in the overcast, chilly midday air, but we were careful not to look like anything more than a casual, friendly couple.

Yielding called two more witnesses after lunch and established the authenticity of John Ed's handwriting on a few documents, one of them a letter to Sarah that he closed with "love."

Bowden derisively dismissed this inference of motive. "Judge," he said, "I think the mountain labored and brought forth a mouse," at which the spectators chuckled.

Bladon Springs's postmaster of fifteen years, Jane Douglas, took the stand at mid-afternoon, Yielding then played his hole card. He showed her a document, asked if she had notarized it for John Ed, and when, and to tell the court what it was.

"Yes, I did, on February 28, 1961," she replied. "It was an application for a marriage license for him and Sarah Robertson, issued in Pensacola, Florida."

Cargile shot a glance her way; Bowden's head jerked up from his legal pad; and furor echoed off the plaster walls and wooden floor of the old courtroom. John Ed's eyes narrowed, and he grimaced. The crowd seized the revelation with loud mutterings and continuous buzz.

Cargile let it run for a minute or two before restoring order with his gavel and a threat to clear the room. The jury stared at Jane Douglas as though dumbstruck.

· · · · · · · · · ·

Chapter 70

Of all the things that could happen in his chosen arena of combat, Strudwick Bowden always said being blindsided was the worst. It had happened rarely over his career because he was nearly always a step ahead of where the prosecution was going and how he could block any momentum. This time, despite his shock and rage, he recovered quickly, as the best in his business did, and counter punched with his favorite expression.

"Objection, your Honor!"

Cargile responded, "Speak up, Mr. Bowden."

The attorney asked to see the application, and Yielding handed it to him. He scanned it quickly but thoroughly, then spoke firmly.

"Judge, no one in his wildest delirium could imagine a court in Florida could issue a license to someone in Alabama and thereafter a legal marriage be performed. There couldn't have been within the confines of the State of Alabama. I don't know who masterminded this, but he must have been the most ignorant fool who ever lived. And I say that without apology to any man. The application was signed during a period of time when there was pending a plea of special appeal, and is a figment of someone's imagination as far as effectiveness is concerned. It was signed in Butler, far removed from Escambia County, which makes this an immaterial matter with no legal effect. To offer it would prejudice the rights of the defendant and inflame the minds of the jury. It is, frankly, a strange incident."

With that, Bowden sat down, thinking, pretty good shooting from the hip.

Sharp counter skirmish, Yielding thought, but pushed his advantage. "Judge, we're not saying this is proof of marriage, but that it shows a continuation of the relationship, a continuation of their passion. Like a brick in a wall built by the defendant himself, it shows a continuation of feeling. The court has always allowed the admission of anything, before or after the commission of an offense, to support or corroborate the state's charges against the defendant. This application is admissible under any consideration."

Bowden responded insistently and belligerently: "They've shown no evidence—not a grain of sand in the great case of the state—that tends to show these two people were bound in a compromising position. And this application certainly doesn't show motive for the consummation of an offense."

Cargile then brought the arguments full circle, back to himself. He said, "I am of the opinion this paper is admissible as evidence. I overrule the objection. Take your witness, please."

All Douglas could add of substance to the fist-fight atmosphere of the previous half hour was what she had said and done that afternoon. She told the court, "A man I hadn't seen before came to the post office about 2 P.M. and asked me to come to the jail to acknowledge a conveyance. I explained I couldn't leave until I closed for the day, 5 P.M. He said, 'Ma'am, John Ed sent me. He wants you to come.' I said, 'I'll just be a minute.' I locked up and went with him."

The jury, judge, both sides, and we lesser participants were clearly punched out by the day. Looked it, felt it, running on fumes. There would be no testimony from the sheriff.

"We're adjourned," Cargile said shortly past 4 P.M. "There will be Saturday court. 9 A.M." He rose stiffly, we stood, and court quickly emptied.

BOWDEN WAS GOOD FOR his usual quick hallway analysis—the state hadn't proved intent, the autopsy had shown it was an accident, and the marriage license application, while in evidence, was from another state and "could not possibly have any legal effect in Alabama."

I missed Yielding, but he and the application had framed the day and would get plenty of copy. Besides, I was too tired to care and just wanted to relax with a drink and Lindsey. This was not wrong, I rationalized. Screw 'em.

We stopped by her aunt's house so she could call her husband and truthfully say where she was, and to expect her home Saturday night. We ate at a Morrison's in Meridian because it would be quick and better than a burger or barbecue. Lastly, I bought a pint of Bellows at a package store—I didn't know good bourbon from bad, but John Ed drank it, so what the hell. We were at the motel by 8 P.M., and I called Claire with the news about Saturday.

"I half expected to hear that. Cargile is on my hit list," she said, then changed the subject. "I got our Christmas Club check today, five hundred dollars, and Sam and I did some shopping. Everybody else was out there, too; it was a mad house; wore us out fast. But we've got a few nice gifts to show you, and, best of all, still have most of the money. Should I hold supper Saturday night?"

"How about dessert and coffee," I said. "I should be home by eight, latest."

"You sound very tired," she said. "We'll be glad to see you."

Chapter 71

Half a plastic cup of bourbon over ice was strong stuff for me, but that's what I held as I propped against pillows at the bed head, the way Lindsey had the night before. She had a Coke from a machine outside, and doused my drink to sweeten the whiskey a little, more to my taste.

"Now you've gotta write," she said, standing by the bed.

"Soon, but this first," I answered, sipping the drink. "It'll loosen me up nicely."

She bent down to kiss me, then smiled. "I've got a better idea."

"Are you sure?" I said, willpower slipping.

She replied, "It's all a risk, Dan. I'll get a magazine from the lobby, and then take a shower; maybe a nap. Will that be enough quiet time?"

"Should be." I drained the glass, resisted another for the sake of a clear head, moved to my portable on the desk, and started writing. With the quotes I had to embellish the day's high drama, the story almost told itself, and I'd wrapped it up by 10 P.M. It would be the best-read story in Saturday's edition, I figured.

I was back from the bus station by 10:30 and could finally call the work day over. But I found her car gone, the room empty, and a note: "Dan, my aunt called and said he had phoned looking for me. She told him I'd gone out to the drugstore and would call back soon. I don't think there's anything new going on, but let's not take the chance. Love you. Sleep tight. I'll see you tomorrow."

The next morning, over waffles and sausage at the Gravy Boat, I glanced at the *Meridian Times,* and missed her badly, as I had through the night. But an inner voice persisted, "She made the right decision."

ALSO ON FRIDAY NIGHT, Sheriff Hutton granted Bill Tomlinson a favor, a meeting in the jail's small conference room with John Ed and Bowden. "Not too long and hold it down," Hutton said as the three men crowded into a tight space, barely big enough for a table and three chairs.

Coldly, voice low, bitterness flavoring his sarcasm, Bill Tomlinson tore into his brother. "Next to shooting Jo Dell, that marriage license business was the stupidest thing you ever did. And us not know about it! You stupid dumb ass!"

Strudwick Bowden lashed out. "What the fuck were you and your mistress thinking? I'll answer that—you weren't! It was the worst move you could make to show motive, and I don't know if my response pulled your ass off the electric chair or not. What I do know, you fuckin' stud, is that the least you could have done is tell us. Pray tell, why didn't you?"

Sitting in a metal folding chair, head bowed, hands on knees, John Ed didn't look up during the tirades. He answered thinly, "I wanted us to be together; it was two years since it happened. I told her not to go anywhere around here, and Pensacola was my first thought."

"But you knew—you had to!—that you'd have to be married in Florida?" Bowden said. "And did you think you could get a furlough out of prison for a nice ceremony and honeymoon? Ride down in a limo or something? Police escort?"

"I thought we'd figure something out," John Ed muttered.

"You prick!" said his brother. "If you had a brain, you might really be dangerous."

Bowden interjected, "What else would you like to tell us? Such as, are you two married? Do I have to defend that, too?"

"We are not married."

Before John Ed could continue, Hutton rapped on the door. "That's all the time I can allow," he said, having stood close enough to hear everything.

"What a fuck-up!" Bowden spoke in a vicious half-whisper. "I'll be here at 8 tomorrow morning."

"Go back where you belong," brother said to brother.

Chapter 72

Saturday morning the state slogged on with more witnesses, one of whom was Missy Pope, Sarah's housekeeper. She said Sarah had told her she was engaged to Robert Whatley. Verified again, I thought. But Pope also put John Ed at Sarah's house two to three times a week in the early morning for three months before Jo Dell's death, and regularly in Sarah's bedroom for a half hour or more. Observant woman.

Annie Wilkes took the stand shortly after lunch, looking resolute and ready for anything that would follow. She wore a solid tan dress, a dark sweater, and glasses. Her graying hair was done up in a bun. Starting with the oath her voice was steady and firm. She described that weekend in detail, including the fish fry, which she heard from a bedroom while keeping the children. She testified of spending two nights at Jo Dell's house, and being told repeatedly that her daughter was all right, just resting for a few days at Dauphin Island. John Ed said it first, then Rose.

There was the phone call, too, from Wilkes's brother-in-law in Mobile, who had gone to the beach house where Jo Dell was supposedly staying. "But Rose answered and I didn't get to talk," Wilkes said. Jo Dell wasn't there, Rose had told Mrs. Wilkes.

Once that weekend, Mrs. Wilkes testified, she had challenged the hollow reassurances. "I told John Ed, 'I'll never see Jo Dell alive again.' He told me I was foolish, and acted mad." About 7 P.M. on Monday, at her daughter's home, she testified of learning the truth from Sheriff Hutton. A deputy had brought her there.

"Just one last question," Yielding said. "What was the state of Jo Dell's health during this time?"

"She was in bad health after the birth of the twins and had to have a hysterectomy. She recovered slowly, like anyone would who'd had that operation."

"Your witness," said Yielding.

"No questions."

"Your Honor, the state rests." Saturday, 4:15 P.M.

Cargile said, "We'll call it a week. Court will reconvene Monday at 9." He smacked his gavel, we stood, and he was gone.

LINDSEY AND I DROVE to Meridian separately, not caring if we were being watched. No indication of being followed that we could see. In the room we drank a Coke and discussed the past two days.

"I think they've got him," she ventured.

I thought back to the second jury and replied, "But you never know."

She said, "I still can't believe John Ed even hoped that somehow they could be married in Pensacola."

"Nothing short of preposterous," I answered, "but nothing about this case surprises me any more." Then I turned to business and knocked out a strong Sunday piece to drop off later that night as I headed home. Lindsey propped herself on the bed and flipped through the morning paper.

Once she broke my concentration asking, "Has your wife ever watched you work?" Before I could answer she continued, "I can imagine doing that from time to time, at the paper or maybe at home, a way of feeling close to you." I looked at her and smiled. I wouldn't deal with the inference of her comment, not then.

We were ready to leave by 7 P.M., but sat together on the worn sofa for a few minutes. Each of us had called home to say we'd be late; my reason, writing my story; hers, supper with her aunt.

"Don't you dare think goodbye." It was a soft command. "I'll be back sometime next week. I've got a few unused vacation days, and I'll tell them on Monday that I'd like to see the end of this epic. Which is true, even if you weren't here. They'll be holding you a room and I'll leave a message at the desk."

I embraced her and kissed her. "I won't think about you not coming back," I said. "I'll miss you a lot." She whispered, "I love you bad. And we'll have to talk about the future, at least a little bit."

DRIVING BACK ACROSS THREE hours of solitude, my only company the country hits from WCMS and its 100,000 watts of nighttime outreach, I felt unsettling emotions piling one upon another. Willie's "Blue Eyes Cryin' in the Rain" didn't help me sort them out. Family, future and everything else of importance in my life all were knotted tightly to Birmingham. I was on an upward track at the *Star* to get more big assignments and the best stories, which made the prospect of a call from Butler about Lindsey scarey as hell.

The worst outcome of such a call would alienate the support and love of my immediate and extended family, my strongest links to stability. My mentors, who continued to guide and encourage me, might doubt I was worth their interest. Friends, too, would wonder. The collapse of these elements of my life was devastating to consider.

But Lindsey was much more than a casual relationship. That was reality, too. In a setting of dangerous turbulence deep feelings had developed that endured during long periods of separation. Although unsure about our future, I knew beyond doubt that losing her would tear a hole in my heart.

For me, still another reality counted greatly. My life was littered with promises that had lost their meaning real fast, broken as surely as a dish that falls to the floor. The truth of that didn't justify what I was doing and I never thought it did. In later years, however, I came to realize that so many broken dishes might explain my casual regard for commitment. For the present, I had let it happen again.

· · · · · · · · · · ·

Chapter 73

By 10 P.M. I was in the newsroom, one hour before deadline, but I had called before leaving Meridian so the desk would expect time to be tight. I delivered the piece, and while it was being edited stayed a few extra minutes to shoot the breeze with the weekend crew.

"Shoulda stayed on, gone to church," one deadpanned. "They'd have tried to baptize you by immersion, but not let you up."

"Naw, they're good Christians down there; do their killing outa church."

I left them to close up: monitor the scanner and check cops once or twice more, then send the last four news pages to composing; page one, jump page, local page, and jump. It was nearly 11 P.M. when I at last headed home to my family, tired into the gut. I had called to say I'd be later than I thought.

Sam was long asleep, so Claire and I had hot tea and the pumpkin pie she had saved from Thanksgiving. I recapped the week, almost all of it, and predicted it would be over by end of the coming week.

"Hallelujah," she said. "You've got to be drained."

"I really am. Then I hope to get a few days off. Swap 'em instead of overtime, if I can."

Claire was ready for bed and so was I after a relaxing shower. She burrowed against me, and by the feel of her gown I could tell it was short and accessible. "I've missed you in so many ways, my husband, but especially this way," she said softly. "This bed wants both of us in it, and I want you in me."

My answer was a kiss with tender passion. Shifting position, I stroked her and entered her deeply. A rush of release swept over her. "Do it hard," she breathed in my ear, holding me tight. "Yes, yes, so good !" Too quickly we finished together, and slept.

Sunday was deserved family time, just us, restful and welcome. That evening, I repacked.

· · · · · · · · · ·

Chapter 74

Seventh day, Monday. Strudwick Bowden's turn, and he considered himself in charge of this trial, fuck the stupid judge and probably the thickest defendant he'd ever represented. He had the only steel balls in the courtroom, and the other side had better know what was coming.

Sarah and Robert—Bowden began calling them as a twosome—had gotten a premarital blood test in Waynesboro, Mississippi, just over the line below Meridian. His witness, Dr. Lucius Martin, testified he met with Sarah in January 1959, gave the blood test on January 31, and completed the certificate on February 3. Cross-examined by special prosecutor Bostick, the doctor said he had seen Sarah "in the past year," and she was still Sarah Davis.

Mary Lois Cox, a practical nurse, became a strong defense witness in telling of living in the Tomlinson house to care for the new-born twins, and seeing Jo Dell decline into poor health and become emotional. "She said her female organs were involved. Most of the time she stayed in the room with the twins, and when I left she took over their care." Cox also described Jo Dell and Sarah as being friendly toward one another when she saw them at social occasions and at school functions. Cross-examined by Yielding, she acknowledged the time frame was 1955.

The defense called fifteen witnesses that Monday, half of whom spoke up for John Ed's good reputation and character. The next day Bowden questioned eight more who did the same. Yielding sometimes asked a question, but for the most part let the character witnesses speak their piece.

One of the Tuesday witnesses was James McKinney, a Marathon Oil Company employee, who said he, too, knew of Sarah and Robert's engagement. He then said they didn't get married because Robert's father came down from Holly Springs, Mississippi, and convinced them "to put it off."

Bowden's last of seventeen witnesses on day eight was Gus Davis, Sarah's brother. They ran the fish camp at Bladon's Landing on the Tombigbee River.

"John Ed and his family came over regularly, and Sarah was there most of the time," Davis said. He mentioned Robert Whatley, saying, "Sarah told me they were going to get married." And Davis added that when he saw Sarah and Jo Dell in the same company they always seemed friendly toward each other.

Called back to the stand the next day, Davis testified of seeing an agitated John Ed on January 31, 1959, who said, "If I don't get it off my mind I'm going crazy."

Bowden's next move was to get into this trial record the statement John Ed made to Bostick that was entered into the second trial transcript: "The rifle accidentally went off and she was shot." He had decided not to risk John Ed as a witness on his own behalf. Cargile allowed it.

Sheriff Hutton, the next witness, ignited a brush fire of intense argument, mostly between Bowden and Bostick, sparked primarily by earlier testimony of his first conversation with John Ed.

Bowden asked, "Did you, on February 3, 1959, in talking with John Ed, make this statement: 'Boy, I want to say this to you, as far as I know now you have told the truth.'"

Hutton answered, "Yes sir."

Bostick objected on the grounds that Hutton, a previous prosecution witness, already had been examined and cross-examined. Overruled. Bostick then tried to get the sheriff to say his "told the truth" statement came after John Ed had lied about finding Jo Dell at a motel and then changing that to a trailer.

Bowden objected to everything Bostick attempted to ask, breaking in before he finished a question. They clawed back and forth at each other, Cargile joining in to allow it or not. The judge did permit Hutton to say John Ed hadn't changed his story when he, Hutton, made his "truth" comment. It was also disclosed that before Hutton testified, Bowden himself had written the "truth" statement based on what he had been told, and Hutton had confirmed it as correct. Bowden orchestrating testimony? I asked myself.

THE COMBATANTS SLUGGED IT out verbally again over where the fatal bullet hit Jo Dell. Reading from the transcript of the preliminary hearing in February 1959, Bostick quoted Hutton as having demonstrated where John Ed had shown him his wife was shot; at the front of the left shoulder. Hutton answered, "I meant to say John Ed indicated her armpit, not forward of shoulder. At no time did he say the bullet entered in the front of her shoulder."

Bitter argument then erupted over the involvement of Bill Tomlinson. Bostick asked Hutton if Tomlinson had told him, "It's true, Lonnie, she was running around." Bowden objected. Sustained.

And Bostick asked the sheriff if both brothers, on the night Jo Dell was recovered, had wanted him to keep the matter quiet, remove the body from the well and take it to Mobile before anyone else knew what had happened. Bowden objected that the question was posed "to prejudice and inflame the minds of the jury." Sustained.

Finally, through Hutton, Bowden confronted Yielding personally: "Has any pressure been put on you by Mr. Yielding not to testify in this matter?"

"No sir," Hutton replied. "I did discuss the case with the prosecutors."

Bowden accused Yielding of thwarting the defense effort, saying, "You didn't go to Barbara Evans and other witnesses and attempt to thwart their testifying by saying they didn't have to testify?"

Yielding jumped up, shouting: "It's untrue! I challenge Mr. Bowden to prove it! No such thing occurred!" The judge directed him to sit down.

"No sir," said the sheriff. "And I never heard Mr. Yielding do it. I was present on two occasions when Mr. Yielding talked to Mrs. Evans's father, and he had the Code of Alabama with him."

Bowden had no other questions for Hutton, or any more witnesses. Damage done. On the ninth day, the god of defense, as he often thought of himself, rested.

THE FEW NEW NUGGETS of information I'd heard were gratifying, a welcome bonus to the repetitious testimony that had carried over from the second trial. I had to keep telling myself, old news to some, but not to this jury or a lot of readers, so keep it lively and fresh. I worked at it. Stan Meyer seemed satisfied.

Happiest of all to get to this point was the jury, tired to the core of sitting in their punishing chairs for endless hours, nine of the past ten days, processing witness after witness, even on Thanksgiving Day. One more step—closing arguments—and they, thank God, could get down to business.

· · · · · · · · · · ·

Chapter 75

Leroy Simmons watched Seth Yielding leave the courthouse, and followed him at a distance in the darkness to his office. "Mr. Seth!" he called. "Can I see ya fer a minute?" Seth recognized Leroy and invited him in, hoping it would be a quick visit. Leroy had mustered up his best courage for what he was about to say. For he knew the possible consequences.

"You needs to know sumthin', Mr. Seth. I been 'fraid to say it fer a long time, but I ain't holdin' back no more. This is what I know. I was cleanin' out Mr. John Ed's roof gutters that day, leaves and pine burrs, ya know. An' through a winda I saw him and Miz Rose pull up a carpet in the den that had a big dark place on it."

Seth interrupted. "When was this?"

"That time Miz Jo Dell went missin'," he replied. "An' I reckon it was blood. They told me to hep 'em get it out the door and inta his truck, which I did, 'cause it was real heavy. I didn't see the big spot no more, but I knows it was there 'cause I had done seen it. Mr. John Ed drove off wid dat rug, an' I ain't seen it no more. It might mean sumthin', and I been wantin' ta tell ya, but I'm scared shitless right now. An' if anybody knowed of this conversation, I'd be a dead nigger.

"Ain't said 'nuther thing, too. A lady friend o' mine who heps out at Mr. John Ed's house from time to time was dere one day and tole me she heard him say that when he first saw Miss Jo Dell layin' there that she was cold already."

Hearsay, Seth thought, but reached for Leroy's hand. "You're a brave man, Leroy, and I won't forget it. I don't know what it means yet, but I needed to know what you've said. Whatever happens your name won't be mentioned by me. Not ever. I promise. Now you slip on out, like you've never been here. Take this twenty dollars for your trouble, but don't flash it around, and be very careful how you spend it."

"Thank you, suh," and Leroy was out the door and quickly vanished into the cold, moonless night, leaving Seth in an excited state of quandary. He had been handed potential dynamite, but he'd have to work out exactly what to do with it, and in a hurry.

TRUE TO HIS WORD, Yielding decided not to tell anyone—not even Bostick— what he'd been told. He would go to Cargile himself before final arguments.

"Your Honor, may I approach the bench?" he asked first thing after court was gaveled into session on Thursday morning, day ten.

"Yes, Mr. Yielding?" said Cargile.

He spoke softly, just out of earshot. "Your Honor, I'd like permission to call one additional witness, based on important information I have only just received. It could be crucial to the outcome of the trial, otherwise I wouldn't ask."

Strudwick Bowden stood silently beside his adversary, his curiosity suddenly piqued.

"My office," Cargile said, then announcing a fifteen-minute recess.

"Judge, someone who claims to be an eyewitness has told me that the weekend Jo Dell was killed, he helped the defendant and Mrs. Rose Tomlinson remove a carpet from John Ed's house that contained a large red stain. The witness fears for his life if he testifies, so I would like to question Mrs. Rose, who is already on the witness list."

Bowden didn't contain himself. "Judge, this is another scheme of the prosecution—absent concrete evidence—to concoct a cock-and-bull story in hopes of influencing the jury. For three trials now, the court has accepted as truth the defendant's statement that his wife died from an accidental gunshot wound in the woods miles down the road from his house."

"But we haven't had this information before," Yielding interjected. "Now we need to determine what led up to this sudden carpet removal, and what bearing it could have on—"

"That's bulls—"

"Hold on, Mr. Bowden," Cargile said, suddenly interested in what the matriarch herself might say. "It's an irregular request, but within the legal bounds of judicial canon, and is at my discretion. I'll allow it with this stipulation, Mr. Yielding: keep it brief and to the point. I'll explain it to the court, then you can proceed."

"The prosecution calls Mrs. Rose Tomlinson," Yielding announced. It was a stinger because the judge had not named the surprise witness. Mrs. Rose, seated at the defense table, looked startled for an instant, then composed herself. She walked rigidly and stone-faced to the chair and swore to be truthful.

A bombshell, maybe, I thought.

Seth honed in. "Mrs. Tomlinson, I'd like to take you back to the weekend of January 29, 1959, to your son John Ed's house; the weekend that your daughter-in-law was said to be at Dauphin Island. Did you and John Ed remove a large carpet from one of the rooms?"

"Yes."

"Which room was that?"

"The den."

"Why did you do that?"

"Objection!" Bowden thundered. "Irrelevant!"

"I'll allow it, but stay on point, Mr. Yielding."

"We did it because it had been stained badly during the holidays and would never look nice again. It was to be replaced while Jo Dell was at the beach, as a surprise when she came home."

"But she never came home, did she?"

"Objection!"

"Withdrawn."

"Mrs. Tomlinson, had Jo Dell picked out the new carpet for her house?"

"John Ed said she had," she replied, glancing at her son, who was watching her intently.

"And you have testified that the carpet was badly stained. What had stained it?"

"A bottle of red wine had fallen off a tray over Christmas and most of it had soaked into the carpet."

"Where is the carpet now?"

"I don't know. John Ed took it away. I haven't seen it since that day."

"Is there new carpet on the floor?"

"No. In all that happened it has not been replaced."

"Just one last question. Mrs. Tomlinson. Do you say with absolute certainty that the rug was stained with red wine? Or was that large red spot the blood of Jo Dell Tomlinson, who in fact was shot dead in her own home!"

"Objection!" cried a furious Bowden.

"Withdrawn. Thank you, Mrs. Tomlinson. Your witness." Yielding walked back to his seat, feeling her hatred knifing into his back, following his every step. The jury hadn't moved during this testimony. It may not have breathed, I thought. They stared ahead, as if unable to process what they had heard.

BOWDEN STOOD BEFORE THE woman who was signing his five-figure checks.

"Mrs. Tomlinson," he said gently, "are you certain of the truth and veracity of your testimony, so help you God?"

"I am," she replied sternly.

"And can you, by chance, identify the mysterious person who allegedly divulged this to Mr. Yielding?"

"Our family uses several helpers around our houses. I don't remember who it was." Rose Tomlinson, expressionless, eyes fixed on the back of the courtroom, was then excused.

· · · · · · · · · ·

Chapter 76

In a manner unheard at the flawed first trial, and exceeding that of the failed second trial, gloves came off and bare-knuckle oratory ricocheted off the plaster walls of the old courtroom during closing arguments. Tag-team combatants fought to either kill John Ed Tomlinson or free him.

Seth had worked the night before to perfect a presentation he knew would finish him with the Tomlinsons as long as he and they were alive. That of a two-timing husband who would stop at nothing to get his way, a scheming mistress with no scruples, and a faithful Christian wife who stood her ground for her children's sake, and suffered murder for doing it.

Bostick would flesh out the rest of the story—the frequent times John Ed and Sarah were seen together, John Ed's letter of May 1959 to Mrs. Sarah Tomlinson, the marriage license application in February 1961, friends who swore he looked normal right after the shooting, and the defendant who blatantly changed his story at will, it seemed, while telling the sheriff his version of what happened.

He would sow another thought in the jury's mind: "Don't look for possibilities, look for what probably happened. Base your conclusion on the evidence that came off the witness stand. I'm sorry this terrible crime happened. But who caused it? Who?"

Yielding looked his longtime nemesis straight in the face and asked the jury to sentence him to die in Alabama's electric chair. "If any man deserves it, it's this man. Let your verdict speak to the world. He saw his brother on Friday, but didn't tell him; didn't tell him on Saturday or Sunday. When he talked to the sheriff on Monday he already had the advice of a lawyer and loved ones, and had whitewashed the whole thing in his mind. It was the perseverance of Mrs. Wilkes that drove him to finally tell it."

Yielding faced the jury as they looked back at him. He didn't shout or smack his fist; just spoke to them, man to man. "I can hear her begging, 'Don't take me from my children!' So can you. But it was too late. You see, it's always back to Sarah Davis. Gentlemen, there isn't any doubt. There can't be. It's simply not there."

"These men heard me," Seth thought returning to his seat. "They'll do the right thing."

Cargile then spoke up "Recess for lunch until 1 P.M. It's a little early but this is a good stopping place. Adjourned."

THE ALABAMA CRIMSON TIDE was undefeated in nine games heading into the December 2 showdown against Auburn, and Strudwick Bowden, looking across the expanse of his creative mind, wasn't beyond comparing himself to another singular field general, Paul W. Bryant—the Bear— who seemed on the threshold of a national championship in just his fourth season as coach at the Capstone.

Bryant liked the biggest games, the toughest arenas and basked in victories and adulation. Bowden liked the biggest tests, toughest odds, the confidence of winning, the adulation. Good comparison, he thought, the night before resting his defense. Henderson County, even the state of Alabama, had never heard the persuasive force he would unleash upon this jury.

THE BIG CONCERTS, AT Birmingham's Municipal Auditorium, Memorial Coliseum in Tuscaloosa, and even the few that played tiny Livingston State Teachers College, in far west Alabama, usually had warm-up acts to prime the crowd for the main attraction. Henderson County's gospel quartets, Sunday singings, and the occasional honky tonk band had never merited a warm-up group. But one would appear, in a non-musical manner of speaking, at the courthouse that Thursday afternoon at 1 P.M.

Spit-polished as only a southern gentleman-lawyer could be, Calhoun Cates, second chair for the defense, opened for the star who would follow. And to those twelve men sitting before him, most of whom he knew by name, he drilled home one question time and again: "Don't you have a reasonable doubt?"

"How could you not?" he asked rhetorically. "Do you think a man of impeccable character, one many of you know personally to be a good father and husband, do you think a man like that would have it in his heart to take his wife out to those woods and kill her?

"He was crazy!" said Cates of John Ed's actions afterward. "He couldn't remember anything clearly except what had happened. And if he hadn't told it we would still be looking for Jo Dell. Her burial in a well, the stories of where she was, the marriage license application—his mind was gone!" Cates shouted as if kneeling at the altar.

He closed his thirty-minute summation by describing in prolonged prose the state's case as a house of cards. "There's only one person in the world, besides John Ed, who knows what happened, and she is not here. How could you help but have a reasonable doubt as to what happened out there?" Cates sat down feeling that he had risen to the occasion. Awaiting his call, the star's slight nod validated his belief.

· · · · · · · · · · ·

Chapter 77

I t's essential to look the part, Strudwick Bowden knew, and he did, starched and pressed in the finest suit Blach's, in Birmingham, could offer: four-point white handkerchief in breast pocket, black patent leather lace-ups, his white mane freshly trimmed by his barber who came and went last night. Walking free of the defense table and into the arena where his only concern was twelve men, he glanced at his fourteen carat Bulova wristwatch: 1:30 P.M.

Speaking softly but audibly, he asked the court reporter to please place all exhibits on the defense table. Then he addressed the jury, saying first that case law gives the defense counsel the right to discuss a case with witnesses; saying next that he would talk to them about testimony "that says without equivocation it was an accident, and cannot be anything else."

He paced slowly in front of the jury box, mostly speaking calmly, but at times bending low and sometimes shouting. "You're not trying a bad man— a killer—an individual who lived a sordid life. You've got a right to say whether he has a single characteristic of a man who would slay his wife. A man who is innocent until guilt is proven beyond a reasonable doubt or moral certainty. Be patient. Act if you can without error. You have more power than you'll have the rest of your lives, the power to give or take a life. You are judges of the facts, one of which is," shouting now, "that this case is wholly based on circumstantial evidence!"

The jury, fresh from a night's rest, intently followed his every move, the gestures, the body language, the expensive bifocals he occasionally removed and held by the stems in his left hand. He wanted undivided attention, and years of practice told him exactly how to get it.

Bowden then shifted emphasis to the case itself, and in meticulous chronological order led the jury through it, one step at a time, embellishing certain facts when it suited him.

"They were in a death struggle when this thing occurred. It was an accident, so says the evidence. It couldn't have been any other way.

"When he put that body in the well, he buried a corpse, the thing that had been her earthly castle before she passed on! That's all he buried.

"The minute that boy saw his wife dead before his eyes, the minute he took her in his arms and said, 'Jo Dell, Jo Dell!' he was in a panic. His mind was burning like molten iron. He didn't know what to do. He was as much surprised as she was, if she had time to be surprised. What kind of a man is it that could have been calm under such circumstances?

"He did things that were eighteen-carat stupid. He used bad judgment. And they want you to put him in the penitentiary, or worse than that. My God, how far can the prosecutor's conscience go?

"Barbara Evans Walker tells our very fine defense attorney, Calhoun Cates,

'I'm not talking. I don't have to talk to you defense lawyers. I'll have none of you.'" Seth Yielding, standing right here yesterday, said that is what he told her to say. God have pity on the people of this county if he does that!

"There's not a Negro bootblack in this county that doesn't know if you obtain a marriage license from Florida you cannot be married in Alabama! This happened because reason took a recess. How would the marriage have been consummated?

"Time's running out on him. He's thirty-eight years old. He's got a right to live, to go to those motherless children. They love him. You've seen it. Can you convict a man to satisfy the desires of certain people who want the whip of the law to lash his buttocks?

"The evidence clearly is not sufficient. Maximum punishment for molesting a body is twelve months in jail and a five hundred dollar fine. But, gentlemen, he is not indicted for that."

IN CLOSING, BOWDEN IMPLORED the jury to remember Dr. Nethery's testimony that it appeared Jo Dell was shot accidentally, that Sarah Davis and Robert Whatley had taken premarital blood tests, and that John Ed himself had said under oath at the first trial that the gun went off as they struggled for it and had never wavered from that story.

Bowden's final words, purposely obscure so they would have to think about the deeper meaning: "You show me a man with a lot of graves in his heart and I'll show you a man who doesn't have to haunt cemeteries."

Bowden slumped into his hard chair and wiped the sweat from his brow with another linen handkerchief. Feet aching, energy spent, exhausted, exhilarated by the conflict. Like the Bear after kicking Tennessee's ass. His gold watch said 3:20 P.M. His tenacious eloquence had consumed one hour and fifty minutes.

CARGILE HIMSELF, IN TWENTY years on the bench, had never before witnessed a mastery of facts and nuances within the context of such a powerful summation. To catch his own breath, he sipped from his pitcher of vodka, then turned his attention to the jury. "They're eager to get on with it, so let's go," he thought; and proceeded to declare their duty with care and caution, covering every phase of their deliberations—evidence, testimony, verdict (innocent, degrees of guilt), and other. "If you have a question, let the court know and it will be answered. When you are ready to report, just tell the deputy who will be outside your door." He did not utter the word, confession.

· · · · · · · · · · ·

Chapter 78

Late afternoon, finally alone, behind a locked door, they were all tired but nonetheless ready to think about the rest of John Ed's life. Albert White, the clean-cut, forty-something sawmill owner from down below Silas, who always looked neat but never overdressed, became their foreman by unanimous vote. Also, he had a degree from somewhere.

White scanned the faces of the six farmers, the accountant, the railroad man, the industrial engineer, the field superintendent, and the truck driver seated before him, then said, "I'll accept because it's my duty to our county, and because you obviously have confidence in me. We must do our job and put this tragedy behind our people once and for all. For nearly three years it's dragged on, and divided our county, even neighbor against neighbor. We'll operate like I do at the mill. Anyone who wants can speak out at any time, say whatever they're thinking. If we happen to disagree, no one should be disrespectful to another juror. Yellin' and cussin' won't get us anywhere. And I will keep us on track, toward a unanimous decision, whatever that is. Some jury in Henderson County has got to decide it. After all this time, let it stop with us."

"Mr. Foreman," said a voice several seats away, "I'm Tony Carlton, and I say we vote to convict and get it over and done. He planned it, did it, and not only lied about that sweet woman, but I'd horsewhip him for leavin' her in that well."

"Hold on," said Billy Tyson, two chairs away from White. Mustering his thoughts, he continued. "John Ed is presumed innocent until proven guilty beyond a reasonable doubt, and the state hasn't proven a cotton-pickin' thing. It's all circumstantial. Yeah, his actions afterward were unforgivable and stupid, and probably he was running around on her. But he's not on trial for any of that. Plus, he's always said it was accidental and the doctor who did the autopsy backs him up."

White responded, "Well, we have a healthy difference of opinion right off the bat. Before we continue, I'd like an indication of where we are relative to a verdict. We can do it by show of hands or secret ballot. Makes no difference to me."

"Raise hands, we ain't got nothin' to hide, or shouldn't have," said Jimmy Hearn.

"Innocent, three. Convict, six. Three, then, undecided," White recited the vote, including his own to convict. To Calvin Long, Herman Jacobs, and David Young, the undecided, he asked if they would say how they were leaning. Each stood his middle ground, mind still open.

"Y'all good for one more vote?" White asked. "Any against it?" No hands. "Okay, the six who favor guilty, who says death penalty?" No hands. "Who says life?" Tony's hand. "Okay, the rest of us want years right now."

"You men undecided," White said, "if the evidence were compelling enough, could you vote for conviction and a certain number of years?" Three hands. "Innocent, we know your position. Good. At least now we have a broad idea of where we are. But by no means have we sighted on a decision. It's 6:30 P.M., so let's quit for the day. We're all weary and need to rest our brains and bodies. Just remember, we cannot hear anything, read anything, or utter a word about the trial or what we are doing. It's in our hands now, and is life—or death—serious.

White, a married man who lived nearly one hour away, ate supper alone to think about his jury. They had made themselves his, and if he led them right it could all be over pretty quick. They knew his feelings and he knew that nine of the twelve would consolidate around punishment that was justifiably harsh. He had to reverse the innocent three—the trucker, a farmer, and the railroader—through common sense reasoning. Each man seemed rough cut as a plug of tobacco and probably could smell bullshit a mile away. But maybe, too, each one was grounded in standards of basic decency under girded by the Golden Rule. Circumstantial or not, some of the evidence spoke strongly to those points, and he thought if one loosened up the others might follow. He would see soon enough.

"Message for you, Mr. Anderson," the desk clerk at the Meridian motel said when I stopped to say hello that night. "Lady named Lindsey called. Said she'll be up on Saturday."

· · · · · · · · · · ·

Chapter 79

White greeted his colleagues Saturday morning at just past 9 a.m. Two urns on a side table held coffee. Two dozen doughnuts were in their boxes. "Gentlemen, you've had the chance to sleep with your thoughts and beliefs. You look fresh and rested. Have any of you had revelations or has anything else new or different come to mind since yesterday?"

One spoke up as if waiting for the chance. "My thinking is that, since most of us indicated yesterday we could vote guilty in some degree, we should examine the hard evidence that is not circumstantial and see where that puts us," accountant Clark Richards said.

"Anyone not okay with that?" White asked, relieved that Richards had stepped up, unprompted. Voices quiet. He wanted these men now to come forth and share their thoughts.

One did. "It's a fact, isn't it, that he made his dead wife out to be a whore? Said first that he'd caught her shacked up at a Citronelle motel. Then changed it to a trailer. Then that she was at Dauphin Island. When, in fact, she was in that well. Damn him for lyin' like that, tryin' to smear her good name!"

Another: "He left her out there, shot dead, overnight, on the dirt. Any one of us, and you know it, would have the sense to lay her in the car or truck and drive like a bat outa hell to the hospital in Butler. But, you see, he knew he'd go back and dispose of her, make her disappear. It was the plan. He was no more crazy than you or me."

Third to speak was the railroad official, Guy Stanford, one of the innocents. "It's a fact he was fuckin' Sarah Davis. Why else would he be goin' to her house before daylight and into her bedroom? And they were seen together almost everywhere. Barbara Evans testified of being with 'em at Nathan's and hearin' 'em talk about being in love and gettin' married. For months he flaunted Sarah Davis before Jo Dell and the whole county. No man should do that to his wife. Hell, he didn't care who knew."

Just what I wanted to hear, White thought.

A fourth juror, an undecided, spoke up, "It's a fact that Sarah Davis and Robert Whatley got blood tests in Waynesboro required for marriage. But it's a fact, too, that John Ed sent Sarah to Pensacola to get a marriage license application, and that both of 'em signed it and had it notarized. We seen it! Which has the most meaning? I say the application. And I'll bet they're married. They used Whatley to front what they were really doin'."

Buzz jumped around the table from man to man. Three or four got fresh coffee. They ate doughnuts, and chewed as well on the man shown to be guilty of deceit and betrayal. White chatted with a few, thinking, we are beginning to draw the net tight.

The next juror made the point of John Ed taking Jo Dell's car to Mobile. "That damn sure wasn't crazy, either. It was calculated all the way as part of his plan to plant the lie of her disappearance."

Truck driver Virgil Sampson, also an innocent, unloaded on the fish fry and whiskey party. "If your wife is dead and you know it, an' you're lyin' about where she is, it's lower than a goddam snake to have friends over to eat and drink like nothin's happened. And to have your wife's mother there, keepin' your babies, to hear and see it all, her sick to death about her daughter, already thinkin' she's dead. Lord have mercy!"

No need to go on, White thought, they were pulling together. So he called a twenty-minute recess. He was the last to pee, and while he waited wrote Judge Cargile a note and sent it by the deputy stationed by the door. It said, "Making progress. Everybody seems to be coming around. Verdict maybe after lunch."

They reassembled and White addressed them briefly. "Gentlemen, it's been very helpful to our process to hear the viewpoints you've expressed this morning. We're making progress. When we'll get a verdict and what it will be—if we do—we don't know. It's too early yet. So let's just keep goin' on what we know are facts."

Someone brought up the well and the picture they had seen. "It's not circumstantial that he pushed that poor woman's body like a piece a shit into that filthy and freezin' well. I know he's not on trial for that, as that fuckin' Bowden likes to tell us, but I know this: I couldn't look my own wife in the face, or live with myself, if we didn't deal with that."

Murmurs of agreement followed his comments. White let them run for a few minutes.

"The stained carpet," another said. "Mrs. Rose swears on the Bible that it was wine, but I don't believe that bitch. She'd do anything and say anything for her boys and to keep those grandchildren. She said it was taken out, but that's the last we know of it. I say she and John Ed could've killed Jo Dell at home, arguin' over the kids, and him carry her out to the well. We'll never know the full story, but we do know there was a red-stained carpet."

The room quieted down after that, and White asked, "Any more discussion?"

Someone answered, "Not for right now."

White said, "Then how about a long lunch? Let's ask to go now and reconvene at 1:30."

These men, he thought, are ready to go home.

. . . .

Chapter 80

I stood to stretch and the first face I saw was a smiling Lindsey. "It's too cold for an outside picnic, but we can go somewhere and eat in the car. I've got all we need," she said impishly.

"Sounds good," I replied. She was alluring in tan corduroy pants and coat, tight navy sweater, and brown loafers. "Let me check with the newspaper. I'll just be a minute. There's an open office down the hall."

Parked in a wooded area near the Memorial Gardens, we had ham sandwiches, coffee and brownies, and talked about our maze of complications, about what happened over Thanksgiving.

"I was desperate to get back to you," she said, holding my hand. "But we were very busy at the office after the holiday and I couldn't get away any earlier. Will there be a verdict today? You know, I hope not. It would mean one more day I could stay, and maybe you could stay over Sunday, too."

"I think the jury will report," I replied. "If it does, we'll have to go from there."

Tears welled in her soft green eyes. "I couldn't face not seeing you again." I held her close for just a moment. We drove back hardly talking. We didn't need to.

THE JURY ATE TOGETHER at the Downtown Café, making small talk mostly about football and the worsening behavior of blacks and their "movement." They strolled leisurely back to the courthouse and relaxed for a short time in a room outside an empty office. As they reassembled at 1:30 P.M., Albert White was waiting for them, ready to test the morning's discussion as being genuine or rhetoric. He said, "Gentlemen, I believe that our discussion of the morning has brought us to a point of advancing toward a verdict. If you're opposed to moving in that direction, please speak up."

"Mr. Foreman, I think we're pretty close to a decision. Let's see what happens," said Jacob Martin, one of the quiet ones so far.

"Anyone else?" White waited. "Hearing none, I'd like to take a secret ballot on guilty or innocent." He passed around half sheets of paper and said, "Write one of those words, fold the paper and pass it to me."

He opened the eleven pieces, plus his own, and read the same word twelve times: Guilty. Although on one sheet the writer had scratched through Innocent.

"Gentlemen," the room was dead silent, all eyes on him, "We are of one accord. John Ed Tomlinson is guilty of something." Heads nodded. Someone added, "Good decision."

"Now the question before us is, but what?" said White. He continued, "I want us to vote again, and again in secret. If it was your decision, what would you say, and ask yourself, how would you justify it?" He reviewed the definitions Cargile had provided.

"First degree murder is unlawful, willful, malicious, deliberate, and premeditated. Second degree murder is unlawful, willful, and malicious. First degree manslaughter is unlawful and intentional. Second degree manslaughter is unlawful and accidentally committed, in that it happened without one's direct intention." He added, "There we are."

. . . .

Chapter 81

The life before them was no one's quick decision. Some stared at their paper. Some paced the room. A few, White could tell, were praying. Some stood at the window, looking out. No questions or comments. Minutes passed. Gradually, they passed judgment. "First degree, three of us. Second degree, six. Manslaughter one, three. Manslaughter two, none."

White then made a bold move. "I think we should try to consolidate around second degree murder. Three of us are on either side of that. If we can do that it will mean punishment of not less than ten years, and no maximum number. As a reminder, first degree manslaughter is one to ten years, and first degree murder is either a life sentence or the death penalty. Let's divide up to try and settle it—manslaughter in that corner, first degree over there, the rest stay at the table. If your two small groups changed your position, what penalty could you live with?"

"I'm of a mind to stay where I am, I spoke my feelings yesterday," Tony Carlton told the other hard-liners. "Life."

David Young and Martin Ezell indicated a willingness to shift if the penalty was forty years. "He'd die in prison," Young said.

"That's a point," Carlton replied.

Billy Tyson reasoned with himself in the other corner. "If it was intentional, as the law says about manslaughter, if he shot her to get her out of his way to a divorce and the kids, then ten years ain't enough, 'cause he'd be out in five, countin' what he's already served. No sir, he's got to do more than that, twenty, at least." The other two said they'd go along with that.

White spoke quietly to his five colleagues at the table. "We can keep the lead in this effort if we'll agree on a range of years. Any thoughts?" The prevailing opinion was twenty to forty years.

The three segments reconvened as one, and Carlton spoke for his group: "We'll shift for forty years." Tyson followed with a question for White: "How does the law define malicious?"

White looked it up in a dictionary on the table: "Malicious means hateful, provocative, and clashing, among other things." Then he read again from Cargile's definitions: "If a killing is malicious, even if it occurs during a sudden heat of passion or rage, it is murder."

"Then at least twenty," Tyson said. "Now what about y'all?"

White answered. "We're in the range of twenty to forty. And it appears all of us are. I'll just ask the question, who could support mid-range, thirty years? Show of hands." He counted six. "Who is less than thirty?" Four hands. "How much higher?" Carlton: "Thirty-five."

"Mr. Carlton," White said, "If the four who favor less than thirty will compromise on twenty, will you do the same?"

"Don't want to, but I'll think on it," Carlton replied.

"Gentlemen," said White, "we're very close to finishing our work. All we lack is a few of us making adjustments. And remember, the penalty we're looking at is harsh, but justifiable, given all we know. So I'll ask again, Mr. Tyson and Mr. Ezell, can you accept twenty years?" The two looked at each other across the table for a long minute. Tyson then nodded.

"Mr. Carlton, I know how you feel because you were the first to speak up yesterday. I also think you're a reasonable man, so I say, can you live with twenty?"

"I reckon," the juror replied.

White moved swiftly to counter any change of minds. "Then this is our verdict: guilty of second degree murder, recommended sentence of twenty years. Show of hands if you agree." Twelve hands.

. . . .

Chapter 82

In his charge to the jury, Cargile had instructed them to write the verdict
on the back of a certified copy of the indictment that charged John Ed
with first degree murder. White took the document from an envelope, wrote
the decision, put it back in, and sealed the envelope. Then he opened the
locked door and gave it to the assigned deputy.

"Verdict," he said. It was 2:50 P.M.

EIGHT MINUTES LATER CARGILE brought in the twelve. They saw John Ed
sitting at the defense table, chin in left hand. He had waited in court all
day, and now stood as the judge directed. He showed no emotion as Cargile
said, "Gentlemen of the jury, have you reached a verdict?"

White replied, "We have, Your Honor."

"What say you?"

White read the verdict.

The crowd that I estimated to be one hundred or more murmured and
whispered one to another, but quelled any other emotions, apparently relieved that after thirty-four long months justice had been served.

Eying one juror at a time, Cargile asked if that was his verdict. Each man
replied, "Yes sir." Next, he wrote the verdict into the court record, saying,
"12-1, 1961—Jury sends verdict of guilty of murder in the second degree
as charged in the indictment, fixing defendant's punishment at twenty years
in the penitentiary. Defendant is adjudged guilty of murder in the second
degree as charged in the indictment and is sentenced by the court to twenty
years in the penitentiary as punishment. Defendant gives motion of appeal
and sentence of twenty years is suspended pending appeal. Appeal bond
filed at fifteen thousand dollars."

Showing no emotion, John Ed, hands on hips, talked quietly with his
mother and brother. His children were not in the room.

Strudwick Bowden quickly confirmed an appeal to the Alabama Supreme
Court. Cargile then announced the sentence was suspended pending the

court's decision, and that bond was fifteen thousand dollars. The bond was paid and John Ed was subsequently released.

Cargile dismissed the jury, first praising them for their diligence over the course of seven and a half hours in arriving at unanimous agreement in such an emotionally charged case. "You are exemplary citizens," he said.

AN EXUBERANT SETH YIELDING told me that the Supreme Court would set a date to hear the appeal and doubted it would be before January. "As it stands today, if the appeal is denied, John Ed will be given credit for the two years and ten months he has already served, and will have to serve several more years before being eligible for parole." He added, "I expected a stronger verdict because I will always believe it was first degree murder. If he had been found guilty of that, he couldn't have tried for parole for ten years. But as representative of the people, I will abide by the decision of these twelve men."

Assertive as usual, but noticeably subdued, Bowden nonetheless took the high road in appraising his defeat. "The verdict did not reflect the strength of the evidence that clearly showed accident, not murder. Still, I am well-pleased that these twelve citizens of Henderson County, who were selected by the defense and the State of Alabama, were big enough to reach a unanimous decision."

"Mr. Bowden," I asked, "in reflecting on these two trials and your approach to John Ed's defense, will you have second thoughts about not calling the defendant to testify in his own behalf and deny the charge against him?"

Calmly, he replied, "Mr. Anderson, that strategy was employed at the first trial and resulted in a life sentence, albeit a flawed verdict that was overturned. Mr. Tomlinson has maintained from the beginning that what happened was an accident, and that statement was entered as evidence through the sheriff. It would have served no useful purpose to put him on the stand. And there are enough flaws in the conduct of this trial to reverse this verdict as well."

"But the marriage license application wasn't part of the first—"

"That's all, Mr. Anderson, thank you," Bowden said, and walked away, out of the building and out of my career. I had no more contact with the most flamboyant and self-impressed person I'd ever met, except to read now and then about high-visibility cases he was handling. But I've never forgotten that twice I was in the close company of the best in the business. That was a high privilege and an education I never forgot.

In my other post-trial rounds, Mrs. Rose wouldn't speak to me, but Bill Tomlinson agreed that keeping John Ed quiet was a sound decision. He, too, thought Cargile once more had made key mistakes, but wouldn't be specific. Nonetheless, I had the elements of a strong story—verdict, good quotes, looking ahead. I just had to put it all together; I told Stan Meyer I would write it here and drop it off by 9 P.M.

. . . .
Chapter 83

Lindsey, knowing I had to write while the story was fresh, stopped to see her aunt for an hour or so, then drove to Meridian. I was almost finished when she knocked at the motel door.

"Don't let me rush you, but hurry," she said breathlessly. "I need you one on one.

"Just hold me," she said as we sat on the sofa. "I haven't wanted to live this moment because a part of me says it will be the end of us. Yet, I want to believe that we mean too much to each other to let go. But I need to know what you think."

I pulled back slightly and replied, "Lindsey, I must see you again; somehow I'll work it out. But I can't say when. Write me at the paper, or call, and let me know what decisions you're making. I'll write, too, but calling is too risky. That's the best we can do, and let's leave it at that for now."

We embraced and kissed with soft urgency. She said, "Just always be honest with me, Dan. Don't ever hold back something I need to know. And I'll be the same." The door locked behind us. She turned south and I drove east. Heart-wrenching symbolism. I just didn't know it.

I NEEDED THE PHYSICAL and emotional distance from Henderson County more than I thought. That relic of a courthouse, the flawed judge, the threats, pompous lawyers, underlying rivalries, on and on. I knew, too, its people were tired of living that murder and wanted to be rid of me and what I stood for.

Of Lindsey and me, I needed distance to put us into reality. The situation that had bound us together and ignited our relationship had ended. What would happen without that fuel was a question whose answer bore great meaning. We could pay a painful price for what we were doing.

Right now, I just wanted time away from deadlines to rekindle family warmth and enjoy the holidays. Meyer agreed. "See you in a week," he said. "But if you leave town, let me know."

· · · · · · · · · · ·

Chapter 84

The New Year 1962 hung darkly in the southern sky; storm clouds forming that would obliterate any full moon of promise, even though some places in the urban South—pushed by business leaders facing buying boycotts—were crumbling under black pressure.

Developing situations across the region dictated demands upon a culture that tended to fight change with blood; demands that would then consume the lives of us who were reporting them. We came to measure hours, days, weeks and months by little else than the next call to get up and go, or that threatened our families. The dozen or so reporters and photographers covering this story were never off duty. Lindsey wrote occasionally, but I was not able to answer. Our relationship, once moored securely, seemed to be loosening and drifting away.

VERY QUIETLY, IN BIRMINGHAM, the Chamber of Commerce began serious discussions with black leaders A.G. Gaston, Louis Willie, the Reverend Fred Shuttlesworth and others. Surprisingly, their talks led to desegregated public bathrooms, and removal of "white/colored" signs at water fountains before the year ended. To our amazement at the newspaper, the Southern Christian Leadership Conference held its national convention in the city in September. Peacefully. We covered the meeting heavily, from welcoming rhetoric to adjournment.

Klan-led unrest, however, was unnerving much of the state, and particularly the University of Alabama. Its president and trustees were shocked by the killings and violence that erupted at Ole Miss in fall 1961, led by mobs opposing James Meredith's enrollment.

Alabama president Frank Rose, feeling that the Capstone's turn was coming, sought to marshal every reasonable voice in the state, saying "this university must never become the scene of mob violence, battle troops, or bloodshed." Rose then froze all applications from black students, which, in the previous few years had numbered 213. At homecoming 1961 the trustees, in a bold stand, stood by the president. Their courage made terrific copy and, more importantly, symbolized thoughtful reason.

THREE MOMENTOUS EVENTS WITH threatening implications formed at the dawn of 1963. The first was Governor George C. Wallace's "segregation forever!" inaugural speech on an icy January morning in Montgomery, which I helped cover and heard firsthand. The second was Martin Luther King's gamble to energize his financially-faltering movement by unleashing a direct action campaign in Birmingham in April. Hard-core retaliation rocked the city, and kept all reporters, among others, on continuous alert. The third was Wallace's orchestrated "stand in the schoolhouse door," June 11, against the integration of the University of Alabama, which occurred despite his defiance.

There was a fourth event, as well, momentous of international proportions in its horror, which no sane person could have foreseen—the bombing of the 16th Street Baptist Church, September 15, which murdered four little girls dressed for Sunday School. I worked until midnight, covering in those twelve hours or more the random killings of two more youths and continuing outbursts across the city.

Will the madmen among us never be stopped, I wondered in the early morning, driving home to Claire, Sam, and Dale, our new second son. My answer came nine weeks later. On November 23, President John F. Kennedy was murdered in Dallas, Texas, where he had gone to make a luncheon speech.

. . . .

Chapter 85

It was just one, I was told years before, on an afternoon in court. But I couldn't get the comment verified. It was the pivotal question of the second trial, which gnawed me and wouldn't let go. I needed the answer for personal satisfaction if nothing else. Reporters don't ever walk away and leave such intrigue lying on the table.

Who had hung the second jury.?

I DIDN'T GO BACK to Butler often, but when I did it was to work old contacts for information and insight that were kept from me when the air was too thick with conflict and fear. Those men and women were more cordial now, although some still spoke cautiously, as if that air would never clear completely.

One man, who wore a suit and tie to work most days, came to trust me enough to disclose a lot of things that were happening then that I never knew. And during one of our meetings, when I asked the pressing question, he gave me a name and pointed me toward a person. But he insisted, "You've got to keep me out of this." I promised.

HE AND ESTHER LIVED at the end of a short chert drive that turned off an unmarked asphalt road maybe three miles southeast of Butler. I knew I'd found it because the black metal mailbox resting on top of a four-by-four read "L. HART." A disheveled pick-up that once was red sat in front of the gray frame house that occupied a small clearing cut from surrounding woods. I never saw all of the house, or around back, but first and final impression was low-end adequate.

I was expected, as I had telephoned to introduce myself and tell him my business. His barking, tan squirrel hound surveyed me suspiciously, and announced a stranger. He opened the door before I could knock and saw me into a small square living room that had green linoleum on the floor and a squat-leg coal heater in one corner. Windows were open and a floor fan whirred in an arc. Curtains fluttered. The room was stuffy hot.

Lester Hart, who my informant had said was the one, shook my hand, and Esther said, "Have a seat." She wore a plain purple print dress, no jewelry or makeup, and tennis shoes. His clothing was coveralls, a short sleeve tan shirt and work boots. They looked to be in their late sixties, the poster couple for a hard life. He'd been an easy mark for the Tomlinsons, I thought.

I gave my name again, showed them my press card, and thanked them for the courtesy of speaking with me. He didn't know that I knew, I was sure of it. If, in fact, my source was right. "May I tape record our conversation, just for accuracy?" I asked. "My notes wouldn't get everything. I realize it's been years now, but since you served on the second jury, Mr. Hart, would you share what you remember about that experience?"

"Hits pretty much gone from memry, I reckon," he answered. "'Bout all I recollect is that we didn't know who done it." Esther added, "And we still don't. There weren't but them two out there, and they've both passed on." He finished: "'Course, aside from the first trial, he didn't testify, but he always said it was an accident."

"They was both well thought of," he said. "So was his brother." For my part, I had figured this to be a slow-going discussion, one thing at a time, like picking one's teeth. To keep them cordial and relaxed, my approach would be soft and patient, repetitious as needed to return them to a point for elaboration, and in particular to keep him talking and catch any nugget he might drop. Time dragged, conversation would dodge its underlying purpose, or often lapse into extended silence. Then I would try again to move us toward the only reason I was there.

"What did you on the jury say to each other?" I asked. He replied, "We wasn't allowed to talk about it; the judge told us not to."

"But you talked in the jury room. You had to, the evidence and all, the testimony you heard," I said.

"We did, but none of us knew for sure if he done it."

"The jury foreman finally reported there could be no verdict, that eleven of you had voted for conviction and the same number of years, but that one wouldn't agree to anything but five years. So you all became a hung jury."

"Hit was somethin' like that. All o' us was for conviction, just couldn't agree on the penalty."

"How did you vote, Mr. Hart?

"All o' us had different opinions from the start. Everybody had to shift around."

"How did you vote, finally, Mr. Hart?"

This sharecropper, who'd never had anything of substance until somehow he came into possession of this low-scale little five-room house in 1962, would not be swayed now, as he wasn't in the jury room in spring 1961. "I didn't know what to say."

"And you don't remember who the holdout was?

"Naw, I don't. I couldn't call his name, ah caint do it. And the ones on the jury I knew, they done passed on."

"Well, if you could vote today, what would you do, guilty or innocent?"

"It'd be hard to say." He'd go no further.

"Were there any repercussions toward you or the jury over the trial ending as it did?"

"Naw. We never heard nuthin' like that."

SLOGGING THROUGH THIS MORASS of platitudes I wanted to shout at times, "Stop it, Lester! You know what you did, you sold out." But I restrained myself by sharing information that I doubted they knew, and circling back to certain points in the hope they would comment about them again.

Esther's calm demeanor hardly changed as we talked, somewhat perhaps when she would inject that she didn't know that back then women couldn't serve on a jury, or that "I just don't think he done it," or that she went to school with Jo Dell and saw her as a loner who didn't have many friends. She casually recalled gossip that named Sarah Davis or John Ed's mother as possibly connected to the killing. Said Lester and she attended the funeral and that she went to the second trial for a day. Also, that they were suspicious of John Ed's story that JoDell went willingly to the woods, saying, "Why would she?"

Esther Hart knew the "I didn't know that . . . I don't remember" game better than her husband. Under her facade, this ordinary-looking person was smart and devious.

We played each other that afternoon, cagey but transparent, like bad poker.

All three of us knew it. They won.

. . . .

Chapter 86

Like the forceful sun merging with gentle twilight, gradually but steadily the forbidden feelings that existed between Lindsey and me faded. Each other's needs that we met and the emptiness of final separation receded into that part of the heart that preserves only certain memories. I thought lovingly of her and us at times, and I knew she did as well. But years passed with no contact.

SOUTHERNERS ARE PRONE TO believe everything happens for a reason. I don't accept that idiom completely, but cannot deny what happened on a fall afternoon at the courthouse square in Butler. Ending one of my rare trips there, I was leaving the stately old building having tracked down a rumor and discovered an informative file in a place I shouldn't have been looking. Across the street, outside the law office of Oscar Cole, stood a woman whom I glanced at and instantly knew by name. Still radiantly pretty, same build I remembered, smartly-dressed as always. No mistaking the woman I had loved. Long dormant feelings flickered with warmth. She walked toward the cafe where we had eaten many times. I fell in behind her for half a block and then said quietly, "Lindsey. Got time for coffee?"

She stopped but didn't look back for several seconds, as if she couldn't have heard that voice. Then she turned to me and whispered, "Dan? My God!"

We moved together and embraced, drawing a few interested looks; something we had never before done in public. We dared to hold hands strolling to the cafe like old lovers not forgotten.

"You first," she said as we combined fresh coffee with still-warm apple pie. And I covered the particulars: marriage, two sons, strong career. Visiting to tie up a few loose ends of the story that I still hoped could become a book.

"Now you," I said. She replied, married to the same husband, no children, law degree University of South Alabama, lucrative little practice in Fairhope, small civil stuff. In town to meet with Mr. Cole about her late aunt's estate, which he is handling. We didn't reopen most memorable Chapters because they were safely stored, ours forever.

Suddenly, Lindsey glanced at her watch and frowned. "Dan, I've gotta go," she said. "I'm sorry. I have to meet my husband in five minutes. We're heading back to Mobile."

I had held her hand so often that it felt natural to grasp it once more, probably for the last time. Looking into those eyes that once entranced me, I stumbled over parting words because I've never liked saying goodbye. "We were good for each other, and still would be. Our feelings were deep, and they are in us permanently."

We stood. She kissed my cheek and was gone. I still have all her letters.

. . . .

Chapter 87

Our very first conversation was slowing, and a perfect April evening was unfolding in a breeze fragrant with all the perfumes of spring. "It's six o'clock," I said to Sarah. "Let me at least buy dinner before I go back."

"You're a gentleman, Mr. Anderson," she replied. "I know an out-of-the way place toward Meridian where the tea's sweet, the barbecue's spicy, and the ice box pie is homemade. You game?"

"Famished. I'll drive."

"We're not finished, you know," she said, navigating toward Sassy's diner, best known to the locals. "I've lots more to say about me and John Ed and our children, and I doubt you know about the further tragedies that struck the Tomlinsons.

"No, I don't. What about it?"

"Later, when we're not so tired. Maybe it'll motivate you to come back soon."

As we ate unnoticed, she told me that Seth, several years after the final trial, had moved his family and law practice away from Butler and across the Tombigbee to another county seat, Grove Bluff. "Did local pressure drive him out?" I asked.

"It was rough for awhile because he had gone after John Ed so hard," Sarah said. "You saw most of it, how he never let up. And everyone knew that a lot of it was personal, the poor man–rich man rivalry he felt toward the Tomlinsons, especially toward Bill and Rose. John Ed just put himself in the center of it. Seth brought them all down several notches, for sure, but mistakenly thought he could ride that verdict into the probate judge's job. Lost a tight race to Bill, the incumbent, in the mid-sixties. Hundred votes, I think. Tomlinson power. But people across Seth's circuit liked him; reelected him twice more as circuit solicitor."

"Did the red-stained rug ever turn up?" I asked. "Or who saw it removed?"

"No. Talk was that it vanished into the quarry that's south of town. And whoever helped take it out of the house was never named. Quite a mystery in itself."

I took Sarah home and thanked her for such a hospitable afternoon of quality time and good information. "I'll be in touch," I said. "I want to come back soon."

"'Till next time, then," she said with a parting smile that bore its own hint of mystery.

TIRED OF THE ACCUSATIONS, the flaming rhetoric and everything else associated with three trials, in December 1961 John Ed told Sarah and the family to withdraw the appeal of his conviction. He wasn't feeling well, either, and wanted to start his sentence. He then spent Christmas and New Year's subdued but free of lockup.

Warden Augustus Mabry greeted John Ed at Kilby Prison on January 9, 1962. "Thought we might be spendin' another Christmas together," he said, chuckling coldly. "Instead, it'll be the next several Christmases. Welcome back. Twenty, ain't it?"

"Can't say it's good to see you, warden," Tomlinson said. "Let's get the preliminaries done with so I can go lay down. I'm tired. Not feelin' well lately. I brought you my doctor's statement about it."

. . . .

Chapter 88

May was dancing to spring's serenade when, five weeks after my April visit, I went back to see Sarah, honoring her invitation for a lunch feast of fried chicken, vegetables, corn bread and apple cobbler. We ate in her dining room, furnished tastefully with what seemed to be fine antiques; table, six chairs, and sideboard.

"Don't know why you went all out, but that was terrific," I said. "Couldn't help but think of John Ed as I enjoyed it. I'll bet you spoiled him."

"Did the best I could after he came home. Our blended family—seven kids, you know—took a lot of work, but we appreciated every day we had. Mrs. Rose was a bitch," she said as we washed dishes. "She had nothing but contempt for me and my three daughters, although John Ed adopted them. She moved into Butler from Silas, and raised the twin boys. We had the two girls, but Rose would have nothing to do with my girls."

"Speaking of . . ." I said, "what happened to your children?"

"Lives of their own," Sarah answered. "Tuscaloosa, Sweet Water, Thomasville. Four granddaughters." We finished the dishes quickly, then Sarah said, "I want to take you for a ride."

"Where are we going?"

"A little farther out in the country. I want you to see John Ed's grave."

THE MID-AFTERNOON SUN HIGHLIGHTED a setting whose pastoral beauty had the perfection of a Hubert Shuptrine watercolor in *Jericho*. On one side stood a tiny, rectangular white church, its modest steeple of perfect proportion to the building. God's quiet presence honored a wide, smooth surface of manicured grass, inset with gray headstones, which stretched to a stand of ancient oaks. A low wrought iron fence bordered the site, and a curved arch inscribed McDowell Cemetery marked the gated entrance.

"It's a private place; the McDowell family made special allowance for us. We've been friends a long time," Sarah said.

A short walk inside brought us to the imposing granite monument that said, in capital letters, TOMLINSON. And beneath the name on one side was the inscription, "John Ed Tomlinson, November 21, 1923–May 23, 1979." Next to it was a blank space.

"That's for me," Sarah said. "I'll be lying beside him, so thankful we'll sleep together forever. Away from all the pain and all the talk, just to ourselves." Tears coursed down her cheeks and mine as she spoke.

"What a lovely place," I whispered, and took her hand. "Thank you for bringing me. I hadn't remembered when he died." We were less emotional riding back as she continued the story about her husband and their time together.

"The conviction, the appeal, then the withdrawal overshadowed the holidays," Sarah said. "And Rose, of course, who tried to alienate the twins from us by doing her best to keep them at a distance. Knowing that he faced prison in January led us to decide, rather on the spur of the moment, to go on and get married. On January 3 we went to Waynesboro, Mississippi, just across the line, and got our marriage license. A justice of the peace married us at his home in Waynesboro on January 6, 1962. His name was Oliver Overstreet. Heard our vows but never saw us. He was blind. My brother, Gus, and his wife were witnesses. It took five minutes."

I couldn't resist saying it; reporters are impertinent beings: "Considering the contention during all the trials that there was nothing between you two, did Strudwick Bowden acknowledge your wedding?"

"Didn't hear from him."

"And your engagement to Robert Whatley?"

"I thought it was real at the time. But soon enough I knew that it was

John Ed and me who were real. I did Robert wrong, and regret it. I believe he went back to Holly Springs, Mississippi. Barbara and I stay in touch. She's still in Birmingham.

"It hurt my heart to have to give up my husband to Sheriff Hutton so quickly after the wedding and see him go back to prison. Ninth of January he left, looking at five years minimum. But he told me on our last night, 'Sarah darlin', at least we're together now, and that'll keep me goin' down there. Hold your head high and be proud that you're my wife. I certainly am.' We'd go down to see him every other Saturday and stay at a motel in Montgomery. Then, on Sunday, after lunch, we'd go to the prison; me and my oldest, Mary Lou, all dressed up, and her little sisters looking real pretty, too."

We were at her house now. As I thanked her again for the day, she said, "It'll take one more visit, Dan. I think then I can finish saying what I want you to know.'"

. . . .

Chapter 89

The State of Alabama ended its confinement of John Ed Tomlinson on October 4, 1965, and released him on parole. He had served three years and ten months, plus the nearly three years during and between the trials. Good behavior was a factor in the shortened sentence. He even became a trustee, but lost that privilege when he was caught drinking moonshine and wouldn't name his supplier.

"The happiest days of my life up to that time had been the birth of my children, and John Ed's and my marriage," Sarah said during our next visit, a few weeks later. "Now I could add my husband's release. Mary Lou went around the house singing, 'Daddy's coming home!' It was almost too good to be true.

"The blended family consisted mostly of our five daughters, ranging from Margaret, John Ed's oldest, seventeen, down to my two youngest. We saw the twin boys from time to time. We first lived at my small house in Bladon Springs while work was done at John Ed's home, which had been closed up for three years. We made ourselves part of county life mainly through church and school, and were pretty well accepted, primarily because of the children, I'm sure."

Sarah continued, "John Ed loved my girls and was good to them. They had become close during our visits to him, particularly Mary Lou, who was thirteen. We didn't try to rush things with his two oldest children, Margaret, who was almost grown, and Melissa, coming into adolescence. We didn't want to add to the turmoil they had known, or the life changes they were experiencing."

John Ed, she said, went back to logging and was welcomed by some of his old buddies. "I overheard him tell one man, 'I ain't got nothin' against nobody. I just want to start a new life and go on with it.'"

Try as he did, Sarah told me, he found a new life hard to manage. She said, "We started drinking too much. I grew to like bourbon. His favorite was moonshine. So it was just a matter of time before the booze affected our health. Especially his. He got cirrhosis of the liver, but still wouldn't stop. He ended up in a prolonged coma at the Mobile Infirmary, and slipped away on May 23, 1979. Just fifty-five. The whole thing, start to finish—Jo Dell, three trials, prison, parole—had taken twenty years out of his life."

She said suddenly, as if she had just thought of it, "I mentioned the Tomlinson's tragedies last time. It's the truth that tragedy has tracked almost everyone who was involved in all of this, directly or indirectly. Snatched them in death in the prime of life. My first husband killed in a tractor accident. Jo Dell. John Ed. Bill Tomlinson died of an illness in 1961, I'm not sure what. Nancy, his wife, was murdered in Meridian, where she and their son, Dickie, had moved. After that, Dickie came back to Butler and lived with an uncle for a long time, but broke his neck in a diving accident and died in his twenties a paraplegic. Seth died of a brain tumor not that long after moving to Grove Bluff. I don't believe in demons, but, Dan, you have to wonder if some infectious evil didn't possess those families; demons of animosity and jealousy."

"Or a common death wish they couldn't escape. Seven! Maybe you're right!"

Chapter 90

The afternoon sun waned into evening. We watched night's slow approach from her porch swing and my rocking chair. Sarah broke the quiet, saying, "There is one last thing, Dan, before I let you go." Happiness tinged her voice, which caught my attention, for it was the exception in our long hours together over three visits.

"I'm surprised you haven't discovered it by now. My husband was pardoned."

I don't get flustered anymore. Seen too much, heard too much, too many surprises. But I leaned forward in the rocker and looked hard into her eyes, which shone with light I'd seldom seen. My astonishment almost stuck in my throat. "You mean the crime was—"

"Forgiven." She finished my sentence as if the word had melody. Then she opened a file folder lying beside her and handed me a sheet of stationery that bore the letterhead, "Alabama Department of Corrections," January 22, 1972, and the recipient, John Ed Tomlinson. The one paragraph message read:

> This letter will formally confirm the official action taken by the State Board
> of Pardons and Paroles at its meeting on January 20, 1972, in granting
> you a pardon for the offense of second degree murder, for which you were
> sentenced to twenty years imprisonment on December 1, 1961.

It was signed by Anthony Adcock, chairman of the board. A copy was sent to Circuit Solicitor Seth Yielding at his office at Grove Bluff.

BY DEFINITION, A PARDON is the official act of forgiving a crime. The conviction is stricken from all records and the person cannot be retried for the same offense It does not mean the convicted person is not guilty, and does not seal one's criminal record from public view. It does mean, under law, that the person is forgiven and no longer deserving of punishment. A pardon is usually based upon a notion of undeserved punishment, but other reasons may be a factor such as acts or behavior proving rehabilitation.

"How did this come about, Sarah?"

She replied, "His determination to live a normal life while on parole, which wasn't easy, but he did it. He showed interest in our children's schools, attended church occasionally, went back to timber business. He became an average citizen and most everybody he saw on the street welcomed him back. Drinking was his main drawback, but he controlled it in public.

Our area's state senator hired him for a timber job and soon developed a high opinion of my husband as a good man who had paid his debt to society. The senator, Irving Fullington, actually approached John Ed about applying to Governor Wallace for an executive pardon. We talked about it, and John Ed thought, why not? This was summer of 1971. Wallace was receptive, but too occupied with national politics, and referred the request to the pardons and paroles board, which has the legal authority to issue a pardon. Mr. Fullington helped us jump through the hoops locally to complete the required application. Then it was in the board's hands to check it out. We weren't in time to make the fall meeting, but were hopeful to be on the agenda in January of '72. And we were notified just after the new year to be there on January 20.

"John Ed's khakis were starched and pressed; he'd had a hair cut; shoes were shined. He almost beamed with confidence that day. But when he was called forward it was not pat-on-the-back-and-done."

Sarah said that she no longer remembered every particular, but did recall the stern approach of board chairman Adcock in asking John Ed about his readjustment into society and family. "He wasn't hostile; just asked pointed questions and expected straight answers," she said. "He also heard testimonials from Senator Fullington and Sheriff Hutton about John Ed's transition and behavior as they knew it, including no run-ins with the law, or an arrest, since his release. Mr. Adcock impressed upon all of us the weight of this decision, and polled each board member for their questions or comments. No one spoke, and the vote to allow the pardon was unanimous. Both of us wept."

. . . .

Chapter 91

Ｎews of the decision spread quickly across the county, but without the flair and flash of all that had preceded it. Town talk mostly agreed that John Ed had accounted for his past sins, although some cynics badmouthed that he was shown undeserved leniency considering what he did, and that the whole thing was a George Wallace whitewash.

The local weekly ran a story, but Sarah said, "John Ed and I both asked them to please not make it a spectacle again. And they didn't. They confined it to a small story inside the paper. The *Montgomery Advertiser* ran something, too, that reported all the activity of the board meeting, which included five pardons. John Ed's was just one line in the story."

"THAT'S IT, DAN. THAT'S everything I know," Sarah said. The earlier glow of her voice now carried finality. "You wouldn't think people still would ask, but they do—did he really do it? As if I know with certainty. My standard answer is, 'I honestly didn't know. I was aware of all the talk at the time and read most of the trial coverage. But I wanted to believe the man I loved so much.' "

She stood then and gave me a going-away smile. I stood, went to her, put my arms around her slender form, and pulled her tight against me. We felt each other breathe but said nothing to let this long moment of closure be as quiet as the evening enveloping us. Then we released and opened just a slight space to better control our emotions.

"Thank you, Sarah. I've never gotten a call that was more meaningful to my life than yours that summoned me here." Voice breaking, I spoke softly. "I can write this whole story now, and will."

She said, "You are in my heart, Dan. I have trusted to put you there." She squeezed my hand. I turned away, walked to my car, and didn't look back.

SARAH CONTRACTED LUNG CANCER several months after we parted, a toll of longtime smoking, plus asthma. Her health declined swiftly, almost as if she was answering her husband's call. Seeking better doctors, she and the girls moved to Mobile. This I learned from Mary Lou years later as I grappled with this book.

Mary Lou was the primary caregiver at the bedsides of John Ed and her mother. She told me, in reflection of their short years together, that in the good times they were loving and thoughtful toward one another, but there were dark chapters of alcoholic binges that turned the relationship abusive, which grew in frequency. She spoke of protecting her mother and caring for her sisters. The Tomlinson children seemed less affected. They scattered in adulthood and only one of the twins chose to live in Butler.

Sarah died in Mobile in September 1993, at age fifty-eight, three years after the phone call that pulled me back to Henderson County. She had prayed for peace, and found it eternally with John Ed at a lovely, isolated graveyard.

Some day, when we meet up yonder, we'll stroll hand-in-hand again through a land that knows no parting. Blue eyes cryin' in the rain.

· · · · · · · · · ·
Afterword

My occasional visits back to Henderson County led me to locals who lived in those times. It's true that few of them still talked about the murder, or visited Jo Dell's grave any more. Most didn't know where John Ed and Sarah were buried. But with decades elapsed and no reason to fear

Tomlinson power, several spoke freely about what they remembered.

The old sheriff, for instance—still full of himself about ridding the county of moonshiners in the 1950s—went on about how Jo Dell's death complicated the local power structure. "We didn't know what to believe," he said, "but I'm sure that she died in the woods, as John Ed always maintained."

What about the stained carpet, I asked. He answered, "There was talk around town that Miz Rose killed her, that blood was on the floor, that John Ed had found her dead and cold, and that so-and-so cleaned it all up. Well, I walked on that floor that night it happened, I was back at the break of day, and I was all over that house. Whoever told that told the biggest lie in the world. There wasn't a word of truth, because I was there."

Actually, Jo Dell had been killed four days earlier. But I wanted to listen, not rile him up.

A woman who had lived in Silas for most of her life absolutely knew that everybody in the county liked John Ed. "I find it hard to believe he could have done anything like that," she said.

"Do you think he was guilty?" I asked. She replied, "Nobody knew what to believe, everybody had their own thoughts. I would like to know, really and truly, but I don't think we'll ever know."

I reminded her of the fact that over three years, at three trials, thirty-six of John Ed's friends and acquaintances were chosen as jurors. "Thirty-five of them judged him guilty," I said.

She looked at me sharply, her gaze fixed with complete confidence in the truth of what she was going to say. "If he had just brought her out of the woods, everybody down here would have stuck by him. He would have never been indicted. Never. Never!"

. . . .
Acknowledgments

This story is built upon the truth of a crime that occurred in southwest Alabama in January 1959. The accounts of the three trials held are based on coverage and research of the first trial, which I did not attend; and my notes and stories from the second and third trials, which I covered as a *Birmingham News* reporter. My work survived legibly a half century of loose storage. For additional information, thanks go to the Alabama Department of Corrections, the Alabama Department of Archives and History, the *Mobile Press-Register*, and the *Choctaw Sun-Advocate*.

I gratefully acknowledge the suggestions, assistance and support of my wife, Hannah; friend and editor Anne Gibbons; Rick Bragg, colleague at the University of Alabama; Goodloe Sutton, editor and publisher of the *Democrat-Reporter*, Linden, Alabama; Attorney Thomas S. Boggs Jr., Demopolis, Alabama; Dee Ann Campbell, editor, *Choctaw Sun-Advocate*, Butler, Alabama; and writer Rheta Grimsley Johnson.

Other true parts of the story (names changed) are the marriage of John Ed and Sarah in Waynesboro, Mississippi; the first marriage license they obtained in Pensacola, Florida; the personal and political rivalry between chief prosecutor Seth Yielding and the Tomlinson family; sustained local tension around the trials; Yielding's move away from Butler; the Tomlinson family's multiple tragedies; the letter to the second jury; the pardon; my career and personal life; and my acquaintance (nothing more) with a woman at the last two trials.

All else is fiction: scenes and dialogue outside of the courtroom and of the juries; the judge's tendencies; my meeting with a member of the second jury; Rose Tomlinson and the stained rug; the Klan's presence and intimidation of Leroy; the Negro community's unrest; Lindsey and I being reunited years after the trials. Also, dialect used in several chapters reflects that spoken at the time.

Cover illustration: Paul Looney, Tuscaloosa.

CPSIA information can be obtained at www.ICGtesting.com
Printed in the USA
LVOW05s1004071114

412462LV00004B/92/P